QUEEN AND BANDIT

Geonn Cannon

Supposed Crimes LLC • Matthews, North Carolina

www.supposedcrimes.com

This book is typeset in Goudy Old Style.

QUEEN AND BANDIT

Chapter One

Most days, Gracie Simon had three hours where she could be herself. The two hours between getting home and going to sleep were private. And the hour after waking up before she had to be at work was safe, too. The window in her bedroom looked out onto a brick wall, and the window in the living room had a double set of curtains, just in case. Those three hours were the only part of her day, not counting when she was asleep, where she didn't have to worry about how she carried herself or how she walked or the timbre of her voice.

Today was not most days, just like the night before had not been most nights. The night before, she'd let a coworker convince her to join "the gang" for drinks. Drinks were incredibly dangerous. Anything that lowered her guard was to be avoided at all costs, and social gatherings were a minefield. But constantly avoiding them was a quick route to being labeled the office weirdo, so she had to say yes to at least some of them. So she decided to sacrifice her nighttime hour of freedom to in the interest of looking like a member of the team.

Gracie hadn't had very much to drink. How she wished she could say the same about Verity Combs, the copy editor currently taking up the other side of her bed. Gracie stayed as still as possible, one hand on her stomach and the other pressed tight against her side, her eyes fixed on the ceiling. Verity was lying on her front, her left arm draped across Gracie's torso, pinning her down.

Instead of sleeping, Gracie had watched the sun rise across the ceiling's cracked brown surface. She wasn't sure she'd even blinked since falling into the bed. She'd looked over at Verity a few times, the other woman's face obscured by a frankly surprising amount of thick blonde hair, wondering if she was asleep or truly passed out. If she was actually passed out, there was a chance she could slip out from under the arm and go to the couch.

But then Verity would snore, Gracie would look back up at the ceiling, and wonder how long it was until morning.

Finally, blessedly, the body next to her slowly resurrected itself. First there was a deep inhale of breath, then the hand pressed down on Grace's stomach, and Verity shifted and lifted her head just enough to get off the pillow. She brought her hand up - Gracie had never before felt such freedom, such relief - and pushed her hair out of her face to see who she was sharing a bed with.

Verity smiled. Her eyes were still half-closed, and her lipstick was horribly smeared across her mouth, but it was still an attractive smile.

"Well, hey there, sailor," Verity mumbled, her voice still cotton-y with sleep.

"Hey." Gracie sounded choked even to her own ears.

Verity wet her lips and raised an eyebrow. She pursed her lips and moved her hand to pinch the sleeve of Gracie's shirt.

"Can't help but notice you're still fully dressed."

"You are, too."

Verity looked down, confirming she was still in the dress she'd worn to work.

Gracie explained, "I was just trying to put you to bed. Neither of us were in any shape to drive, so I thought you could sleep it off here, and I... I was... I... you kind of fell on me."

"I think it was more than that." Verity scooted closer. She reached for the highest button on Gracie's shirt. "Couldn't have been comfortable. You oughta lighten up, Gracie."

"I-I'm fine," Gracie said, shrinking away from Verity's hands. "But seeing as we're both up now, I think I best be... I should, um, get... to..."

Verity was practically lying on top of her now. "What's the hurry? It's Saturday. Neither of us has to be at the office today. Why don't we just stay here for a little while?"

"I shouldn't, um, I... I do actually have an assignment..."

"An assignment?" Verity said. "Well, then we'll just have to hurry."

Gracie closed her eyes and swallowed, wishing for a car to slam into the front of the building or the ceiling to cave in, anything that might save her from what was happening. Verity's hand was sliding down the placket of Gracie's shirt.

"You know, if any of the other men had taken me home last night, I would definitely not have woken up in these clothes."

That was basically what Matz had said when Gracie was walking Verity out of the bar, one arm slung heavy over her shoulder. *"Pace yourself, Gracie! She's taken down men twice your size!"* Toland had added, *"While twice as drunk!"* and both men had collapsed in laughter.

"I know," Gracie said. "That's kind of why I decided I should be the one to make sure you got somewhere safe."

Verity batted her eyelashes. The effect was somewhat diminished by the fact her eyes were uncoordinated and turned it into more of a disastrous blink.

"My knight in shining armor."

Before Gracie could counter, Verity had stretched up and pressed their mouths together. Gracie choked back a yelp of surprise. She put her hands on Verity's shoulders and tried to cringe away but the mattress was too firm to provide her any escape. She squirmed and twisted, but Verity put a hand on Gracie's belt to pull her back in place.

"Stop," Gracie gasped when the kiss ended. "You don't have to do this."

"You deserve a reward, don't you think?"

Gracie's face was burning up. "No! No, I didn't... this wasn't anything but consideration. I-I don't, I..." She managed to get Verity's hand off her belt before it traveled lower. "I don't want this."

Verity sobered and leaned back. "You don't *want* it?"

"I'm sorry. You're beautiful. Don't get me wrong, i-it would... it would be..." She cursed her awkward stutter. "I just... I'm not looking for anything. I just wanted to make sure you were safe."

Verity looked away, lips pursed and brow furrowed. The sleep and the drunk haze were clearly still fogging her mind, preventing her from connecting the dots.

"It's not about you," Gracie said. "Honest."

"Okay."

Verity scooted to the other side of the mattress, taking a second to adjust her skirt before she stood. She looked around, spotted the bathroom, and headed toward it.

Gracie sat up. "I'm sorry."

"You don't have anything to be sorry for." Verity didn't turn around.

"Still. I don't want you to think you're not... you're very... um..."

Verity stopped in the bathroom door and looked back at her. She was smiling sadly, her eyes mostly veiled by her still-sloppy hair.

"Don't worry, Simon. I'll tell everyone you were a gentleman."

She went into the bathroom and closed the door.

Gracie dropped her head back onto the pillow and grunted with frustration.

"If only I was, V," she muttered under her breath. "It would solve a lot of damn problems."

The problem was that Gracie definitely wanted to give in

to Verity's flirtations. As soon as the apartment was empty again, Gracie jumped out of bed and ran into the bathroom. She stripped out of her clothes and turned the water on hot, stepped in before she was completely undressed, and angled her face so the cold spray pounded her eyes and forehead. A whole night next to Verity Combs. Smelling her perfume. Being weighed down by her.

Gracie moved her feet apart and braced them against the edge of the tub. She was still wearing her boxer shorts and she pushed her hand inside. She tried not to think about what would've happened if she had really let Verity's hand get this far, then surrendered and focused on what she hoped would've happened. She had been strong all night and now she could give in without repercussions. She bowed her head so that the water was hitting the crown, flattening her short copper hair. Her head was shaved on the sides, long in the front, so the tendrils hung down over her face as she masturbated. She watched the water pool around her curling toes and moved her hips against her hand until she came.

When she'd caught her breath, she turned off the water and peeled off her sodden underclothes. She left them in the tub and went to the sink. She was tall and slender, lean like her mother with big hands like her father. She wasn't flat-chested but close enough that she didn't have to worry much about anyone noticing, especially if she wore undershirts a size too small. There were enough masculine traits in her features - strong jaw and thin lips, an aquiline nose, and thick eyebrows - that people just assumed she was the person she presented as.

And the person she presented as was Simon Grace. It was an extremely easy change, swapping her first and last names, and so far it had worked a treat. Of course there were people at the paper like Verity who insisted on giving everyone a nickname, and through some cruel twist of fate, they'd dubbed her Gracie within a few weeks of the job. So after carefully crafting a false identity, half the people she worked with called her by her real name anyway.

The irony was enough to make her sick to her stomach.

She brushed her teeth, combed her hair, and retrieved a dry outfit from the closet. She hadn't been lying when she said she had an assignment, though she was dreading it.

Gracie put on her eyeglasses as she left the house. She didn't need them to see, but anything that helped obscure the shape of her eyes or face was an extra layer of protection.

Her car was parked at the curb. It was her pride and joy: a 1940 DeSoto Coupe, forest green with white interior. It gleamed in the sun, and she ran her hand possessively along the shapely back fender. Her apartment was shoddy and every item of clothing she owned had been mended at least once, but her car was the one extravagance she'd allowed herself. It still had its issues but nothing that got in the way of how absolutely free she felt when she climbed behind the wheel.

The dashboard was real wood with chrome trim. She sometimes spent her Saturdays polishing every inch of metal on the thing until it looked brand-new. The engine might cough a little, but her baby definitely turned heads every time she took it out.

She really hadn't been able to afford it. She got her first big paycheck as a writer and, on the way home she passed a lot where the car had practically been shouting her name. She justified it by saying she needed a way to get around, to follow leads, to investigate stories. A reliable vehicle was as much a necessity as her apartment. More so, really, because if she lost her apartment she could spend a few nights in the car until she found a new place.

But the actual reason she walked into the dealership and dropped more money than she'd ever paid for anything was much simpler: she really just wanted a nice, cool car. And it was green. And she loved green. And she couldn't bear the thought of anyone else driving this gorgeous car.

Gracie loved the car so much she actually looked forward to the long drive to work. In addition to giving her extra time behind the wheel, it also gave her a chance to slip more fully into her character. She'd been play-acting maleness for so long that it was almost second nature to her, but it was still a cloak she had to put on every morning. One slip could be forgiven. Maybe she hurt her back and it made her walk strange, or she had a cold so her voice was a little odd. But enough slips would add up, whispers would start, questions would be asked. She couldn't risk it.

The office of the Los Angeles *Mercury*, the Merc, was a dull brown building in Van Nuys, part of a nondescript cul-de-sac of three buildings that faced each other around a shared parking lot. Gracie pulled into her usual spot near the street, cutting down on the potential of anyone dinging the finish. The office was usually quiet on Saturdays, and the lack of other cars in the lot gave her hope as she headed inside. Maybe she could just get what she needed and get out, two minutes, no muss or fuss.

The lights were on, but that wasn't unusual. She just needed her press credentials and the tape recorder she kept in her bottom drawer. She reached her desk and pulled out her chair, ignoring the memos littering the blotter as she grabbed what she needed. She was just standing up again when a door at the far side of the bullpen open. She didn't have to turn around to know her editor, William Swain, had just stepped out of his office.

"Sorry, chief, just on my way out." She hurried away from her desk as if moving quickly enough would erase the fact she'd been there.

"You're just who I was looking for, Simon. Come here. I have a story for you."

She reluctantly turned to face him. He looked like a panda bear, round and soft with salt-and-pepper hair. He was bald on top but made up for it with a thick beard that gave him the impression of a muzzle. Today he was wearing a dress shirt that was only a little rumpled and sweat-stained at the collar. He had one beefy paw on the jamb of his office door like he was dangling from it. He motioned her closer with the other hand.

"I'm actually on my way to a story. Councilman Atwater. He agreed to talk to me about being forced to resign, but this was the only time he would agree to talk to anyone."

Swain shook his head and waved more emphatically. "Bray can handle that. Come on."

"You can't give my story to Bray. He can barely handle the obituaries. Besides, there's no time. I'm supposed to meet with Atwater in..." Two hours. "...half an hour."

"Bray is quick and he's good enough for a story most people will barely skim. I'm offering you something everyone's going to be jealous of come Monday morning."

Gracie stared skepticism at him, but his bushy eyebrows were up and his cheeks puffed out in a smile. The City Council story would be front page. But her curiosity was going to be the death of her. She sighed, slumped her shoulders, and finally changed direction to join him in his office. He chuckled and ushered her inside. He picked up a piece of paper, turned it around, and held it out to her like a prize.

"What's this?" It was a glossy photograph of a woman's face with the name EVELYN WADE written out in the bottom margin.

"That's Evelyn Wade," Swain said.

"I gathered that much," Gracie said. "Why am I looking at her face?"

He stared at her with disbelief. "You don't know her? Everyone knows her. *Over Red Rocks? The Night At Sea? Chicago Canary?*"

Gracie shrugged and looked at the back of the headshot. "Sorry. I don't get out to the movies very much. Is she any good?"

Swain snatched the photo away. "Who cares if she's any good? Look at that mug! She's going to be the next Greta Garbo. And the director of her current flick has agreed to let one of my reporters come on-set for a~"

"Oh no."

"~profile of her."

"No!"

"Just a quick interview, a couple pictures~"

"I have to be the photographer, too? Come on, Swain!"

"~and a few hundred words about where she's from, who she's sweet on, something to give the readers a taste of the woman behind the silver screen. The next big thing from Universal!"

"I'm not a photographer."

"You told me you have a dark room at your place."

"It's a hobby, but~"

He waved her off. "It'll be fine."

"You have professional photographers on the payroll who could do this."

Swain gestured at the empty bullpen. "Do you see any of them around? You're selling yourself short, Simon. You'll do great."

Gracie glared at him. "Of course I'll do great. I'm a good reporter. It's not about whether I'm capable, it's whether this nonsense is worthy of my time. You're pulling me off front page political corruption for a fluff piece on some starlet? You have to be joking."

"No joke. I told you, no one is going to care about Atwater a week from now. But Evelyn Wade is immortal. Or she will be, soon, and you're going to help her get there. This is LA, Simon. Celebs like her are the real power, not whatever politician is currently occupying some random office."

Gracie closed her eyes. It didn't seem like there was a way out of this, so she tried to find the positive angle. She hated Atwater, and believed him to be the worst kind of slimy politician, and part of her had been dreading the idea of sitting down to talk with him. It would've been worth it for the front page. For the prestige of seeing her name, however mangled, connected to such an important report. It could have been a stepping stone to even bigger stories.

"When do you need it?"

"It's tomorrow's top story."

Her eyes popped open. "*Tomorrow...?* As in~"

"As in twenty-four full hours. Like you said, it's a fluff piece. No one's expecting Shakespeare. Just a little thing to make the bobbysoxers buy our paper. Just go talk to her and write up something that won't get her dander up, I'll approve it, and you have a byline on a very popular story. It's a cake walk of an assignment, Gracie. Be grateful."

She decided arguing was pointless and surrendered. "Where do I have to go?"

"Attaboy," Swain said, handing over the picture again. "You don't even have to go very far. They're out in Bronson Canyon right now shooting some nonsense about the Trojan War or something, I think." He searched the papers on his desk and handed one of them over to her. "Directions. Just take your press pass, tell 'em you're with the Merc. They'll let you on."

"Fine. But if I do this, I want automatic approval for my next three stories. I don't care how dry you think they are."

"Sure, sure, whatever you want. But Evelyn Wade first. This is going to be it. This is going to be the interview that turns her from a star into a... a..."

"Icon."

Swain grinned wide enough to show his teeth, and he aimed one finger at her. "That's it, Simon! That's why you're my go-to guy. Go. Go, my boy, turn that girl into an *icon*."

Gracie pressed her lips together and turned her back on him, scanning the directions as she left the office. The Bronson Canyon location really wasn't far away at all; it wouldn't even take ten minutes to drive there. She folded the papers length-wise and slipped them into her back pocket. She tried not to be too upset about losing the Atwater story. Corruption would always be around, and maybe someone more important would screw up in a bigger way later. Still, it would've been nice to get a story like that in her scrapbook.

No use crying over spilled articles, though. She was out of luck and might as well try to make the best of it.

Maybe the movie star would have something interesting to say.

CHAPTER TWO

EVELYN WADE didn't want to come out of her trailer. It was barely even noon and it was already well past ninety-five degrees out there. The wind was blowing just enough that she knew she would end the day with grit in her eyes. And if she went out there, she knew she would just end up sitting under one of those big umbrellas that didn't do a damn thing to keep her cool while Joe and Barry flubbed their lines. So she was content to stay inside until she was actually needed.

Not that the trailer was much of an improvement. The couch cushions were about as thin as a newspaper, so she had taken them all and stacked them on one side. It didn't leave her much room to stretch out, naturally, so she had her shoulders on the stack of cushions with her legs propped up on the wall. With the arm of the couch under her butt, it almost felt like she was sitting on a chair that had been turned on its side, which made the whole world feel topsy turvy.

She didn't mind. She liked the dizzy feeling it gave her. She had her script in front of her and tried to focus on her lines, but she kept looking past the pages at her toes, letting her mind wander. She was wearing sandals with straps that climbed up her legs in an intricate crisscross pattern. She wasn't allowed to take them off because the process of retying all those damn leather ribbons was such a pain. She didn't mind; the sandals were comfortable enough that she could forget she was wearing them after a while.

This would be her fourth film with Universal. Her first had been moderately successful, and the next two did exponentially better. Everyone believed this was the one that would seal the deal and confirm she was actually a star and not just someone who got lucky a few times. It was a lot of pressure on what she had to admit was just a mediocre film.

Evelyn lifted the page again and tried to focus. The film was called *Olympus*, a fantasy adventure about sailors in 1915 caught in a storm in the Mediterranean. They wash up on an island where the Greek gods have been in hiding for centuries. When they hear that the world is at war, they decide the time is right for them to make their presence known again. It ended in a big battle between gods and mortals which ends, of course, with the mortals victorious and the gods retreating back to their hidden isle.

The movie was only being made because the studio thought RKO was going to make a killing with *Sinbad the Sailor*, something she couldn't quite fathom. She'd seen the flick when it first came out and hadn't been impressed. Okay, she'd liked Maureen O'Hara. She had liked Maureen O'Hara a lot, actually. But even a woman like that wasn't enough to make a movie profitable. The fact she was practically alone in the theater when she saw it didn't exactly bode well.

But once the execs decided the next big thing had arrived, it was a fool's errand to try changing their minds. So what if *Sinbad* didn't set the world on fire? That just opened the door for *Olympus* to be the vanguard.

The director originally wanted her for Aphrodite. While it was technically the bigger role, Evelyn had her agent fight for Artemis instead. Aphrodite was in almost every scene with the gods, but she was eye candy. She had a dozen lines in the entire script, and when everyone else was talking, she was "lounging seductively" in a "gauze-thin wrap that leaves just enough to the imagination."

Artemis also had a revealing outfit - a chiton that left her right shoulder and upper chest exposed, with a hem that ended mid-thigh - but she also got to take part in the battle. She had a bow and arrow, a shield, and a sword, and she used them well. Evelyn had been training with a combat instructor to make sure she didn't embarrass herself. She'd gotten good enough to fake it, and was almost good enough to believe she could hold her own in a real fight.

Someone knocked on the trailer door. "Evie?" The production assistant, a young man named Howie with acne scars and a permanently terrified expression on his face. "You ready in there?"

She rolled her eyes and dropped the script onto her chest. "Be out in five."

"Mr. Auer told me to remind you that the *Mercury* is sending over their reporter today. He's supposed to be here any minute."

"Bully for him," Evelyn muttered. She swung her legs down and adjusted her costume. Her hair was probably flat in the back, but someone would plump it up for her before they started rolling film. She put on her sunglasses - a ridiculously large pair with lenses that made her look like a bug - to keep the sand out of her eyes before she opened the door.

Howie took a step back, almost tripping over his own feet. Evelyn ignored his clumsiness and climbed down out of the trailer, squinting until her eyes adjusted to the nuclear sunlight reflecting off the sand. Only a handful of scraggly trees marked the hills in the distance but they did nothing to break up the monotony outside of their filming location. It was hard to believe there was a major city just a mile or so over the hills.

"Have you ever been to Greece?"

"Ma'am?"

"Or anywhere in the Mediterranean?" she asked again. "Do you think it looks anything like this?"

Howie looked around as if he'd just arrived. "Uh. Well. I think, um, most people who watch the movie won't know any better than I do."

She raised an eyebrow and shrugged. "You're probably right. Where do they need me?"

He pointed and scurried off toward the scrum of people standing a little distance away, and she followed him.

There was a small village set up just outside an invisible perimeter which marked the difference between "Greek island in 1915" and "Los Angeles desert thirty-two years later." The director, writer, a producer, and two cast members were sitting in canvas chairs underneath a white tent that flapped in the breeze. Extras milled around wearing either sailor uniforms or togas and chitons similar to hers. The girl who had eventually been cast as Aphrodite, an ingenue who swore up and down that she'd been born with the name Adora Bell, was wrapped in a thick terrycloth robe to conceal the tissue paper that made up her costume. Evelyn sympathized with the girl; she had to be sweltering in the damn robe, but she supposed it was a fair trade-off to avoid everyone ogling her.

The director, Solomon Auer, saw her coming and unfolded himself from his chair. "Goddess of the hunt, I've been hunting for you all morning."

"Well, here I am, Sol," she said, hands on her hips. "Where do you need me?"

He held up his hands to frame the scene in front of him. "We're doing the initial meeting between the two factions. You'll be up on those rocks with your bow drawn, ready to draw blood, while the rest of the gods confront the interlopers to the island."

Evelyn cupped a hand over her eyes to examine the landscape. A scaffold had been set up behind the rocks where she was supposed to stand. It was a shaky, dangerous-looking construction of metal pipes and boards, but it was better than trying to get up there by climbing. She nodded and took off her sunglasses. She handed them to Auer, who hooked them on his vest pocket.

Now that her eyes had fully adjusted to the brightness, she was aware of someone else standing in the shadows of the tent. Rumpled shirt and suspenders, sleeves rolled up past his elbows, lank red-brown hair falling down over one eye. A camera strap was slung around his neck, the object itself hanging down mid-chest. He had a strong chin, thin lips, and big eyes that were currently magnified by a pair of glasses.

He was also a woman.

Auer saw her staring. "Oh! I might as well introduce you now. This is Simon Grace, the reporter from the *Merc* we mentioned. He just got here and I invited him to watch you film the scene."

"No skin off my nose, as long as he knows how to keep quiet."

Simon nodded. "I won't be a nuisance."

Evelyn gave him her best, shiniest smile. His voice was fantastic. She wondered how long he'd worked on it. "Well, then. Aces!" She turned back to Auer. "I just need a little brush and fluff and I'll be ready."

He was already gesturing toward hair and makeup. "Can we get a touchup for Miss Wade here, please? Thank you!"

Evelyn stepped away and, seconds later, was flanked by two elves from the Pretty Posse, what she called the people who made her look good for the cameras. One fussed with her hair, and the other dabbed and patted at her lips and eyes to make sure everything looked perfect.

"You've gotta stop lying on your back in the trailer," the hair girl muttered. "You're ruining all our hard work here."

"Telling an actress to stop lying on her back is like asking a fish to stop swimming, darling," Evelyn said, adding a pout to her voice.

The hair girl snorted and shoved her shoulder. "Go, you're gorgeous."

"Thank you, elves," Evelyn called as she strode toward her position.

The other actors began to migrate toward their marks. Evelyn climbed the ladder on one side of the scaffold and walked across to where her bow and arrows had been left. She slung the strap of her quiver over one shoulder and carefully stepped from the shaky security of the board to the sloped and hazardous surface of the stone. The sandals slipped a little but not enough to worry her. She braced herself against an outcropping and swung the bow out from her waist in a wide arc.

A few feet below her, Joe Singer puffed out his chest and stretched his arms out to either side. He was a picture perfect movie star, from the strong chin to the shining blue eyes. He looked like he had stepped directly out of a recruiting poster to play Henry King, the heroic captain of the shipwrecked mortals. Standing next to him was Barry Denton, olive-skinned with his hair slicked back to draw attention to the slant of his forehead. He had a goatee to frame his square jaw and high cheekbones. Barry was their Ares, the main antagonist of the film, and no one had to wonder why he'd been cast as a god.

Barry's outfit was similar to Evelyn's, but cut lower to reveal his pecs and a hint of his abs. It was probably the only time her male costar had been more exposed than she was, she realized with a smirk.

Auer shouted to be heard by everyone. "Let's get this one in the can, people. Places!"

Joe and Barry moved so that they were facing each other. Joe telegraphed a punch toward Barry's jaw, Barry responded by waving his head from side to side in a cartoonish daze.

"Stop clowning around, fellas," Auer scolded.

Evelyn raised her bow and nocked an arrow. She aimed it at Joe's chest. She'd accidentally fired the arrow on their last run-through, and they were all relieved to discover the plastic tips weren't hard enough to do more than bruise. Luckily Joe hadn't held the slip against her, but she was determined it would be the last mistake she made on this set.

"First positions! Clear the frame! Everybody ready…"

The cast moved to where they were supposed to be and held.

"*Action!*" Auer called.

"We have no quarrel with you," Joe said, his voice projecting as if he was standing on a stage. He raised his hands in a placating gesture as he scanned the extras flanking Barry. "We just want to get home."

"They are warriors!" Evelyn barked, holding a scowl on her face as everyone turned to look at her. "Their ship bears weapons of war."

"We do not seek out battle," Joe said. "Our country is at war, that is true. But you are not our enemy. There is no reason for us to fight."

"And even less reason for us to be allies," Barry countered. "Leave this land before we are forced to send you to po-sigh-a-done."

"Cut!" Auer said.

Joe dropped his hands to his sides and rolled his shoulders. Barry brought up a fist and racked it against his forehead a few times.

"I know, I know, I know," he said. "Poseidon. Poseidon."

"You got it?" Auer said.

"I have it," Barry said, reassuring both director and his costars.

Auer said, "Okay, let's take it again from the top."

Everybody reset. They went through their lines, and Barry sailed past the word he'd flubbed. The scene continued perfectly until the gods decided they would take the mortals back to Zeus for judgment. When they reached the last line, Auer called cut again and asked them to do one more take. "Poseidon, Barry. You also hit your mark a little hard. Try to make it smoother this time. And... *action!*"

They went through one more time without a hitch, and Auer declared the scene complete.

Evelyn lowered her arm and rubbed her shoulder. She returned to the scaffold and carefully climbed down, leaving her props at the foot of the ladder so someone could secure them somewhere until she needed them again. Close to half an hour standing on a rock in the blazing sun so she could say one line. It could've been worse, she reminded herself as she watched Adora Bell slip back into her robe. She could've gone through all of this just to be eye candy in the background of the scene while everyone else got to work. She almost felt bad for the kid. *There but for the grace of God,* she thought.

"Wonderful," Auer said when she was back in the tent's shadow. "Just fabulous. The way you held that bow, it's like you actually know how."

"I do know how."

He ignored her and waved over the reporter. "Let's get a shot of you in the costume. That'll look great with the interview, right?"

"Um, sure," the reporter said. He awkwardly moved into position and fumbled a little with the camera.

Evelyn stepped back into the sun and put her hands on her hips. She squared her shoulders and lifted her chin for a heroic pose.

"What are you doing, sweetie?" Auer said. "Men don't want that. Right?" He slapped the back of his hand on the reporter's shoulder with a laugh. "Come on. Give 'em a good shot."

Evelyn raised an eyebrow at him. Auer raised his eyebrows and gestured.

"I don't~" The reporter stammered.

"It's all right," Evelyn said. "He's right." She bent her knee and turned to the side, raising her shoulder so it touched her chin. She plucked at the hem of her chiton and lifted it just enough to show almost all of her thigh. She pursed her lips and widened her eyes, sucking in her cheeks. The reporter watched her, looked at the director as if confirming this was what he wanted, and then raised the camera again.

"Say cheese, doll," Auer said.

"I already took the picture," the reporter said.

"Quick on the trigger, ey?" Auer laughed and slapped the reporter's shoulder again. "Who can blame you with a dame like this?"

Evelyn smoothed down the front of her chiton. "I'm not

in the next few scenes, Sol. Why don't I take Mr. Grace back to my trailer so we can have the interview?"

Auer and the screenwriter exchanged grins. Evelyn pretended not to know what they were thinking. She plucked her sunglasses from Auer's pocket and slipped them back on.

"Sure, sure. Take your time, sweetie."

Evelyn smiled warmly at the reporter and motioned for him to walk with her. He turned on the ball of his foot and fell into step beside her, walking quickly as if he was just as eager to escape the tent as she was. When they were almost to the trailer, he looked back to make sure they were out of earshot before he leaned closer and whispered to her.

"I took the first picture."

"Pardon?" Evelyn said.

"The first one?" Grace clarified. "Arms akimbo, like Superman from the comics. That's the picture I took. The second one I just pretended."

Evelyn said, "You did? Well, Mr. Grace, there might be hope for this interview yet."

She opened the door to her trailer and motioned for him to lead the way. It wasn't gallantry, rather just habit to prevent anyone from peeking up her skirt as they followed her inside. She had half a theory that trailers were elevated for that very reason, to give a reason for stairs that allowed stares. Grace didn't hesitate as he went up. She went in behind him and closed the door, grateful for the relatively cool air of the interior. She put her sunglasses down on the counter and patted her hair to knock out any sand that might have gotten caught in the waves.

Grace was standing by the couch, eyeing the cushions. "You can just rearrange those however you want and have a seat. Can I get you something to drink? I have tea, lemonade..."

"Ice water would be great, if you have that."

"Oh, I most certainly do." She went into the kitchenette at the back of the trailer. "I have a question I want to ask you, but it's not something one just blurts out. Normally I would preface something like this by saying something along the lines of 'I hate to be rude', but given the reason you're here, I don't think that's necessary."

"No, I mean, of course. I'm going to be asking you questions so it's only fair that it goes both ways." He sat down on the couch and put his camera down on the cushion next to him. He fumbled in his pockets and produced a notepad and pencil. "Ask away."

Evelyn brought him the water and looked him in the eye. "Are you hiding who you are or being who you are?"

Grace blinked. A line appeared between his eyebrows. "What? I, uh... I don't... what?"

"Should I treat you like a man, or are you a woman who is just doing what she has to do in order to get hired in this town?"

She put the glass in Grace's hand. Grace looked down at it, then looked back up.

Evelyn smiled.

"Take your time, sweetie. It's a big question."

CHAPTER THREE

GRACIE'S FIRST thought upon seeing Evelyn Wade was that she was a goddess.

She literally was at that moment, the goddess of the hunt, but the effect would have been the same even if she'd been stepping out of the grocery store instead of a trailer on a movie set. There was a glow about her that had nothing to do with the sun currently beating down on them. She wore a white outfit that looked like a toga, just tight enough across the chest to reveal the curves without looking intentional. The hem of the gown was trimmed with gold and swished across her thighs as she walked with long, confident strides toward the tent.

Gracie had just arrived and introduced herself to the director when the actress appeared. Gracie tried hard not to stare, but apparently she hadn't done a very good job. The director laughed and bumped her with his elbow.

"She has that effect on folks, pal."

Gracie had chuckled and adjusted her glasses, then tried to be as invisible as possible when she was actually introduced. Evelyn barely paid any attention to her before she headed out to take her place for the scene they were shooting. Gracie backed up until her shoulders touched canvas. She hoped the shadows under the tent were deep enough to hide the fact she was blushing.

When Evelyn ascended the ladder, the wind caught her chiton and blew it up almost enough to reveal her underwear. Both the director and screenwriter made quiet noises Gracie couldn't parse, but the childish laughter that followed left no doubt that they'd both been watching. She wondered how vital it was for Evelyn's character to be up high for this scene. The rock looked dangerous as hell, and if they'd only blocked it that way to get a peek at her ass...

After a sweltering half hour spent shooting the scene, and then Evelyn suffering through the ridiculous posing the director made Evelyn take, they had retreated to the relative safety and privacy of her trailer.

And then the question. And what a question, what a dangerous can of worms. She could either admit who she was or start off the interview by lying to someone she was asking to be open and honest. But telling the truth put her at enormous risk. Her entire life would be blown up if Swain or the owners of the *Merc* found out she was a woman. But the way Evelyn asked the question made it clear she already knew the answer, so she was only asking for confirmation.

"I'm doing what's necessary to do the job I want."

"Works for me. So I guess your name isn't Simon."

Gracie felt the tension fading from her shoulders. "Actually it is. Grace Simon. I go by Simon Grace at the paper. A lot of people call me Gracie."

"Clever. Sit."

They sat down on opposite ends of the couch, a full cushion between them.

"Can I ask how you knew?"

Evelyn laughed, draping one arm across the back of the couch. "Honey, I've spent my whole career putting on masks and costumes, and watching everyone around me become a whole new person when they hear the word 'action.' If I couldn't spot an amateur actor like you through a cheap costume, I would be in the wrong profession." She held up a hand. "Not that it's a bad disguise. Far from it. You actually look damn convincing. Sound good, too."

"So what gave me away?"

Evelyn considered her features, then held out two fingers. "Your eyes. The nose. There's something feminine about the way they swoop. You look... you know, you actually look like one of those people in a Renaissance painting. Sort of androgynous. It's an excellent look. With that red hair? And your skin... is it always gold like that?"

Gracie put her hand on her cheek. "Gold...? I don't..."

Evelyn grinned. "Gosh. I've embarrassed you. I'm sorry." She waved her hand as if clearing smoke. "We don't have to talk about that anymore. I'll keep your charade going while we're around other people, but in here? Just between us girls? I'll go ahead and call you Gracie. Would that be all right?"

"It would be great, Miss Wade."

"Evie."

Gracie nodded. "If you insist. Evie. I guess we should start with the simple stuff. Where you're from, who your parents are, that sort of thing."

"No one cares about that."

"Sure they do," Gracie said. "I can't say I understand why, but that's the stuff that sells papers. That's kind of the business I'm in here."

Evelyn sighed. She raised her other arm and raked it through her hair. "Well, I'm here to sell tickets. Get people out to the theaters, spend two hours watching some nonsense about sailors fighting gods on a Greek island. I want them to believe I'm really Artemis. It doesn't help me if they know my parents' names or where I grew up, or..." She waved her hand. "Anything like that. They don't *want* that, even if they buy the papers and pretend to care."

"You think your fans don't care?"

"I think it doesn't matter to them one way or the other, honestly. They take whatever we give them."

Gracie pressed her lips together. "I thought you agreed to do an interview."

"I did. I'll tell you everything you want to know about *Olympus*. You can hang out and see how dreadfully dull the whole affair is. That's what the public is really after. A peek behind the curtain. Backstage."

"Part of that is understanding you."

"Is it? I don't think so."

Gracie looked down at her pad, then looked past Evelyn at the window. The blinds were drawn but open enough to cast stripes of sunlight across the floor. She hadn't wanted to do this damn story in the first place but, if she was going to put her byline on it, she didn't want some stupid fluff piece about 'the magic of the silver screen.'

"I could have been talking to Councilman Atwater right now."

Evelyn laughed. "Oh, then you're welcome! I have to be more interesting than that."

"No. No, you aren't. I could have been grilling him about corruption in the city government, digging up a conspiracy, maybe making a real difference. But I was pulled off that story and forced to come here instead. I thought, okay. Okay, I can do a profile on an interesting woman that girls can look up to. But no. You want to be a dolly that puts on fun outfits and prances around in front of a camera. All sparkle and no substance." She stood up. "I'm sorry, Miss Wade. I'm annoyed, I'm irritated, and it's made me rude. But I resent having my plans for the day thrown into a wood chipper just to come here and write about people playing pretend in the sand. I won't take up any more of your time."

She walked to the trailer door.

"Roger and Marjorie."

Gracie turned around. "What? Who are they?"

It was Evelyn's turn to look out the window. "My parents. Roger and Marjorie." She looked at Gracie and raised an eyebrow. "Well? Are you going to write that down or what?"

Gracie hesitated at the door for another second, then

walked back to the couch to take her seat again. She already felt guilty for pushing this hard, and she tried to move back to safety. "We don't have to go into anything you're not comfortable with. I don't need a biography going all the way back to childhood, just a little bit of an insight to you as a person. And you'll have final approval of anything before it goes to print."

Evelyn waved her hand dismissively. "Sure, sure. Let's just start talking and see where this goes."

Gracie poised her pen over her pad and realized she didn't even know where to begin. She had no prepared questions or, despite her promises, even an idea of what kind of profile this was going to be. She pressed her lips together and looked around the trailer for any hint of inspiration. Evelyn rested her fist against her temple and raised an eyebrow, assuming the reason for Gracie's hesitation.

"Maybe you want to come back another day, or...?"

"No! No, I'm here now. My editor probably already has a section of the paper cut out for this. I just don't usually do these kinds of profiles so I'm not exactly sure where to start."

Evelyn adjusted herself on the cushion and struck a pose. "Most interviews start with describing me in a ridiculous amount of detail. What I'm wearing, how I'm sitting, if you can see my curves."

"That doesn't seem necessary."

Evelyn shrugged. "It's how the game is played. There are a lot of things about how the game is played that aren't necessary, but they're just what's done."

"Like what?"

"Nothing." She pushed her hair up away from her face, let it fall, and sighed heavily. "Damn, what I wouldn't do for a cigarette."

Gracie said, "I don't mind."

"No, I'm not supposed to. Bad for the teeth." She pulled her lips back in a grimace to show her pearly whites. "My agent would murder me."

"Would it help if I smoked so you could at least smell it?"

Evelyn's eyes widened. "Oh, goodness, *would* you...? I hate to impose."

"It's fine."

Gracie began patting her pockets, though she was pretty sure she didn't have any cigarettes on her. Evelyn was already up and retrieved a pack from the desk drawer. She brought it back and presented it to Gracie as if it was on a pillow.

"Why do you have a whole pack if you're supposed to stay away from them?"

"Because I try to be a good girl, but no one can be a saint. And you can quote that in your article."

Evelyn produced a lighter. Gracie took a cigarette, placed it between her lips, and leaned forward. Evelyn clicked the lighter and touched it to the end, and Gracie inhaled. She blew out a line of smoke as Evelyn dropped back onto the other side of the couch. Evelyn sighed and rolled her head back.

"That's heavenly. Thank you."

"No problem. I haven't had one in ages." She looked at the end table and pulled an ashtray closer. The initial buzz from the tobacco was making her feel more relaxed. "Okay. You don't want this to reveal too much of yourself, and I don't want it to be some silly fluff piece. Let's make it about something that matters."

Evelyn said, "You saw what we're filming out there, right? In act three, Joe is going to call down thunder and lightning to scuttle the hero's ship. Talking about things that matter isn't going to sell tickets to this flick, and that's what my real job is here."

She reached out and took the cigarette from between Gracie's fingers. She did it so smoothly, with such confidence, that she was already taking a drag before Gracie thought to be surprised by it. Evelyn closed her eyes and tilted her head back to blow out a solid stream of smoke. It dissipated above her as she held her arm out to give the cigarette back. Her lipstick had left a faint red ring around the butt, which made Gracie feel self-conscious about taking another drag.

"Just outside the hustle and bustle of downtown Los Angeles," Evelyn recited, "a tiny piece of desert has been transformed into a Mediterranean island. It is here that gods and mortals will clash for the upcoming Universal blockbuster *Olympus*, but today glamorous starlet Evelyn Wade is sitting in a comfortable trailer enjoying a break from the heat and the sun."

Gracie stared at her. Evelyn waved at the notebook.

"You can use as much of that as you want."

"I don't want you to just dictate the article to me."

Evelyn laughed. "Well, there seems to be a lot you don't want, Mr. Grace. I don't particularly want to be here, if we're being completely honest with each other. But it's an obligation. It's part of the job, and we can't just do the parts of the job we like. I'd much rather be in here than sitting around out there so everyone can ogle me."

"You know they're ogling?"

"Oh, honey," Evelyn said with something like true disappointment. She plucked at the hem of her costume. "Even Adora Bell out there knows they're gawking. At least she has the excuse of putting on a robe so she won't get sunburned. Poor thing. They'd have her walk around completely topless if they thought they'd get away with it."

"That's terrible."

Evelyn made a noise but didn't comment further.

Gracie tapped her pen on the page. "Okay. So how about we, um, talk about the future? Optimism sells, right? What are you going to do when *Olympus* wraps?"

"Sit in my apartment, call directors, and stalk auditions. Hope that this won't be my last film. You always have to kind of cross your fingers and hope in this business."

"Sounds nerve-wracking."

Evelyn shrugged and looked toward the window. "It's a small price when you consider what I do when I have work. I'm doing what I always dreamed of. This is the job I always wanted to do growing up. A little uncertainty is a small price to pay."

"That's a nice way of looking at it. What would you be doing if you hadn't made it?"

"Ooh. Now that's a scary thought. Let's see. I would probably still be back home. Chicago. That's where I grew up. I was a member of the Great Water Playhouse. That was where I played my first villain. I was Iago. Played the hell out of that role, too. I fell in love with the idea of acting, so I think no matter what happened, I would always be an actor in one way or another even if I wasn't making a living at it. I'd figure out how to pay the bills by taking whatever job was flexible enough to let me make it to rehearsal. Grocery store clerk? Probably that."

Gracie said, "So it's all about the acting for you? The passion for acting?"

"Well, the money is very nice." She winked and shook her shoulders, then stood up and went to a cooler tucked under the kitchen cabinet. "Are you still okay with water?"

"It's fine."

Evelyn came back with a bottle and took her seat again, tucking her leg up under her. "It wouldn't be a terrible life, you know? Acting for the fun of it and skipping all the nonsense that comes with being famous. And I could..." She made a quiet sound and jerked her head to the side, stopping whatever she was about to say by taking a swig of her drink. She held it in her mouth, puffing out her cheeks for a few seconds until she finally swallowed. "No, it wouldn't be a bad life."

"What were you going to say?"

"It doesn't matter." She gestured at the cigarette and Gracie handed it over. "You like to play the what-if game, huh?"

Gracie shrugged. "It's a defense mechanism, I guess. If the wrong person figures out, you know..." She gestured at herself. "I could lose everything. My job, my house. So I have to think about what I'd want to do if all this went away."

"Hm. Well. If you put it like that, if I knew the world was ending tomorrow, I know exactly what I would do. I'd tell the truth."

Gracie furrowed her brow. "The truth about what?"

"Everything." She took another drag off the cigarette and held the smoke as she passed it back to Gracie. "You want to talk about real things? You were standing in the tent while I shot my scene. How many times did they mention my ass? Or maybe these?" She patted her chest with her free hand.

"I, um... I didn't exactly pay very close attention..."

"Mm-hmm. They don't always bother waiting until I'm out of earshot, so I can make a pretty good guess. The only reason they might have held back is because you were there, but you're just one of the fellas, right? So just boys doing what boys do. It's like that on every set, for every studio. There are some good eggs, but there are some really rotten ones. And all kinds down the middle. If I knew the world was going to end tomorrow, I would give you a list of all the worst ones and let you put them in the newspaper for everyone to see."

Gracie raised her eyebrows. "Wow. I'm not sure what good that would do if everyone you name wouldn't face any consequences. What with the world ending and all."

Evelyn laughed. "Oh, they won't face consequences no matter what. You publish the article, there will be a few days of hubbub, and then it'll all die down and everything will go back to normal. Maybe one or two guys will get blacklisted to make a show. 'United Artists cares about its actresses,' that sort of thing." She rolled her eyes. "But by my next flick, I guarantee you, the director would be asking me to put on a bikini and give him a twirl in his office."

"That's terrible."

"That's the business." She sighed and took another drag, then looked at her cigarette. "I seem to have stolen your smoke."

"That's all right.. I'm not too keen on it anyway."

Evelyn held it out to her. "Still, you should hold it so I can claim it was yours."

Gracie took the cigarette and held it. "This might be a silly question, but if there aren't going to be any long-term consequences, then what's to stop you from just going ahead and doing it?"

"No *long-term* consequences," Evelyn said. "You can't forget about the short-term. As soon as that article comes out, there would be a fire storm and I'd be right there at the center of it. I'd have to keep coming to work and have them shooting daggers at me. They might retaliate by locking me out of this trailer, or make me stand around in the heat for hours when they don't actually need me in a scene, or who knows what else. I know it would be brief in the grand scheme of things, but I'd rather just go along and keep things sailing smooth, you know?"

"I suppose," Gracie said, her voice quiet.

Evelyn looked at her. "You better not be thinking about writing the article anyway."

"What?" Gracie was genuinely surprised. "No. No, I couldn't do that without you giving me the okay. And no one would print it without names and details. I wasn't thinking about that at all."

"Then what were you thinking about?"

"You'd be willing to give me that information if you could just remove yourself from Hollywood for a few days after it goes public?"

Evelyn just stared at her.

"Even if it just gets two or three of the worst offenders out of the business, that would be something. And naming names would let other actresses know this sort of thing was going on and that it isn't right. Or, or maybe some of the guys would be scared enough to think twice about trying anything. I'm not saying one article will change the whole industry completely, but it's something I do think would be a very good thing. And if the cost of that is you have to skip town for a week, well..."

"Well?" Evelyn prompted.

"Well. We could do a second article a week or so after the first one. We'll make it a full profile of you, really in-depth, the kind of thing that lets your fans know who you are. Like they know you. So you'll be more than just that lady who said all those controversial things. That way the message gets to the public, but the messenger doesn't get killed in the process."

Evelyn looked intrigued. "That's still a pretty hellish week between the two articles. Los Angeles would be an absolute hell for me."

Gracie shrugged. "I got a car. Where do you wanna go?"

Evelyn pursed her lips and raised an eyebrow. She reached out and plucked the cigarette from Gracie's fingers and took a long drag. She blew the air out in a single solid plume and then flicked the ashes into the ashtray on her side of the divan.

"Huh," she said.

Then she looked at Gracie and smiled.

"Where should we start?"

CHAPTER FOUR

THE FIRST time Evelyn read for a producer, he invited her to his office on a Saturday so she could read some scripts he had in production. "I don't know where I need you until I see what you can do," he said. "Shame I can only put you in one movie. You'd be a star in any of them!" She was excited enough to ignore how odd it was that his secretary wasn't there; she just told herself it was Saturday and she was probably off. She arrived on time and the producer asked her if he could take a few pictures "to show around to a couple of directors." She agreed and, to his credit, he probably did show the pictures around. But not for the reasons he claimed.

She read the first script. She gave him a breathy voice, she posed against the arm of the divan, she sang. Looking back, she cringed to think how much she had acted like a trained puppet.

He was also producing a beach movie, so he had to see what she'd look like in a bikini. So if she could just pop off her sweater, he could get a couple more pictures...

"His name was Reed 'Doc' Phillips. He never cast me in a damn thing, but those photos he took got into the hands of another producer who passed it on to the director of *Chicago Canary*, and after that, my career was on its way."

Gracie bent over her pad to scribble down the story. Evelyn took a deep breath and wished she could justify lighting another cigarette.

"How many more names do you need?"

"How many more are there?"

"Oh, honey." Evelyn sighed and closed her eyes. She scratched her eyebrow with the nail of her little finger. "I could probably fill your whole paper if I just talked about rumor and whispers in the powder room. But I think we'll stick to the ones I can personally corroborate. Even so, there are plenty to fill as much space as you have."

Gracie leaned back and blew air out past her lips. "Okay. Whenever you're ready."

"Two different directors asked me to spend the weekend at their house in the Hills. I don't want to name them because both of them backed down when I politely refused, but I want people to know it happened. Those aren't the only invitations I've gotten. Of course they're not. I even accepted a few."

"You did?" Gracie seemed legitimately shocked. "I-I thought... I'm sorry, I just assumed you were fending them all off."

"I've done what I can," Evelyn said, "but you can't fight them all off. You just have to choose your battles. The ones you can actually stomach giving in to, you grin and bear it. That's when you get in cast in a big movie with a lot of buzz. That's when your name gets passed along to the right people. If you're just slapping away hands all the time, you get labeled as difficult."

Gracie said, "I think I'd prefer that label to the alternative"

"Good for you. Enjoy sacking groceries in Lake Forest."

Gracie furrowed her brow. "But you're talented. You shouldn't have to sleep your way to the top."

Evelyn laughed. "Of course I'm talented! But do you know how many talented girls there are in this town? Throw a script and you'll hit seven of them. Talent doesn't mean squat if you can't get in the room. Talent doesn't ring your telephone. The men who make the decisions care about talent, sure, but only once you get far enough in the process."

"It's still rotten."

"As rotten as a five-day banana. But you already knew all of this, *Mr. Grace*. If you didn't, you would have tried writing for your little paper under your real name. I bet you have talent, too. But if your publisher knew you were a dame, you'd still be on the household tips page back wherever you came from. You want men to see your talent, you've gotta make them stop thinking about sex. So you put on those suspenders and cut your hair. I went to bed with a couple of men I might not otherwise have given the time of day, and we both get to do what we want in life. Everybody wins. Having sex with a lousy partner is not the worst thing in the world. Thousands of women do it every day for free."

Gracie said, "So you just accept you're going to sleep with men you're not attracted to in order to keep working?"

"That's what this article is all about. Putting it out in the open. It won't change anything, but at least more people will know it's happening. Shining a light is the best way to make the cockroaches scurry."

"And you're not afraid of what they'll do to you when the article comes out?"

Evelyn said, "It might be hard to find a job for a little while. Or maybe this will be my last movie. Who knows? It has to happen sometime. But actresses have made a fuss before. I'm sure there's a silent movie starlet who tried to spread the word but no one listened."

"Then why bother?"

"Because if we say it enough times, eventually someone will hear. And eventually it will stop being news and it will just be something people know about. I don't know if that's enough. And I don't know if it will make these jackals behave themselves. But I was always taught that ignoring bad behavior was the same as condoning it. I want it on the record that I may have played the game, I may have done things I'm not proud of, but I know the difference between what's acceptable and what isn't."

Gracie said, "You know, you never answered me. Where do you want to go?"

"Chicago," Evelyn said softly, her voice catching slightly at the end of the world. She looked away from the reporter and focused on the burning tip of the cigarette. She didn't want to say more than that, not yet, not until the wheels were all in motion. She still had to get Sol to give her some time off from the picture. They could move around scenes if she made a good enough argument. "There's some... there's something I can do in Chicago to make the trip worthwhile."

"Okay. Well, I think my car can~"

There was a knock on the trailer door. Evelyn snapped out of her thoughts and looked at the clock. "Oh, goodness, we've really been talking for a while, haven't we?" They both stood up and Evelyn swept her hand through the air to disperse the smoke. "If he smells anything, just say it was you."

"Mum's the word."

She opened the door to reveal Howie on the top step. She smiled down at him, which only seemed to make him more uncomfortable.

"Sol needs me back on set?"

"If you're finished in here," he said. "He just wants to try and get one more scene in the can before we lose the light. But if you're still busy~"

Evelyn cut him off and turned back to Gracie. "You'll stick around 'til the end of the day, right?"

Gracie nodded. "Sure. I don't have anything else on my plate today."

Evelyn was surprised at the shift in the reporter. Her posture when she stood up wasn't drastically different, but now it was somehow more masculine. Her voice was deeper, too. Not too deep to draw attention, of course. She'd somehow sharpened the soft edges of the words.

"Faboo," Evelyn said and looked back at Howie. "I'll be

out in a sec, dear."

Howie nodded and spun on his heel. Evelyn closed the door and faced Gracie.

"You have to give me lessons on character work, darling. That was uncanny."

"Years of practice." Gracie said, still manlier than she had been a moment ago. "It's a survival tactic. I don't even really think about it anymore. I just do it."

"Well, it's a keen talent, and one a lot of people in this business would kill for. I barely recognize you." She went to retrieve her sunglasses. "Are you sure you can convince your editor to go through with this?"

"It'll be controversial, but that will just sell papers. That's the only thing he'll really care about when the dust settles. And when said dust is back on the ground, we have the profile. That's a double-whammy. Two straight editions of the *Merc* that people can't keep on the shelves. The paper will be the talk of the town. He'll go for it. I'm sure."

Evelyn nodded. "That's good enough for me. We can sort out the details after I'm done."

They walked out of the trailer together and headed back to the tents. Sol met them halfway with a script in his hand.

"We're doing the big chase scene, all the gods chasing the mortals back to the beach. You're going to have a little bit of a scuffle with one of the extras, is that okay?"

"That's fine, Sol, whatever you need." He started to turn away. "Uh, real quick. There's a favor I need from you. It's kind of a big favor, but I'm hoping you can swing it."

"Sure, sweetheart, whatever you need."

"I need a week."

He was still examining the script. "A week?"

"A week off."

Sol's head snapped up. "What? No, that's not possible, honey. Starting when? No, it doesn't even matter, a week is..." He turned and looked toward the hills. "We've got the Grand Hall scene coming up. The feast is scheduled for, for, for Thursday. You've got to be there for both of those."

"This is important, Sol. I just need one week. From tomorrow until next Monday."

"That's *eight days*." He looked like he was on the verge of a panic attack. "In my world, a week is seven. What's so important that you have to skip out in the middle of filming?"

Evelyn said, "It's personal. An emergency. It just came up."

"Personal?" He swept a hand over his face. "Look, I'm sorry, sweetie, I am. But if you're not on set tomorrow morning, we're going to have to recast you. We can't afford to lose a week."

"Of course you can," Gracie said.

Sol and Evelyn both looked at her. Sol said, "What do you know about my budget, pal?"

Gracie shrugged. "Nothing. And I don't really know much about movie-making in general. This isn't my beat. But I can guarantee it would take a lot more than a week to find a new actress to play Artemis."

Sol said, "I have a dozen headshots on my desk of actresses who could be here in twenty minutes."

"I don't doubt that you could. But how long would it take to reshoot everything you've already filmed with someone else in Evelyn's place? More than a week, I bet. Not to mention how expensive it would be to have the rest of the cast do it again. The more I think about it, the more it makes sense to just shuffle around a few scenes that you were probably going to shoot in a studio anyway."

Sol narrowed his eyes at her and chewed his bottom lip. He looked down at the script, looked over his shoulder at the other actors, and then looked at Evelyn.

"A week?"

"One week."

He made a sound that was somewhere between a grunt and a growl. "I'll see what we can do. For now I need you to chase a couple of dummies across the sand. Can you do that, or is your vacation starting early?"

"Might as well get it out of the way while I'm here."

Sol started to walk away, then turned back and aimed a finger at Gracie. "If you ever decide to get a new agent, don't hire this son of a bitch!"

Evelyn smirked. She waited until he was out of earshot before she leaned closer to Gracie. "That was masterful. I now fully believe you can convince your editor of any damn thing you want."

Gracie smiled bashfully.

Evelyn followed Sol across the sand, taking the opportunity to get into character. She needed to stop being Evelyn Wade and become Artemis. Usually that wasn't a very hard task, but being so open and honest with Gracie had her struggling. She felt brave, she felt like she was doing something important and necessary, but at the same time she was quaking in her historically-inaccurate sandals. What if the second article was canceled? What if the wrong people got angry and stayed that way? She didn't know if she was cut out for the daily grind.

She reached the edge of the filming village. Adora Bell was standing a few feet away with Joe and Barry, neither man disguising the fact they were ogling her curves and the amount of skin revealed by her costume. Adora threw her head back and laughed at something one of the men said, and Barry took the opportunity to brush her arm from shoulder to elbow. When Solomon shouted for them to take their places, Joe put his hand in the small of Adora's back to guide her to the place she needed to be. They had only take a few steps when his hand drifted lower to cup her ass.

Evelyn saw the girl tense. Adora turned her head toward him and she flashed a smile, swatted his arm, and said, "Don't get fresh!" in a tone that indicated she didn't really mind. But Evelyn knew she minded, and she was unsurprised when Joe kept his hand right where it was for the remainder of their walk. He only took it away when he had to go to his own mark. He gave her one final swat before he left her alone completely. Adora adjusted her costume, shook out her curls, and brushed one hand over her backside as casually as she could.

He walked past her on his way to his mark and winked, smiling exactly the way he did in all his posters. "Be careful where you're aiming those arrows, Evelyn. I don't want to get hit on accident."

"Oh it wouldn't be on accident, Joe."

He laughed and kept walking. Evelyn set her jaw and looked away. Consequences be damned, she wanted that article to come out. She wanted everyone on every set to know they were being seen and wouldn't get swept under the rug. She wanted Adora to know Evelyn wasn't the kind of woman who would just dismiss stuff like that as 'boys being boys.'

They were men, and she was going to do everything in her power to make sure they started acting like it.

***

While the actors were getting into place, Gracie resumed her apparently invisible position in the tent behind the director's canvas chair.

"You won't believe what Evelyn asked me to do," he muttered to the screenwriter next to him. Gracie knew the director was named Solomon, and she'd heard someone call the writer David. Daniel? Something equally Biblical, she was sure. "She wants a week off. Just out of the blue. Apparently some kind of emergency."

"A week?" The screenwriter flipped open a binder and started going through pages. "Can we lose Artemis for a whole week?"

Sol sighed heavily. "Of course, yes. We're going to be in the studio for the next few weeks anyway. We shoot the stuff with Joe and Adora, focus on the romance subplot, save the crowd stuff for when she gets back. But the audacity! Shifting around our entire schedule like this just because she wants to go flitting off with some new boytoy."

"Boytoy?"

"That reporter," Sol said.

The screenwriter looked over his shoulder and confirmed Gracie was standing right behind them. Before he could say anything, Sol continued.

"It's all just a test, you know. She's starting to get a little attention so she's seeing what she can get away with. She's lucky I'm nice. That I like her. She tries that shit with Huston or Wyler, you know how fast she'd be on a bus back to Kansas?" He shook his head and checked his watch. "All right, we're losing the sun. Let's get this thing back on track."

The screenwriter settled back in his own chair, facing forward, apparently deciding not to tell Sol that everything he'd said had just been overheard.

"Everyone, places!" Sol shouted. "We're rolling... and... action!"

Gracie watched as five men in sailor uniforms started running across the open area in front of them. A man who seemed to be riding a massive camera rig followed the action, then turned as a group of gods and goddesses appeared in pursuit. Evelyn was one of the pursuers, and she dropped down and nocked an arrow in anticipation of firing.

She looked amazing, the absolute epitome of a Greek goddess brought to life. It was hard for Gracie to believe this was the same person she'd just been chatting with in the trailer. The hand which had so casually plucked a cigarette from Gracie's hand released the tension on her bow and let loose the arrow. It arced across the distance between her and the men, landing in the sand near Joe Singer's feet.

Behind the chase, Barry Denton used both arms to lift an impressive-looking staff high above his head. His muscles flexed and gleamed in the sun, oiled specifically for this moment, and he held the pose for a few seconds longer than necessary to be certain they caught it. Then he brought the staff down hard on the ground in front of him. It made a quiet *poof* sound, but Gracie could almost hear the sound effect they were going to put in later.

"These heathens will not leave this island!" he bellowed as Ares. "They must not reach their vessel!"

The gods shouted a battle cry and continued their pursuit. Evelyn caught up to one of the sailors and swung her foot out, knocking his leg out from under him. He fell hard enough that it made Gracie wince. She hoped the poor man was wearing pads under his costume. Evelyn pounced onto him and pulled a blade from her belt. She brought the weapon up over her head and then swept it down across his throat.

The sailors were almost out of sight behind a rock formation. One of them stopped and took cover, raising his rifle and firing toward Evelyn. Someone behind the camera shouted "BANG!" and Evelyn rocked her body as if she had been hit. She turned slowly toward the gunman and threw her knife. It fell short by about ten feet, but the sailor flopped back as if it had been a killing blow.

Sol shouted, "Cut! That was beautiful. Let's run it again."

The entire cast reset, everyone moved back to their original positions, and they did it all again. Gracie couldn't imagine doing this sort of wash, rinse, repeat on every single section of the script. It would be like writing a paragraph, then deleting it to write it again from scratch. She shuddered at the thought even as Sol called for a third take, and then a fourth. By the time he was satisfied, every actor was panting and sweating from their repeated sprints across the sand. Gracie realized it actually looked like they had just been running for their lives.

Evelyn took a canteen from an assistant with a breathless 'thanks,' and tilted it back greedily. For a moment she was backlit by the sun, which glistened off the sweat on her skin and highlighted the muscles of her shoulders and upper arms. She looked golden and unreal and for a moment Gracie cursed the inability of a movie camera to capture the power she was seeing right now.

When Evelyn finished drinking, she swept an arm across her mouth and caught Gracie staring. "What did you think?"

"I think..."

Gracie glanced over at Sol where he had already huddled up with Joe, Barry, and the screenwriter. She looked back at Evelyn, the goddess in the flesh who was prepared to put her head on the chopping block to protect herself and others who might come after her.

"I think I have an article to write."

CHAPTER FIVE

FOR ONCE, Gracie was happy to see that Swain was still in his office when she got back. The door was open and she rapped on the wall as she leaned in.

"I need you to be here in an hour or two when I'm finished with the article."

He looked at the clock. "Is this for the fluff piece? I don't care about that. Just log it when you're done and it'll go to the printers with everything else."

"You're going to want to run your eyes over this one before it goes out, trust me."

Swain raised an eyebrow. "You bring me a scoop, Simon?"

"Just stay here until I get it written."

"I'll be here."

She went to her desk, checked her typewriter, and dropped the notepad next to the blotter. She'd practically written the entire article in her head already. All she needed to do was get it down on paper, fill in a few details, and it would be ready. She cracked her knuckles and threaded a sheet into the typewriter. She chewed her bottom lip for a moment as she debated how and where to begin. When she decided, she leaned forward and began writing.

At some point, Swain came out of his office and asked her if she'd ever stopped for lunch. She gave a non-answer and kept writing. When he passed by her desk again a half-hour later, he left a wrapped sandwich next to her pen jar.

"Thanks, boss," she said, suddenly starving. She unwrapped it and started eating with one hand, the other lifting the paper so she could proofread what she'd written so far. When the sandwich was gone, she brushed the crumbs from her face and went right back to work. A fluff piece was supposed to be three hundred words, maybe five hundred at the outside, but this was going to be easily twice that. She didn't care, and she didn't mind convincing Swain it deserved more room.

True to his word, Swain was still at his desk when she finished. She took the page and carried it into his office, slapped it down in front of him, and settled herself in the chair across from him. His eyes widened when he saw the size of it, and then his brows knit together as he picked out certain words. He sat up straighter and put on his reading glasses.

"What is this?"

"Read it."

Gracie folded her hands on her stomach and waited. She paid close attention to his expression and the emotions that crossed over his face. Confusion dominated, but there was also a touch of anger.

"This was supposed to be a fluff piece," he said when he finished.

"Something else came up."

He looked at her over the rims of his glasses. "You know we can't print any of this. Not a word. We'll be sued for libel."

"Only if it's a lie. Which the accused have to prove, which would mean calling attention to the accusations. They won't sue. She didn't make it up, Bill. I saw the behavior with my own eyes. These guys were pulling this crap right in front of a reporter, so I can only imagine what they get up to behind closed doors. Now, I could go back to my desk and write a neat little profile about the movie they're filming, which is probably going to be a disaster, or we can print this and get some people talking."

Swain worked his lips for a moment as he skimmed the article again.

"You have her approval for all of this? Even if we don't get sued, it's going to come down on her pretty damn hard."

"She's on board. With two caveats."

"Of course. What is she asking for?"

Gracie said, "One week after this runs, we do a full profile of her. You're right about her, Bill, she's going to be a huge star."

"Then it's idiotic of her to do this!"

"It's why she's the only one who can. She's too good to be shut out forever, no matter what dirty laundry she decides to air. But a big part of the recovery will be making sure people see her as more than a troublemaker. We can help her make that happen. I'll volunteer to write the profile myself."

"And the other?"

"To write the profile, I have to get to know her. We have to spend a lot of time together. And it will help if she's not in town for the bulk of the firestorm. I want to get her away from the line of fire, conduct an in-depth interview where no one can find her to yell at her or try to make her pay for telling everyone's secrets."

Swain took off his glasses and pinched the bridge of his nose. "You get her out of town. Which I assume means you want a stipend, since this will be for a story."

"A hundred oughta do it."

He laughed and shook his head. "Is this revenge for taking you off the Atwood story?"

"Atwater," Gracie corrected. "And no. Unless that would help sell you on the idea, in which case, sure."

"Teach me to do a favor for you," he muttered. "No one would've read that political nonsense, you know."

He looked at the article one more time, shook his head, and then opened one of his desk drawers. He dropped a pad down, took out a pen, and quickly scribbled down a receipt. He passed it across the desk to her. While she signed her name - Simon Grace - he turned his chair around and opened a small safe on the floor next to the filing cabinet. He took out five twenties and placed them on the desk, then took the receipt from her.

"If this thing catches fire in a bad way, we're issuing an apology and a retraction. No profile, and the name Evelyn Wade will never again appear in this publication. We serve the people of Los Angeles. Not one single movie star with a bone to pick. I told you, Hollywood is the real politics in this town, and I'm not getting on their bad side. If that means we have to pick a side, we're going to pick the one that keeps us in business. Am I understood?"

"Completely, Mr. Swain."

"Then get the hell out of here before I change my mind."

She stood up and started to leave, then turned back. "No major edits."

He waved her away. "Fine. Fine, whatever, get out."

She saluted him and left the office. She'd had a knot of anxiety and worry tightening between her shoulder blades ever since they came up with the idea. Now that it was written and out of her hands, she felt that tension starting to relax. She went to her desk and dropped into the chair so she could take a second before she left the office and figured out what she needed to do next. Probably go home and pack, and make sure the car was ready for what she was going to ask of it. They could probably make it to Chicago in three days without pushing the engine too hard. Do whatever mysterious task Evelyn had in mind there, then three days back. A solid week, during which she was supposed to be writing a profile that could be thrown into the next edition.

"Busy week," she murmured.

She pushed her hands through her hair and stood up. The article was in Swain's hands. She could either trust him to publish it unchanged or go crazy worrying about what edits he might make.

She opted for sanity and went home. She would pack a bag, get to bed early, and hope that she still had a job when she got back in a week.

Evelyn ached all over when Sol finally released the cast and crew. It wasn't immediately clear if he was punishing her for screwing up his schedule, but it seemed like she was suddenly in every scene. She fought, she ran, she was forced to cram learning her lines for new scenes in between shooting others. By the time someone finally convinced Sol that they'd lost too much light to continue shooting, everything in her ached.

She had just enough energy to get to her trailer and change out of her costume, back into her slacks and a normal button-down shirt. Her driver was waiting by the car and she poured herself into the backseat so she could catnap for the drive home. She pillowed her head on her hands, eyes open just enough to watch the streetlights sweeping by the windows.

The driver didn't try to make conversation. He never did. He seemed to be the only person in Los Angeles who didn't care about the Hollywood part of it beyond being paid to transport people from one place to another. That was why she always requested him above everyone else at the agency.

She thanked the driver when they arrived at her house. She lived in Silver Lake in an ugly little house that she'd spent too much on. She only bought it because someone who expected to be a star someday was expected to live in a place like this. There was a gate, made less imposing by a veil of flowers that tangled in its iron bars. The house was blue, which she liked, and it had a lot of windows, which meant she could either see her neighbor's roof or a lovely wall of privacy shrubs depending on what room she was in. But it was home, and it was conveniently located to the studios, and it served the purpose of impressing her guests when she deigned to invite anyone over.

But in a larger sense, it *wasn't* home. She felt like a guest on her good days, an intruder on the bad ones, and could never quite get comfortable enough in the house.

She went upstairs and stripped off her clothes as she went. There was still sand in her hair, caught in the folds of her clothes, baked into her skin. She turned on the cold water and stepped into the stall, letting the spray hit the top of her head before she leaned back so it could pelt her face. She was washing off not only the makeup, not only the whole day out in the desert, but the entire personality of Evelyn Wade. The glamorous star who posed whenever she stood still, who always had to represent the studio in the best light, who could never let her fans see her angry or tired.

When she felt like a human being again, she toweled off and walked naked and shivering into her bedroom. The only light she turned on was the lamp next to the bed. She dressed in a nightgown from her closet, a floor-length sheath with lace at the bodice and cap sleeves.

A less than reputable magazine had once theorized about what female celebrities wore to bed, and she'd made the list: "A birthday suit." The readers of that drivel would have been very, very disappointed by the matronly reality, but it made her feel cozy. She couldn't imagine anyone actually slept in the nude. It was unnatural and it would be far too cold.

She stretched out on the bed on top of the blankets, one hand on her stomach and the other at her side. Her head rolled to the side and she looked at the darkness of her closet, the barely-visible clothes hanging within. She really should be packing a bag. If "Simon Grace" was true to her word, the article would already be written and ready for printing. Hell, it might already be at the printers ready to go out. She could barely believe the things she'd said. So many stories she'd sworn to never say out loud.

She had been warned her almost immediately. On the last day of filming her first movie the female lead, Betty Childress, had taken her aside. "I've been watching you, kid, and I know where you're heading. If you really want to get there, you'll have to put up with some shit. Understand? It's call paying your dues. It's something we've all done. It's just part of the dance. Don't let nobody hurt you, and don't do anything without getting something in return. Watch out for yourself, 'cause no one else is gonna do it for you. Hear me?"

She'd said yes, and she'd followed that advice to the letter for the rest of her career. So why spill the beans now? Was it just because Gracie had looked so innocent? Those big doe eyes hiding behind her glasses, that suit, the gangly arms. She was a fairly plain woman, but a handsome man, and the elements of her male costume suited her very well. Evelyn had a feeling she would've looked odd in makeup or putting her hair up in curls. But the dress shirt, the slacks, the suspenders... yes, that was a style that fit.

If Evelyn had any regrets about hitching her wagon to this idea, it was that she hadn't read anything Gracie had written. Who knew if she really had the guts or the oomph or whatever was necessary to make a story like this really catch fire? What if Evelyn had just lit the fuse on a dud? It was enough to unsettle her stomach, thinking that she may have only succeeded in torching her own career.

And then there was her hiding place.

Cheese and crackers, what on Earth had she been thinking when she said Chicago? That was more than just a can of worms. That was a whole smashed terrarium with a few ant farms thrown in for good measure. The storm awaiting her back home was almost scarier than what she would be facing in Los Angeles if she stayed to ride out the backlash.

She sat up and put her feet back on the floor. She went to the bathroom, retrieved the Pepto, and took a swig with as much desperation as an alcoholic with a bottle of whiskey. She went into her bedroom and looked between the bed and the closet.

She knew there was no point in trying to go back to sleep. She turned on the overhead light, squinted in its brightness, and took out her medium-sized suitcase. She'd forgotten to ask what kind of car Gracie drove, so she had no idea how much room there would be for their luggage.

But a week of travel, living out of a vehicle and motel rooms, required certain amenities she couldn't be without.

She put the suitcase on her bed and set about filling it.

CHAPTER SIX

THEIR FIRST argument was the suitcases.

Gracie woke up minutes before the sun crested the hills, showered and dressed in time to greet the first glow of morning. She wet a comb and ran it through her hair then headed out to her car. She had maps in the glove compartment which she'd used to draw out what she assumed would be the best route. South was quicker and wouldn't take them through the Rockies, but it was a *lot* of desert. She didn't know how much Evelyn planned to drive, if at all, so she wanted to be sure there was enough scenery to keep her awake.

It was just after six thirty but, though the *Mercury* was usually delivered around that time, she didn't see it in any of her neighbors' driveways. Maybe there was a delay. Maybe Swain had decided to cancel that morning's edition. There were a thousand maybes, but she couldn't worry about them at the moment. She was just going to be glad no one had read the story yet. With any luck, it wouldn't be seen until they were already on the road.

She drove to Evelyn's address in Silver Lake. The gate was

open so she was able to pull up into the driveway and park in front of the entrance. The house was imposing, to say the least, and Gracie felt like she should have some kind of permit to justify her presence.

She had just gotten out of the car when the front door opened and Evelyn swept out, pausing to turn and lift two clamshell suitcases from the entry hall. She was dressed in a sleeveless button-down shirt and high-waisted white slacks. She had a neckerchief tied at her throat, and her hair was pinned back in what Gracie could only describe as a 'normal' style. There was very little flash about her outfit, which Gracie appreciated.

"You're right on time!" Evelyn said from the porch. "Help me with these, would you?"

Gracie stayed where she was. "Where do you expect we're going to put those things?"

Evelyn straightened and looked at the car. "Trunk."

"We might be able to fit one of those monstrosities in there," Gracie said. "But I have my own suitcase that has to go somewhere."

"Then we can put it in the backseat."

Gracie gestured at the suitcase. "That thing standing up in the backseat will block half the window. You can take one."

Evelyn said, "I can't just take one."

"Your choices are one bag or not going at all." She held her hands out to either side. "It's up to you, but you better decide soon. The *Mercury* is going to be dropping in driveways all over town any minute now."

Evelyn twisted her lips and she looked past Gracie at the open gate as if she could see a fleet of delivery trucks idling at the corner. Finally, with a stamp of her foot, she relaxed her shoulders and threw her hands up.

"Fine. But I'm going to need a second."

Evelyn moved the suitcases back inside and crouched down to snap open both cases. Gracie sighed and came closer, standing just inside the threshold. She watched as Evelyn pulled clothes from one case to make room. She just tossed them on the floor, a mess to clean up later. Gracie saw a gown, she saw jewelry, she saw outfits that wouldn't look out of place on a red carpet.

"Where the hell do you think we're going? Where could you possibly wear any of these outfits?"

"A star is always prepared."

Gracie said, "Well, for the next week, you're not a star. And you'll be better served by being as invisible as possible. So just bring... normal clothes. You don't even need a wardrobe for a whole week. We're bound to find a laundromat somewhere along the way."

"And if we don't?"

"Heaven forbid you have to wear something twice." She bent down and took a pair of high heels out of the suitcase. She dropped them on the pile. "Bare essentials only."

Evelyn said, "Why do I feel we have very different definitions of essentials?"

"Don't make me regret this trip before we've even started. I'm putting my neck out for you here."

"Oh *you're* putting your neck out," Evelyn snapped. Before Gracie could even register offense, Evelyn was holding up a hand. "No, no, that's not fair. You're obviously risking a lot. Forgive me. It's just that when you feel the fire all around you, it's hard to acknowledge there might be other people in there with you."

"I understand."

Evelyn moved quickly after that, emptying out enough of one suitcase to pack the essentials from the other. It wasn't pretty but at least it would fit in the trunk. She snapped it shut again and, to make up for being such a grouch, Gracie stepped forward and offered to carry it to the car for her. Evelyn managed a quiet 'thank you' and followed her out, stopping to lock the door behind her.

Even getting one of the suitcases in the trunk was a tight fit, and Gracie was forced to move her bag up into the backseat. Luckily it was small enough that it wouldn't obstruct her view. She pulled out of the driveway and waited for Evelyn to close and lock the gate. Once everything was secure, Gracie headed for the interstate.

Their trip had officially begun.

"I want you to know I'm not usually that stubborn," Evelyn said after a few minutes of silence.

"It's early," Gracie said. "It's fine."

Evelyn said, "There's a place just up the road that serves great waffles and coffee."

"You want to stop already? We literally just got on the road."

"Or another way of looking at it," Evelyn said, "is that we haven't technically started yet. We can start the clock after we've had a bite to eat."

Gracie tried to keep her irritation at bay. If she let every little thing get under her skin, it was going to be an agonizingly long week.

"So that's where you want to be when the news hits? Sitting in a crowded diner eating waffles, surrounded by members of the public?"

"We've still got to eat."

Gracie drummed her fingers on the steering wheel. "We'll get breakfast to go. I don't usually like eating in the car, but I think we can make an exception this time. I'll go in and get it. You stay in the car and try not to draw attention to yourself."

"I can be inconspicuous."

"Sure," Gracie said.

About a mile down the road, Evelyn pointed out the diner. By some stroke of luck, it didn't seem to be very busy yet. Gracie found a parking space at the far end of the lot, out of the way and not likely to be spotted by anyone passing by. Evelyn gave her some cash and, since breakfast was her idea, Gracie didn't argue.

"Scrambled eggs, waffles, very crispy bacon, sausage, grits, black coffee." She saw Gracie staring at her. "What?"

"You eat that kind of thing regularly?"

"A couple of times a week."

Gracie looked down at Evelyn's body, unable to help

herself. "Where do you keep it?"

Evelyn smirked and flipped her hair. "Acting is more than just striking a pose and looking pretty. You saw that for yourself yesterday."

"Yeah, I suppose that's true. Okay. I'll be right back."

She got out of the car and hurried across to the diner's entrance. As soon as she was out of the car, she was Simon. She walked like a man, with a long stride and arms swinging as she crossed the lot. The switch was as easy as putting on a pair of sunglasses or slipping a mask over her face before she crossed the threshold. She didn't even have to think about what voice to use once she was inside.

The counter filled the center of the room, all chrome and shine, ringed by stools that looked like tall mushrooms with red vinyl caps. Five men were stationed at various points around it, each focused on their own newspaper. She didn't think any of them were reading the *Merc*, but it was hard to be certain. She walked up to the counter and a man in a white T-shirt and apron approached her from the other side.

"Mornin'," Gracie said in Simon's voice. "Can I get two breakfasts to go?" She repeated Evelyn's order and decided to get the same for herself. The cook listened intently, nodded, and gave her the price as he turned back to the stove.

Gracie went to one of the booths and sat down to wait.

A bell chimed over the door and two men in suits came in. They were mid-conversation, the one in the lead turning to face his friend as they claimed a pair of stools.

"I'm just saying, what does she expect. You know? You ever heard of the term 'casting couch'? These girls want to be stars. They come out here and throw themselves at producers and directors to get what they want, and then suddenly they decide to change the rules. Men expect a certain exchange."

"Probably sour grapes. She put out, didn't get the job, and now she thinks she's owed something."

The cook put a bag on the counter. Gracie got up, handed over the money, and risked glancing at the men who were talking. She didn't recognize them, but that didn't mean much. The more talkative of the two caught her looking and raised an eyebrow.

"What do you think, pal? You read this stuff in the paper about what's-her-name, Evie Wade?"

"I try not to read the paper before my coffee."

The other man laughed. "Probably a wise rule. Me, I just don't bother at all." He jerked a thumb at his friend. "Why pay for my own paper when I got this fool to read it all to me anyway?"

Gracie managed a smile and took her order. She hurried back to the car and put the to-go bag on the seat between them. While she'd been gone, Evelyn had taken off the scarf which had been tied around her neck and spread it out across the upholstery. It was a small gesture and Gracie wished she had the mental space available to appreciate it.

"It's out."

Evelyn tensed. "And?"

"And nothing so far. Just a couple of loudmouth nobodies blabbering in a diner. Nothing to worry about." She started the engine and pulled out of the slot. "But it's probably a really good thing we're not sticking around any longer than we already have."

"Yeah..." Evelyn seemed to shrink, twisting to look out the window at the diner. Gracie wondered if she was saying goodbye to a place she'd once considered a safe haven. She faced forward again. "You were right."

"It's not about being right."

"Still." Evelyn cleared her throat and put her sunglasses on. "Let's get the hell out of this town."

There was no sharp line to mark the end of Los Angeles but, at the same time, no one could claim there was a gradual transition between the city and desert. One minute they were driving past rolling green lawns and palm trees in tidy little neighborhoods. The next there was nothing but scrub brush and rocky foothills with vast expanses of desert. Gracie's breakfast was on the seat between them, while Evelyn had hers on her lap. Every now and then Gracie would glance over to see the actress take a massive bite of eggs or see her tear a sausage link in two with her teeth. It was a savage affair and nothing she would have expected from someone with such a trim waist and a job with a series of revealing costumes.

Once they were on the other side of the San Gabriel Mountains, Gracie felt like they'd passed a barrier. Los Angeles and all the hellfire they'd released was on the other side of a wall. Now they were in the desert, out of reach of anyone who might want to come after them for the story.

Evelyn rolled down the windows and let the air howl into the car. After a few minutes of that, she reached down and clicked on the radio. Gracie warned her the mountains would make reception sketchy, and Evelyn searched the dial until she found a station that came in with relative clarity.

She heard a scratchy and staticky Tex Williams speak-singing for people to smoke, smoke, smoke their cigarettes, which made Gracie crave one. She kept one hand on the wheel as she used the other to take out a pack, pull one out with her lips, and fumble for the lighter on the dash. When it popped out, Evelyn took it for her and pressed the burning tip to the end.

"Thanks."

"I was hoping if I helped out, you would share."

Gracie nodded at the pack. "Help yourself. The more you take, the less there is for me to smoke. I'm trying to cut it out. Smoking one yesterday seems to've given me the itch again."

"Anything I can do to help," Evelyn said as she lit her own cigarette.

Las Vegas was something like two hundred and fifty miles away. Gracie had never been, but nothing she'd heard about the place made her very keen to check it out. She wasn't the sort to throw away her money in a casino and chorus girls only interested her from a distance. It was a nice little oasis in the desert, though, and a good place for their first pit stop. Four hours on the road would give her a good idea of what kind of road trip partner Evelyn would be while still being close enough for her to call the whole thing off and go back home.

"So I suppose if we're going to be in the car together for the next week or so, we might as well make conversation. It will be helpful for that profile you're supposed to be writing about me."

"We can hold off on that until I'm able to actually take notes," Gracie said. "We're going to stop for the night and we can talk then."

Evelyn nodded. "Where are we spending our first night?"

"Grand Junction."

"Where in the world is that?"

"Colorado. It's about five hundred miles past Vegas."

Evelyn twisted to stare at her. "That's crazy. How long will it take to get there?"

"We're stopping in Vegas first," Gracie assured her. "We'll have to, in order to gas up and grab something to eat. That will be about four hours unless we keep making good time. Then it's another seven, eight hours to Colorado."

Evelyn made a sound of disbelief. "You're going to be cross-eyed by the time we get to Chicago at that rate."

"You can always take a few shifts behind the wheel."

"I don't know how."

Gracie looked over at her. "You don't know how to drive?"

Evelyn lifted a shoulder in a shrug. "Never had to learn. Ever since I came to LA, there's been someone to drive me."

"Must be nice," Gracie said. "And that's definitely information you should have shared before we set out on a three day drive together."

Evelyn said, "I could always give it a go during one of these long, empty stretches."

"That's fine. I kind of suspected you wouldn't be much of a partner with this."

"What's that supposed to mean?"

Gracie shook her head. "Nothing."

"I pull my weight. I *will* pull my weight. And I have! Who paid for your breakfast?"

"I didn't say you weren't pulling your weight. And I appreciate you paying for the breakfast. I do, really. If I didn't say thank you, then thank you. It's just that I would have liked to know for sure if I was going to be responsible for all the driving."

Evelyn crossed her arms and looked out the window. Gracie rolled her eyes and focused on the road. Nothing but dust, desert, and the occasional metal shack for miles.

After a few more miles, Perry Como's voice was overwhelmed by a burst of static. No amount of fiddling with the dial would bring him back, and Evelyn couldn't find any alternative stations coming in clear enough to trust for an entire song. Finally she clicked the radio off entirely and slumped back against her seat with a heavy sigh.

"Well, if you don't want to do my profile, let's get yours out of the way."

"Mine?" Gracie said. "I'm not the one being interviewed."

"You're the one I spilled my secrets to. I basically put my entire career in your hands when I gave you all that dirt. I think I deserve to know a little bit about the woman to whom I've tied my fortunes."

"That..." Gracie pressed her lips together. "Okay. That does make a lot of sense. But there's really not that much to tell."

"Sweetie, you're out here pretending to be a man. There's got to be some kind of story there. It's only boring to you because you lived it."

Gracie sighed. "Fine. Uh, I always wanted to write. When I was in elementary school, I would write little stories about my friends. When I was a teenager, I joined the school paper. I enjoyed writing about the news as much as I liked writing stories, so I started to focus on that. I went to college. I got a journalism degree. And then, when I started looking for work, every editor I talked to wanted me to be an advice columnist. Either that or fashion. One of them told me to my face that no one of either gender wanted to hear a girl talk to them about war or politics.

"So I convinced the editor to publish me as Simon. He had a crush on me and I'm a little ashamed to say I exploited that. When I started applying for jobs, I thought I might as well keep the name that had gotten me that far. I didn't even really think about what would happen if anyone actually hired me. I just wanted to take gender out of the equation to see if I could have made it on my own merits. I never faked any credentials. Everything Simon Grace had, Grace Simon had earned fair and square."

"Good for you."

"I just wanted to do my job. The job I'd learned to love, the one I'd earned. I always imagined that I would wait for someone to offer me a position and I'd stand up, slap my hand down on the desk, and reveal the truth. But when Swain hired me, I... I just..." She shrugged. "There it was. Exactly what I wanted, right in front of me. I wasn't brave enough to risk that just to make a point. So I shook his hand, thanked him, and I went to work."

Evelyn whistled. "Must be hard. I get exhausted playing a character for a few minutes at a time. I can't imagine doing it all day, every day."

"It really isn't that bad. Once you've set up a base reference in someone's mind, you can let your guard down a little. Not much. But enough for it to matter. People don't analyze you as much as you think, day to day. Think about it like this... who is someone you see every day?"

"The elves from the Pretty Posse. A bunch of women who do my hair and makeup. They're usually the first people I see every day."

"Have you ever seen one of them wear a red shirt?"

Evelyn frowned. "A red shirt?"

"Or how about this: how many of them wear glasses? How many of them are blondes?"

"Uh..." Evelyn rubbed her forehead as she tried to remember. "There are two blondes, I think. A redhead. Glasses? Boy, I don't think so. I think I would have noticed..."

Gracie said, "Okay, the defining question. Keep your eyes

on the road."

Evelyn faced forward.

"Which side is my hair parted on?"

"Uh... the... th-the right side." She held up her hands as if that would help her remember. "Yeah. Yes, it's parted on the right side."

"What color are my eyes?"

"They're..." Evelyn blinked. "Huh."

Gracie said, "People don't look harder than they need to. So I establish who I am in their eyes and, once that's done, I can relax a little. Any slips I make can be explained as a bad day or maybe I'm sick or hungover or something."

"Huh," Evelyn said again. "That's pretty good advice. I might have to keep that in mind the next time I want to go somewhere incognito."

"Use it well," Gracie said.

They drove for a few more minutes in silence. There hadn't been any other cars on the road for the past few miles, and Gracie was already starting to feel the isolation. The country between California and Sin City was a whole lot of nothing. The asphalt hummed under their tires.

"What color *are* your eyes?" Evelyn asked.

Gracie looked at her, and Evelyn looked back. They held each other's gaze for what felt like way too long before Gracie finally looked back at the road. Before she turned her head she had seen the first trace of a smile tugging at the corners of Evelyn's lips.

"Blue," Evelyn said under her breath, almost like it was a secret that she'd been entrusted with. She turned to look out the window and then said 'blue' again, this time like she was locking it into her memory.

CHAPTER SEVEN

TWO HUNDRED miles and four hours without a radio was enough to test Evelyn's patience. Distance was hard to tell out here in the middle of nowhere. The car was constantly in motion, maintaining the same speed. If she picked out a landmark - scrub, stone, hill, whatever - it eventually grew in size and then swept past them. But at the same time she felt like they were just standing still. She prayed the rest of their trip was through more civilized territory or else she would go mad. Her attempt to get a biography out of her driver had been a start, but the story hadn't ended up being very long. Of course there was probably much more to be told, but Evelyn didn't know what questions to ask or how to prompt Gracie to divulge more than she already had.

Maybe Gracie was suffering the same madness. Maybe she would allow singing. Evelyn had played a singer in *Chicago Canary* and all the reviews had praised her voice. And all those performance scenes might have been the result of multiple takes over the course of a week, but that was just because of movies and perfectionist directors. She could sing well enough for the car.

They spoke at the same time.

"Do you know the words to~ oh..."

"We're~ what?"

Evelyn shook her head. "No, you go ahead."

Gracie pointed through the windscreen. "We're almost to Las Vegas. It's right up ahead."

Evelyn looked, but all she could see were the sharp-edged hills that had been on the horizon for ages. They had just taken a turn to head... east? North? She'd lost all sense of direction even though they'd been driving in a straight line for the past few hours. She leaned closer to the window and angled her head up to the sky, trying to use the sun to figure out which way they were going.

"How long do you figure until we're back in a proper town?"

"We're about ten miles out," Gracie said.

The sun came out from behind a cloud and seemed to shine a spotlight on the town, finally revealing it to Evelyn's searching eyes. The buildings popped out against the landscape and she could see it easily.

"Well, what do you know," she said. "I've actually never been."

"Really? I thought you Hollywood types spent every weekend here."

Evelyn shrugged. "Maybe the real Hollywood types. I'm usually too exhausted on the weekend to do anything but curl up on the couch with a good book."

Gracie said, "Can I quote you on that in the profile?"

"Sure. But be sure to say I only do it naked, or wearing only a robe. Something sexy and glamorous. We have to titillate the masses."

Gracie smiled. "Fine."

Their first stop was a gas station to top off the tank. Evelyn went inside to get snacks, water, and to use the ladies' room. She was proud of herself for not complaining about needing to pee during the drive, but she was aware that they'd just finished what would probably be the shortest leg of their journey, and it *had* almost been an issue. She had to hope Gracie was equally affected by bladder size and wouldn't make her beg for every pit stop.

When she finished in the restroom, she checked the newsstand next to the cash register for copies of the *Mercury*. She didn't think it was circulated much outside of Los Angeles, but one could never be too careful. While she was scanning, she became aware of the clerk staring at her. She'd put up her collar and was still wearing her sunglasses. It wasn't much of a disguise, but she didn't think she was well-known enough to need one in a place like this.

"Hot day, isn't it?" she said.

"Been hotter."

"Mm, I'm sure that's true."

She gathered some snacks and soda pops and took them to the counter, paying for them as she tried to keep her face turned away from the boy ringing her up.

"You come through here a lot?" he finally asked.

"No, can't say I do. First trip."

He furrowed his brow and counted out her change. "I could've sworn I've seen you somewhere before."

"It's probably just my hair," she said. "Everyone wants to be Lynn Bari, but no one has the face to pull it off like she does."

"Heck, ma'am, I think you do a fine job."

Evelyn grinned and waved the compliment out of the air. "Don't be fresh, young man!"

She took her purchases out to the car while he was still blushing.

Gracie was leaning against the back end of the car, arms crossed over her chest, legs stretched out in front of her and crossed at the ankles. She was still wearing her sunglasses and her hair had fallen loose over one side of her face. She looked up and Evelyn fanned her face in an exaggerated show of arousal. It was just a show to cover up the reporter really did look *extremely* sexy posed that way.

"Do you prefer root beer or orange?"

"Root beer," Gracie said.

"I had a feeling you'd say that." She handed over the bottle as she passed around to the other side of the car.

Gracie placed the bottle under a metal hook on the side of the pumps, swiping down with her other hand to knock the cap off. It clattered to the pavement and Gracie put the bottle to her lips and tilted her head back. Evelyn stopped with her hand on the door, unable to stop herself from staring. Sweat on Gracie's face, her throat working as she swallowed, her eyes closed as she enjoyed the cold soda. When she stopped to take a breath, she pressed her wrist to her lips and turned to see Evelyn staring at her.

"What?"

"Little thirsty?" Evelyn hoped any flush in her cheeks could be attributed to the sun.

"It's a hot day."

All Evelyn could come up with was, "Been hotter."

The pump clicked. Gracie removed the nozzle and went inside to pay. Evelyn got into the car and exhaled sharply, patting her cheeks and forehead with a napkin.

"Goodness, girl. You act like you've never seen a handsome man before. Woman. A handsome..." She closed her eyes and shook her head. Goodness, it was like that picture she'd seen in the funny pages. Two faces in profile or a vase? An old spinster or a bunny? It was easy to see one, then the other, and then your eyes panicked and tried to see both at once.

Gracie got back into the car. She'd bought another root beer and let it on the seat between them. Her lips were tight, her eyes cold.

"What's wrong?"

"Nothing. All set?"

"Sure."

Gracie pulled away from the pumps and got them back on the road. "I think we should find somewhere here in town to have lunch, then continue on to Grand Junction. Holler if you see anywhere that looks good."

"Lunch? I'm still full from breakfast."

"Breakfast was four hours ago."

Evelyn blinked. "Surely not." Her watch confirmed the truth, and she looked out the window at the town as if it had just exploded up around them. "How has it been four hours?"

"Lots of unchanging scenery," Gracie said. "It's hypnotic. That's why it can be dangerous for one person to do the bulk of the driving."

Evelyn flinched. "I'm willing to give it a shot~"

Gracie waved her off. "No, it's fine. I'm just..." She sighed heavily and pressed her back against the seat, arms rigid in front of her. "If you're really not hungry, we can push on. Check the map and see how many towns are between here and Grand Junction. We can stop in one of those and have a late lunch, gain some ground at the same time."

Evelyn unfolded the map and found Vegas, then trailed it north along the pen mark Gracie had made to show their route.

"Bunkerville is about, um, eighty miles north of here. Then St. George about one hundred and twenty."

"We'll aim for St. George, I think."

"Fine by me." She refolded the map and put it back in the glove compartment. They were passing the Flamingo, the hotel casino that Bugsy Segal was gambling so much on.

"They say this place is going to be a boomtown soon. Big casinos like that all over the place. That's when this will really turn into a playground, I bet."

"Uh-huh."

Evelyn glared at her. "Did I do something wrong?"

"What? No."

"Why're you so pissy, then?"

Gracie sighed and relaxed her arms a bit. "I'm sorry. I'm not angry at you. It's that..." She hooked her thumb to indicate the road behind them. "The hick at the gas station. When I went in to pay for the gas, he asked if we were traveling together."

Evelyn whistled. "Boy, if that's all it takes to get you into a snit…"

"He… suggested…" She shook her head. "Look, forget it. It doesn't matter what exactly he said. Just know that he was lewd, and offensive, and it took all the restraint I have to keep from bouncing his head off the counter."

"Gosh, Mr. Grace. You would commit that kind of violence just to protect my honor?"

Gracie shifted uncomfortably. "I didn't like the way he implied you were property, that's all." Her cheeks had become deep red. "We can just move on, okay? He's not worth the time. And I apologize if you thought I was annoyed with you."

Evelyn said, "Well, we've got a few hundred miles ahead of us. Give me some time and I'll definitely rub you the wrong way at some point."

Gracie tried to stifle a laugh, but it broke free. "I have faith in you."

Evelyn rolled down the window to let the cool wind rush inside. She didn't care too much about whatever comment the gas station clerk had made about her. Men had certainly said worse things behind her back. Hell, they'd definitely said worse things to her face. The only thing she was taking away from the situation was that Gracie had been so offended for her. She'd been willing to stand up for Evelyn's honor, and that wasn't something she was accustomed to. And considering the bridges that might be currently burning in Los Angeles, it was kind of nice having someone in her corner.

***

They cut the corner off the top of Arizona on their way to St. George. Evelyn kept track of their path on the map, or watched the scenery pass by outside the window. There still wasn't much evidence of life around them but they started picking up clear radio stations which remained static-free for long enough to hear a few songs. Gracie looked over in the middle of a Dinah Shore song and saw that Evelyn had fallen asleep, her head lolling forward and swaying with the motion of the car. She turned the radio down so the music and eventual static wouldn't disturb her.

Evelyn had soothed her irritation at the gas station clerk, but there was still a tiny spark of rage simmering at the back of her mind. She couldn't forget his smirk when he nodded out the window.

"That your beauty?"

Gracie thought he was talking about the car. "Sure is."

"Wouldn't mind taking her for a spin sometime," the clerk said. "If you're willin' to let another fella have a crack at her."

"I, uh, I don't think we'll be in town long enough for that."

"I don't need long, man." He was still staring out the window. Gracie slowly realized he was watching Evelyn, not the car. "Twenty minutes in the back. Maybe just ten, if she's a wild cat."

Gracie's ears burned red. "How much?"

"Oh, does she have an hourly rate?" He laughed at his own joke.

"For the gas, shit bird."

The clerk snapped back to his job and told her the total for the groceries and the gas. Gracie dropped the money on the counter. She gathered her things, stepped back, and hooked her foot on the edge of the wire tower displaying their selection of chips. She pulled and the whole thing collapsed with a clattering crash.

"What the hell, man!"

Gracie had fled. She was grateful the son of a bitch hadn't chased her out of the store, but regretted she hadn't done more damage. She wasn't typically the 'defending a woman's honor' type of lady but, after hearing Evelyn's account of men in Hollywood the day before, she couldn't bear to watch it play out in real time right in front of her. The clerk was just lucky he didn't have to clean up the chips while also nursing a broken nose.

"I checked."

Gracie looked over at Evelyn, who shifted in her seat and let her head fall back. Her eyes were still closed. "Sorry, what?"

Evelyn murmured quietly. Her head rolled toward her shoulder. "I already checked," Evelyn said again, louder this time. "It's okay. It's fine."

"Okay," Gracie said, holding back a smile as she faced the road again.

They were almost to St. George when Evelyn woke up. She straightened in her seat and folded her arms over her head, touching the roof. She extended her legs to press against the far end of the footwell and stretched as best she could while still sitting down. She tried to be subtle about wiping her mouth to rid her lips of any drooling she might have done while asleep.

"Where are we?"

"Just about five minutes from town," Gracie said. "Hungry yet?"

"Half-starved," Evelyn said. "I'm in the mood for a cheeseburger, maybe."

It was almost five o'clock, and Gracie was about ready to eat whatever food was served at the first restaurant they passed. Fortunately for Evelyn's cravings, the first sign she saw was for a place called Gertrude's Burgers and Shakes. Her stomach growled as she parked, and she looked around to make a note of how full the lot seemed.

"Do you think this place is safe for you to go in and eat?" she asked.

Evelyn said, "Do you mean do I think I'll be recognized? I don't know. I never really know. Sometimes I can go a whole week in Los Angeles without anyone paying any attention to me."

"Wow, a whole week?" Gracie muttered under her breath, still scanning for potential spotters.

Evelyn glared at the back of her head. "What about you? Does your little newspaper get out this far? I kind of doubt the story has made much of a splash outside of its circulation area."

Gracie shook her head. "No, it's pretty much just the greater LA area."

"Then we should be fine." She opened the door and got out. "C'mon, I need to eat."

They both took advantage of the bathroom, grateful there were multiple stalls. Afterward, when they were seated in a booth and had made their orders, Gracie took out the map and unfolded it on the table between them.

"We can make it to Grand Junction by ten or eleven o'clock tonight if we push it a little," she said. "We'll find a place to spend the night there and head back out in the morning."

"What if we can't find anywhere with vacancies?"

Gracie shrugged. "You can sleep in the backseat and I'll stretch out behind the wheel."

"Oof. No fun for you. Fingers crossed we'll find a place, then." She opened her menu. "Doesn't seem fair to you, though. Spend all day driving and then sleep in the driver's seat."

"Well, the backseat is only wide enough for one person even if we wanted to share."

Evelyn said, "Oo, sounds cozy."

Gracie made a point to ignore that comment, since she had no idea how to respond to it. A waitress came over to take their order, so Gracie put away the map.

"Since we're stationary," she said, "maybe we can lay a little groundwork for the profile. Tell me about where you came from."

She saw something pass across Evelyn's face, but it was gone too quickly for her to identify it. Evelyn swept her hands across the table as if clearing away crumbs, then linked her fingers and lifted her chin to look across the table.

"Chicago."

"Wow, that was a lot of preparation for an answer I could've guessed."

Evelyn's lips quirked slightly, whether a flinch or a smile, again Gracie couldn't guess. "Okay. I'm actually from a suburb west of Chicago called Cicero. It's a wretched little town that was basically owned by the mob for a long time. When I was seven, Al Capone and his goons killed my father while he was volunteering at a polling place."

Gracie flinched. "Holy cats. Al Capone?"

"Yeah." Evelyn picked up her water and took a sip. "Well, I don't know if Capone actually pulled the trigger or if it was one of his goons. Probably the second one. But it was madness, so I wouldn't be surprised either way. Daddy wasn't particularly political, but he wanted to make sure the election was fair. The mob, for some reason, didn't agree. So they basically terrorized the entire town to make sure things went their way."

"I'm sorry."

"Well," Evelyn said softly. "I was young. I didn't really understand what was going on. Mama kept me inside until everything quieted down."

They were quiet for a moment, during which their food was delivered by the waitress.

"Can I include that in the profile?"

"Add whatever you think is interesting," Evelyn said, salting her fries.

Gracie said, "Father killed by mobsters trying to steal an election seems pretty interesting."

"I guess."

"So what happened after that?"

"I don't know. Things kept going like normal-ish, I guess. I was seven. I didn't really know much beyond what my mother told me. One day Daddy was there, and the next day he wasn't. We moved out of our apartment because we couldn't afford it anymore and we moved to a smaller one on the ground floor. We had this big picture window in the living room that looked out on the front of the building. I used to sit there for hours watching people walk by. I made up conversations for them, and I mimicked the way they walked. When Mama would get home from work, I would tell her about everything I'd seen that day. She was my first audience."

"That's sweet."

"Yeah, I guess." Evelyn picked up the top bun of her burger and examined the contents underneath, then picked it up and took a big bite.

They ate in silence for a few minutes. Gracie watched the other customers, while Evelyn seemed more focused on everything happening outside the window.

"So that's where your love of acting began?" Gracie asked when they were both halfway through their meal.

"In a way. The real love came a little while later. My school had some dumb little play every year, and I figured I'd try out for it. I wanted to be Wendy Darling, but my teacher thought I was good enough to be Peter Pan. She wanted me to be the star of the play. I didn't understand why Wendy couldn't be the star, just because the play was named after the boy. I still don't get that, honestly. Wendy is more interesting, by far."

Gracie smiled. "I have to agree."

Evelyn looked hard at Gracie, narrowing her eyes. "You know, you kind of remind me of Peter Pan. They usually have girls play him, because of the whole 'never grown up' thing. So it's usually very fit young women with their hair cut short pretending to be boys."

"Keep your voice down," Gracie said, looking around to see if anyone might have overheard.

"Sorry." She also looked for anyone who might have taken notice. Then, before the moment could become awkward, she shifted the conversation. "You know, I noticed something on the map. We're not that far from the Grand Canyon."

"We're pretty far."

"No, look." She pulled the map back to her side of the table. She unfolded it, then folded it again to show Gracie their part of the state. "Look. See? North rim, right there."

Gracie leaned closer. "That's three hundred miles."

"Not that far, considering the whole trip."

"Pretty far. By the time we got there, it would be pitch black and we wouldn't be able to see anything anyway. It would add a whole day to our trip."

Evelyn said, "Would that be so bad?"

Gracie said, "We're pushing it as it is. Three days to Chicago, then a day there, and three days back. I need to be back in LA in time to write the profile so it can be published in the next edition. We don't have time to go running off to see some big hole in the ground.'

"Have you ever been?"

"No."

"Well, I haven't, either. But I know it's not just 'some big hole.' Everyone who has ever been says it's magnificent. It seems like a crime to be this close and not take advantage of it."

Gracie shrugged and ate a fry. "I'm sure I'll survive somehow."

"You really don't want to go see it."

"I don't care either way. And for someone who isn't doing the driving, you're being awfully cavalier about adding another four hours to my time behind the wheel. This trip isn't supposed to be about sightseeing. It's about keeping you moving and out of the spotlight for a few days while the heat dies down. And about whatever it is you've got planned in Chicago."

Evelyn's face changed, her expression becoming guarded as she averted her gaze.

"Still don't want to go into details about that, huh?"

"We can talk about it when we get there. Or not. Maybe you can spend the afternoon writing the article."

Gracie nodded slowly. Evelyn's voice was flat, and she was looking around the restaurant rather than meeting Gracie's eye. Scolding her about the driving, and then needling her about what awaited them in Chicago, seemed to have put up her walls.

"If you need your space when we get there, I'll give it to you. We're guaranteed to be sick of each other by then."

Evelyn just nodded.

The mood didn't seem conducive to further pressing about Evelyn's biography, so Gracie focused on her meal. Evelyn got up to pay before the waitress brought their check over. Gracie didn't say anything about it until they were walking back to the car.

"You don't have to pay for everything, you know. I have a stipend."

"But not an endless one," Evelyn said. "I have the money and the majority of this trip is for my benefit. It makes sense that I pay more than you do."

"As long as you think it's fair, I won't complain. But the motel room is my treat."

"I can live with that."

Back in the car, Gracie made a note of their current mileage and estimated how far it was to Grand Junction.

"We should get there around eleven. We'll shower, get some sleep, and then head out tomorrow after breakfast. Around seven, I think."

"Seven? Again?" Evelyn sighed. "We're making our own schedule here. And we have to pay for a whole night at the motel anyway. We might as well treat ourselves."

Gracie took a deep breath and let it out slowly. "Again... we have a pretty tight schedule. It's a lot farther to Chicago than it looks on a map. After today, we have twenty more hours of driving ahead of us. That's ten hours a day, which is... quite a task. But it's doable as long as we don't go off on wild eight-hour tangents or lay around wasting time."

"Sleeping in isn't 'wasting time.' It's giving your body a chance to recharge. It's vital to your health. Like you said, ten hours a day on the road is pretty daunting. You need to refresh your eyes and your brain."

"You're right. But I think we should cover as much distance as we can now, and we can relax a little tomorrow if we're in a good place. You have to earn your reward, you can't just hope you have time for it later on."

Evelyn said, "If you insist."

Gracie glanced away from the road at the same time Evelyn turned to look out the window. If she didn't know better, she would swear Evelyn wanted to delay their arrival in Chicago as much as possible.

What, or who, could be waiting there that scared her so much?

CHAPTER EIGHT

THEY DROVE into the sunset, which meant darkness seemed to sweep over the mountains ahead of them like a storm cloud. There was enough ambient light from the moon and the occasional other cars for Gracie to get glimpses of rolling hills with grass that looked dead and a few hardy bushes that probably could have survived on the Moon. There were enough small towns around now that the radio was coming in quite consistently, and they'd kept it at a low volume for the past few hundred miles.

"There's so many roads," Evelyn murmured at one point.

"What?" The interior of the car was so dark by the time they reached the state line that Gracie could have very easily forgotten Evelyn was there. She looked over at the silhouette of the woman next to her. "What did you say?"

"All these roads." It almost sounded like she was talking in her sleep again. "Out here in the middle of nowhere. There's so many roads going all over the place. And there are people on most of them. Look." She pointed at a car on another road going the opposite direction, separated from them by a wide expanse of empty scrubland. "That's someone else just off to do... whatever business they have in the west. Someone built all these roads. There's roads everywhere..."

"There sure are," Gracie said, unsure what to say. "That means there's always somewhere to go."

"Hm," Evelyn hummed. "That's nice. I really like that."

Gracie spotted a motel with its vacancy sign lit as soon as they arrived in Grand Junction. They were a little ahead of schedule, which she was grateful for. Two or three hundred miles back she'd realized the moment they entered Utah, they lost a whole hour due to time zones. They would lose another hour in Nebraska. They'd eventually get those hours back going the other way, but she couldn't help but feel like it was a major blow to her entire schedule.

Gracie checked them in at the front desk and drove to their room. The motel was shaped like a horseshoe and their room was in the middle of the right arm. They carried their bags into the room and Gracie told Evelyn she could have the first shower. Evelyn didn't waste time pretending to argue; she dropped her bag on one of the beds and took her toiletries into the bathroom, slamming the door shut behind her.

Gracie sat on the second bed and pulled the phone closer. She dialed Swain's private number and listened to it ring as the shower came on full-force on the other side of the wall.

Swain finally answered on the fifth ring. "No comment."

"It's me, Bill." Her voice slipped easily into its male timbre without her thinking about it.

His breath came out in a loud whoosh. "Well, great. Where are you? No, wait, don't tell me. I need to be able to say I don't know if anyone asks."

"What's going on?"

Another heavy exhale. "You wanted to get a rise out of people with that article? Well, you did it, kid. My phone didn't stop ringing all day. When you called just now, I assumed one of the jackals had gotten my home number. You got a lot of people steaming today, Simon, I hope you know that. Powerful people. People who can make a real stink."

"How bad is it?"

"How bad…" She heard the sound of him dropping into a chair. "One of the actors you name in the article threatened to sue. And one of the producers claimed the whole article was entirely made up just so you could use it as a smoke screen."

Gracie frowned. "A smoke screen for what?"

"They're saying that Evelyn Wade can't be reached for comment. They're saying it's peculiar that she dropped off the face of the world as soon as the article dropped. Even the director of her current project has no idea where she is."

"That's bull hockey!" Gracie said. "She asked him for the week off. I was standing right there."

"Yeah," Swain sounded uncertain about saying the next bit. "Some people think you kidnapped her."

Gracie shot to her feet. "They what?" She put her hand over her mouth and looked toward the bathroom. The water was still running, but Evelyn could still have heard her. "Tell me you're setting them straight on that, Bill."

"I'm doing what I can, but what else would I be saying if my reporter snatched a movie star and hightailed it out of town? I really only have your word that it's not what happened."

Gracie rolled her eyes. "I didn't kidnap Evelyn Wade, Bill. I'll swear on whatever you want me to that she's here willingly."

"Okay, okay. I trust you. Just do your best to not get spotted out there, huh? I don't need stories with Evelyn Wade sightings to start pouring in over the wire from Kansas or wherever."

"Thanks, Bill."

She hung up and put her head in her hands, pressing the heels into her eyes. Unbelievable. Of course everything would be settled once they got back to California, even if Evelyn's reputation was tarnished by the first article. The police couldn't do anything if the alleged kidnappee refused to press charges. But until that happened, was she technically a fugitive? Was there a chance the police would send her information out to cops around the country?

Was there a chance they'd somehow discover she wasn't who, or what, she claimed to be?

The bathroom door opened a crack and Evelyn leaned out. "Hey, is everything okay?"

"Everything's fi-fine." She stuttered when she looked up and saw that Evelyn was apparently nude. She was pressed against the door frame, only her shoulder and bicep visible. Her skin was still wet. It reflected the pale yellow light of the bathroom and made it look like she'd been gilded. Her hair was slicked back against her head, giving her the look of a femme fatale.

"You sure?" A line appeared between Evelyn's eyebrows. "You look pale."

"I'm fine. We can talk about it later." *When we're both less naked*, she added silently.

Evelyn shrugged and ducked back into the bathroom, shutting the door. Gracie looked away from the bathroom and squeezed her eyes shut, cursing herself for getting distracted. She flexed her fingers, curled them into a fist, and repeated the move three or four times until she felt the tension in her shoulders fade.

The bathroom door opened and Evelyn came out. She was only wearing a towel, the terrycloth very loosely tucked up under her arms.

"You're a little underdressed, aren't you?"

Evelyn stopped and used both hands to push her still-wet hair behind her ears. Doing that made the towel dip dangerously low.

"I thought you'd want to get in there as quick as possible. So I figured I would just get in my pajamas out here while you were in there."

"Oh. That makes sense." Gracie stood up and grabbed her bag off the foot of the bed. "I was just... I wasn't thinking."

Evelyn chuckled softly under her breath. Gracie shut the door before she could be tempted to look back. She undressed and stepped into the shower, the slick floor of it still wet from

Evelyn's shower. She twisted the cold water tap all the way on, flinching when the spray hit her in the face like a slap. She let it pelt her forehead and closed eyes for a moment, then cupped her hands under the water and splashed it up onto her cheeks, patting her fingers against her skin as she bowed her head and let the water wash over her hair and run down the length of her spine.

One day on the road and she was already potentially wanted by the police. She dreaded to think what tomorrow might bring.

***

Evelyn, having changed into her favorite silk pajamas and turned out the overhead light, laid in bed on top of the covers and stared up at the ceiling. She wanted a cigarette. She wanted to know why Gracie seemed so stressed out over what was supposed to be just a simple check-in phone call. Maybe Gracie was just the type to get stressed out easily. She had been jumpy after the gas station, too, and that hadn't seemed like anything to fuss over.

Gracie ended up spending a half hour in the bathroom. When she finally came out, she paused by the door with her hand on the wall.

"Do you want the bathroom light on?"

Evelyn lifted her head off the pillow. "Why?"

"Sometimes it helps when you're sleeping in a strange place."

"Oh. Yeah. That would be fine."

Gracie left the light on and walked to her bed. Evelyn had been too distracted by the strange question to notice what Gracie was wearing, but now she took note of the outfit: a white sleeveless shirt and white briefs. She sat on the edge of her bed and picked up the alarm clock to figure out how to set it.

Evelyn propped herself up on her elbows. "You even dress like a fella when you go to bed?"

"Yeah," Gracie said.

"Why?"

Gracie looked up at her to see if she was being series. "I don't have a heckuva lot of women's clothes. Barely any, really. Every time I go out, I have to be Simon Grace. If there's ever an occasion where someone sees Simon without his pants on, he'd have a lot of explaining to do if there was any lace or frills on 'em."

"I think if someone's looking at your unmentionables, the jig is already pretty much up. Especially in those tighty-whiteys. They don't leave much to the imagination."

Gracie shifted uncomfortably on the mattress. "Well, it helps me stay in character. I'm setting this for seven. That should give us time to get some breakfast before we head out on the road. Sound good?"

"If you insist."

Gracie set the clock and put it back on the nightstand between their beds. She moved the pillows up to make a cushion against the headboard. Then she swung her legs up and stretched out on top of the blankets. She had left the map on her mattress and she picked it up, holding it close to her face so she could examine the route. Evelyn laid back down as well, but she kept her head turned toward the other bed.

Gracie had one leg stretched all the way out, but the other was slightly bent, so Evelyn could see both. The legs were long and thin, well-muscled. She was wearing socks, white with black stripes at the top, that ended mid-calf. Her whole body was long, lean. Her breasts were small and more obvious in the tank top than they'd been in her normal clothes, but even then, it was easy to see how she could conceal them without much trouble.

"You can turn on the lamp if you need to," Evelyn said.

"No, I'm just double-checking." Gracie folded the map and put it next to the clock. "Long day ahead of us tomorrow."

"For you. I'm starting to feel like dead weight."

Gracie chuckled. "Just keep me from falling asleep and I'll consider it even."

"Deal."

They lapsed into silence. Evelyn stared at the ceiling some more. There was a crack in the corner and some water damage. They were close enough to the highway that she could hear the occasional vehicle passing by. The hum of their engines made her think again about how many roads she'd seen during their trip. Out in the middle of nowhere, no signs of civilization in any direction, but those reliable strips of grey running to all points of the map. She couldn't imagine how much time and effort had gone into making all those roads to tie the country together.

On the bed next to her, Gracie sighed and shifted onto her side. Evelyn looked over and saw that she'd apparently fallen fast asleep already. Her lips were slightly parted and her hand was loosely curled in front of her face like she was trying to play a trumpet.

She rethought her earlier comment about Gracie being a plain woman. She was handsome despite her gender. She had soft, deep-set eyes. Evelyn narrowed her eyes and tried to imagine Gracie with long, flowing hair and makeup. She would have been a knockout if she put in the effort. But even without that effort...

It was strange. Evelyn had been attracted to women, sure, but she'd always figured it was different than how she was attracted to men. With men, it was sexual. With women it was something else. Pure and innocent, sweeter. But looking at the optical illusion across the motel room, she could see how easily the lines could be blurred. The mask of Simon Grace gave her subconscious mind permission to be attracted to this person, even though she knew it was really Gracie.

"Strange," she whispered.

"What is?" Gracie murmured.

Evelyn tensed. "Nothing. Sorry. Go back to sleep."

Gracie didn't respond, didn't even move. Evelyn wondered if the question had even been fully conscious. Either way, she decided to keep any further thoughts to herself.

CHAPTER NINE

GRACIE WOKE before dawn. She'd promised Evelyn they wouldn't leave this early, and she wanted to be true to her word. When the need to use the bathroom finally became too much to ignore, she got up and moved to the bathroom as stealthily as possible. When she finished and came back, Evelyn hadn't moved an inch. She was lying on her right side, facing the window, cradling her pillow with both hands. The blankets were tangled around her legs, which looked like she'd been frozen mid-run.

The sun was starting to brighten the window. Gracie put on her pants and a shirt she didn't bother to button up, retrieved her camera, and left the motel room. She walked out to the parking lot and scanned the area for good shots. Flat-topped hills rose up on the other side of the highway. She waited until there was a lull in traffic and brought the camera up to take a few pictures. If the profile mentioned this road trip, Swain would probably want pictures to add zest.

She thought about what was waiting for her back in Los Angeles. It wasn't really a threat, since there was no way Evelyn would let them arrest her for kidnapping. But if the police took the accusation seriously, if they sent her description out over the wire to other departments... but how would they even know where they were? She doubted the Los Angeles Police would bother sending a flare up to every cop in the western United States to find her. Of course, celebrities were treated differently...

She didn't know if she was going to tell Evelyn about it. She probably deserved to know before they got back home, but there was nothing she could do to fix things at the moment. Trying to call someone to set the record straight would only risk exposing their location. It was better to just let her stay in the dark for the time being.

Gracie went back to the room to find Evelyn sitting up, the pillow in her lap, the blankets wrapped around her like a shawl. She was wearing a full pajama set, but the collar was wide enough to reveal most of one shoulder and a wide span of her upper chest. Her hair was a horror show; two tangles were fighting each other on one side of her head, and a particularly vicious twist of curls had fallen over her forehead to shade her eyes.

"I thought maybe you were out getting breakfast," Evelyn said.

"Just taking pictures."

"Of me?"

Gracie stopped and her smile faded. "No. Why would..." She shook her head. "No. Of course not. I wouldn't take pictures of you while you were asleep."

"You wouldn't be the first."

"God, that's creepy," Gracie said.

Evelyn shrugged, apparently unfazed by the revelation. "Do you want to take some now?"

"Of you?" Gracie wasn't aware she had echoed Evelyn's question. She didn't know why the offer made her uncomfortable. Or rather, she knew, but she didn't want to acknowledge it. "You're not exactly looking screen-ready right now."

"Are you saying I look unattractive?"

Gracie looked down to hide her blush, chuckling softly. "No, ma'am, not saying that at all. I think you look adorable. But there aren't a lot of people who would be willing to be photographed first thing in the morning."

"Well, I'm not most people. I don't mind people seeing me like this. It's natural. Real. I'll make you a deal. Show the photos to me when you've gotten them printed. If I don't like how they look, I'll have you burn the negatives in front of me."

"Fair enough."

Gracie brought the camera up. Evelyn flipped her hair, reached up to fluff it out of her eyes, and leaned in with her lips pursed. Gracie lowered the camera.

"Don't pose."

"I'm not posing."

Gracie said, "Yeah, you are. You're whole body changed when I put the camera up."

Evelyn said, "Well, I want to make sure you get my good side."

"That defeats the purpose, doesn't it?"

Evelyn rolled her eyes and looked away. She dropped one hand down onto the pillow and brushed the other across her face. Gracie didn't lift the camera, but she snapped three exposures. Evelyn looked toward her at the sound of the first snap, eyes wide and lips pressed together.

"What was that?"

"I just took them."

"You didn't..." She lifted her chin and raised an eyebrow. "Well. I'll have to keep my eye on you, Sneaky Simon."

Gracie smiled and sat on the edge of her bed. "I'll keep to our agreement, though. You'll see them before I show anyone else."

"I appreciate that." She scooted to the edge of her bed and put her feet on the floor. "So what's the plan for today."

"I'll let you shower first and I'll go get us something to eat. Then I'll shower if we have time." She checked her watch, nodded. "Then we drive to Denver, gas up, get lunch. And from there it's on to Lincoln. Should be something like eleven and a half hours on the road."

Evelyn shook her head. "You sure you can handle that?"

"I don't have much of a choice."

"Sure you do. Teach me how to drive."

Gracie smirked. "I don't see that happening. For one thing, we don't have the time."

"If we skip the showers and eat breakfast on the move like we did yesterday, we have enough time for you to give me the basics. Just enough that I can take a little of the weight off your shoulders."

Gracie said, "Sorry. I'm not going to let you drive my car four hours based on a couple minutes of instruction. It's special to me."

"It's *green*."

"Yeah?" Gracie wasn't sure what that had to do with anything.

Evelyn seemed taken aback. "Oh, you did that on purpose?"

"What's wrong with green?"

"Nothing. It's a fine color. Just not what I'd have chosen..." She touched her hair again. "Fine. If you won't give me a lesson, I guess I will take a shower." She started to shed her bedding to get out of bed.

"And I'll find something to eat." She stood up and retrieved her wallet. "Are you planning to eat like you did yesterday morning?"

"Yes, please."

"I don't know where you pack it all away."

Evelyn had gotten up and cocked her hip toward Gracie. "Treat me right and I'll let you look for it sometime, handsome."

Gracie ducked her head and hurried to the door. "I'll try to be back before you're out of the shower..."

"No rush."

Outside, Gracie stood in front of her car and ran her hand over the curve of its side. She moved her hand up to the centerpiece of the hood, of the whole car really: the shining chrome ornament shaped like a goddess stretching out into the wind. Most people thought it was a train at first glance, but closer inspection would reveal the unmistakable shape of breasts and a head tilted back as if savoring the breeze. Gracie ran her thumb over the tiny woman's features. The profile of a woman's body was obvious, her hair and arms combining to create a wing shape that ended in a point.

"Don't worry, baby," she whispered. "I'm not going to let her hurt you."

She smiled at herself, patted the hood, and stepped around to get into the driver's seat so she could go track down something to eat.

***

Two hours later, Grand Junction was a memory in the rearview mirror. It hadn't taken long for the gentle desert hills to explode upward and become the Rocky Mountains. Evelyn had been distracted by the water running alongside the road. It was the Colorado River, according to the map, which would continue rolling south to carve out the Grand Canyon. She ruminated on that missed opportunity for a while and, when she looked up again, the entire horizon had disappeared behind massive rocky hills. The road led directly between two particularly large cliff faces that seemed to close behind them, and suddenly all she could see were vertical walls of stone on either side of the car. The curve of the road also prevented her from seeing how far they would have to travel like this, so she looked down at the map.

"You wouldn't think mountains like this could sneak up on you."

"They do just seem to pop up, don't they?" Gracie agreed. "Pretty, though."

"I guess."

Evelyn didn't want to admit the way the mountains closed in on either side of road was making her feel claustrophobic. It wasn't normally a problem for her, but this was intense. She slipped on her sunglasses so Gracie would be less likely to notice when she closed her eyes and kept them shut. She crossed her arms over her chest, suddenly grateful Gracie had refused her offer to drive this leg of the trip. They would have gotten to this part, the mountains closing in, and they wouldn't have been able to pull over to switch seats and...

Oh god, they couldn't pull over. What if something bad happened? What if there was an emergency? Were there cars behind them? There was no way out...

"Hey, what's wrong?" Gracie asked suddenly.

"I don't know." Evelyn's voice was shaking, and her arms had constricted around her. It was more of a death grip than a hug now. "I can't breathe."

Gracie said, "You're breathing too much, actually. I think you're going to pass out. Listen. Breathe in through your nose, then hold it. Don't let it out until I get to ten, okay?"

Evelyn did as she was told. Gracie counted.

"Purse your lips. Breathe out real slow, okay? Don't breathe in. I'm going to count again, and when I get to ten, I want you to breathe in through your nose."

She did. When she got to ten, Evelyn inhaled. Her shoulders rose, improving her posture, and she held the breath again. This time she counted with Gracie and let the air out in a long, slow exhale.

"Better?"

"Mm-hmm." Evelyn flipped her hair out of her face and looked down at her lap, not willing to look out the windows yet. "Do you have a magic trick for humiliation?"

Gracie said, "There's nothing to be embarrassed about. Keep your eyes closed. I can tell you when we're in a more open stretch of road, if you'd like."

Evelyn started to argue, then nodded. "Yes please." She kept her chin down and closed her eyes. "I don't like feeling trapped."

"No one does, I reckon," Gracie said. "I'm scared of the water."

"Water?"

"Big water. Lakes are usually okay, but the ocean... I went

to the beach when I first got to California, and I almost wet myself. There were people just going out into it, and the waves would go over their heads, and they'd just... it was so big and so much more powerful than they were. I almost threw up. I ran back to my car and I haven't been back since."

"Never?"

"I don't want to see it."

"You should try the breathing thing. Works wonders."

Gracie chuckled under her breath. "We're in a bit of a more open area now. Still closed in, but the mountains are further away, if you want to try."

Evelyn opened one eye a crack and looked through her lashes. There was more sky visible, and now she could see there were actually shoulders on either side of the road where they could pull over if necessary. She lifted her head and opened her eyes fully, cautiously relaxing.

"I think I can handle it now. Thank you."

"You're welcome. If we're ever by a large body of water, you can return the favor."

"That seems like a reasonable swap."

Gracie nodded. "Then I'll consider us even."

Evelyn remained calm for the rest of the mountain pass, even when the cliffs started to close in again. She breathed deeply and closed her eyes when necessary. She only relaxed when the horizon was visible again and the mountains on the horizon were a more reasonable height.

"You didn't do much writing last night," she pointed out.

"We didn't have time," Gracie said. "Besides, my eyes wouldn't have been able to focus on the page anyway. I was shot. We'll do some when we get to Denver."

Evelyn looked in the backseat, then got up and twisted around, her knees in the seat so she could rummage in the bag behind Gracie.

"Hey, now, that's not safe! What the heck are you doing?"

Evelyn retrieved the notebook she'd seen Gracie pack, along with a pencil, and dropped back down in her seat.

"If I can't help you drive, then I can be your secretary.

You ask what you want to know, and I write down the answers so you can refer to them when you write the article."

Gracie looked at the notebook, back at the road, back to Evelyn, and then finally back to the road. "I-I guess that would be okay."

"Okay! So let's see." She tapped the lead of the pencil against her tongue and flipped the notebook to the first blank page. She read Gracie's scrawled writing. "I told you about Daddy getting killed and growing up with Mama in Cicero..." Her voice trailed off as she read what Gracie had written in the restaurant.

"*Cicero IL. Father killed by Capone? Small apt, grnd floor. Ppl watching. PPan. Evasive!*" The last word was underlined three times.

Evelyn looked at Gracie. "What's this supposed to mean? Evasive?"

"It means you gave me two lines of a biography and then started talking about the Grand Canyon. How many articles has that Al Capone story appeared in?"

"I-I don't... I don't know, one or two."

Gracie said, "I'm sorry for being so blunt. I didn't think you would ever see the notes. You can't deny you changed the subject immediately after things got personal."

"Well, I'm opening the door now." She tapped the pencil against the page and then waved it at Gracie like a wand. "What do you want to know next?"

"I don't want to talk too much about the accusations in this profile, since it's meant to separate you from them. You told me about watching people out the apartment window. Was that when you decided you wanted to be a movie star?"

"No, that's when I decided I wanted to act. I didn't want to be a movie star until I saw Jane Wyatt in *Lost Horizon*."

"Jane Wyatt..." Gracie sighed. "What a beauty."

Evelyn looked at Gracie and tried to read her profile. The way she'd said the actress' name was the same way most women said Clark Gable or Cary Grant. How far did she take her masquerade? She wanted to push a little further, but she didn't want to risk Gracie calling her evasive again. So she just made a mental note to touch on the fact again later and wrote down "*Jane Wyatt, Lost Horizon.*" She kept writing, speaking aloud as she did.

"I was twenty years old when it came out. It was the first movie I'd ever seen. I had been doing plays around Chicago for a while, but I don't think I'd really considered it as a career path until our director took us to see the movie at the Tivoli Theater. Oh, it was a palace. It was probably the most magnificent building I'd ever been in at the time. Heck, it might still be. I walked into the building and it felt like another world. I felt rich. I felt fancy. Then we went in and sat in these utterly divine seats, and the movie started playing.

"I couldn't take my eyes off of it. And then Jane Wyatt showed up and... it was like a religious experience. I don't even think I paid attention to the rest of the movie. I saw everyone in that theater staring up at the screen and I realized I could do that. I could do it, easy. So I made up my mind that I was going to make my way to Hollywood and become a big-time star. And look at me now!"

"You certainly seem to be on your way. My editor bent over backwards to get your profile. Seemed like it was a pretty big coup. Of course that was before I turned it into a tinderbox. But I think he's still happy to have your name to sell papers."

"Hopefully the studios will feel the same about pushing tickets." She looked out the window and tapped the pencil against the pad. "I know I'm not going to change anything with this article. I want to be clear about that. I'm not naïve enough to think all the bad men are going to be punished and kicked out so good people can take their place. I just wish there had been something like this waiting for me when I got to town. A big flashing warning sign so I could have opted in, eyes open, knowing how the game was played."

Gracie said, "No one warned you?"

"Oh sure, lots of women did. I think I told you that when I first brought it up. They would take me aside and tell me to avoid being alone with certain men, and taught me how to fake a laugh when I'm groped instead of going with my natural slapping instinct. But a whisper campaign only works once you're already on set, and assumes you're on the set with the right people. This will make sure everyone sees it and everyone knows. If I have to sacrifice my career to make that happen, then so be it."

Gracie's voice was soft. "That's very noble."

"Hogwash. I'm just doing the right thing. There's nothing noble about that." She cleared her throat and adjusted her fingers on the pencil. "Now, I don't want to be accused to deflecting you again so what would you like to know about next?"

"Um." Gracie furrowed her brow, clearly trying to change gears back to the interview. "You told me about being cast in *Chicago Canary*, but were the rest of your casting experiences like that?"

"No, not really. Once I had my foot in the door, I got an agent and things became much more professional. They still ask me to do a turn for them in the office, of course. And it helps if I wear something low-cut."

"And you're fine with that?"

Evelyn said, "Regardless of what this article does, it's still part of the game right now. I either have to play along or go back to Chicago auditioning for the lead in *Our Town*. But just because I play the game doesn't mean I have to let them make all the rules." She looked at Gracie, winked, and reached out to elbow her arm. "That's something you and I have in common, 'Simon.'"

Gracie smirked, nudged her back, and focused on the road.

CHAPTER TEN

WHEN THEY arrived in Denver, Evelyn spent a few extra minutes in the rest stop's bathroom to freshen up. She was impressed with herself for not begging Gracie to stop more often. There had been restaurants, shops, gas stations, places they could have pulled over for a few minutes to relieve themselves if the need got to pressing, but they'd only done that once or twice because of her. The ability to hold her water might come in handy on a movie set one day, and it was nice to know she could go the distance if necessary.

She finished in the bathroom and stepped outside, squinting in the sun. She had expected Gracie to have gone to get them something to eat, but she spotted her instead at the far end of the parking lot. She had her camera up in front of her face, aimed north, and Evelyn followed her line of sight. The sun was still high in the sky but seemed low due to the mountains. All the rocks and trees were golden and shining like they were made of diamonds. It was a shame the camera wouldn't be able to pick up all those colors, but she knew a picture would be better than memory. She was glad it would be saved.

Evelyn shifted her attention back to Gracie. She was dressed as she had been every single day of the trip: button-down shirt, suspenders, tan pants ironed so they had a crease in the front. There was enough wind that the shirt flapped around her flanks, like it was a flag tangled around its pole. Her hair was also caught up in the breeze.

Gracie finished snapping pictures and came walking back, glancing up to see Evelyn was watching her. She let the camera hang from its strap, bumping her chest, and slipped her hands into her pockets. She nodded for Evelyn to follow her when she was close, and Evelyn pivoted and matched her pace.

"They have a couple of meal options. I thought I'd let you take a look instead of making the decision for you."

"What a gentleman."

They settled on chicken sandwiches and a large bag of chips, and they were back on the road in under an hour. They had arrived early as well, and Evelyn spent the first few minutes of their drive calculating when they would get to their stop for the night.

"If we keep up at this rate, we could be there by eight o'clock. Basically early evening. We can see the sights! Go to a nightclub."

"I don't think Lincoln, Nebraska, has much of a nightlife."

Evelyn clucked her tongue. "Don't say that! You never know what these farmers get up to when the sun goes down."

Gracie rolled her eyes, but there was a smile on her face. "All right. I'll keep an eye out for any hot dancing joints when we hit the city limits."

"Attaboy," Evelyn said, slapping the seat next to her thigh.

They ate slowly over the next few miles. Evelyn continued to search for radio stations, stopping when she found something good. At first Evelyn was only humming along with each song; Tommy Dorsey and the Andrews Sisters, Frank Sinatra, Perry Como. Eventually she started singing along, quietly to give Gracie a chance to tell her she should cut it out.

When no admonishment came, she sang louder, at a full voice.

In the lull between songs, Gracie said, "I had no idea you were such a good singer."

"Eh," Evelyn said. "Good enough for a car."

"You sang in *Chicago Canary!*" Gracie pointed out.

"I was too young and dumb to say no. It's one reason I can't bear to watch that thing. God, what was I thinking? What were those critics thinking? They all must have wax in their ears."

Gracie shook her head. "I haven't seen it but, based on what I've heard the past two days, you've got nothing to be embarrassed about."

"Well, thank you. How about you?"

"Oh, no. Definitely not."

Evelyn grinned, showing her teeth. "Oh, now I have to hear it. The next song, you take the stage."

Gracie cleared her throat and shook her head, eyes locked on the road ahead. The next song played, and her shoulders slumped.

"Oh, no. I love this song."

"It's fate!"

"You set me up somehow."

Evelyn turned up the radio. "The song's slipping away from you, babe, let's hear it!"

Gracie started singing on the next line. The song was 'Swinging on a Star,' Bing Crosby at his best, his voice at its most resounding. Gracie dropped her voice and mimicked the singer almost exactly, surprising Evelyn into a loud, "Well!" before she joined in on the verse. After the first chorus, Gracie had loosened up enough that she was swaying in her seat. Her thumbs drummed on the wheel as her voice became more like Bing's, even picking up his accent.

Evelyn's voice trailed off on the last verse, and she just watched Gracie. The way she sang, the way her face changed when she smiled, that deep Bing Crosby voice coming out of her mouth... Her sleeves rolled up to show off those fine forearms, her hair fanned across her forehead...

Oh hell's bells, I'm sweet on Simon.

She snapped her mouth shut and turned her head away as if she was afraid the image of Simon Grace would get burned onto her retinas forever if she looked for one more second. She brought her hand up and pressed her curled fingers against her lips as she looked out at the rocky landscape they were speeding past.

"Hey, what's going on?" Gracie asked when the song ended, still chuckling. "I thought we were doing a duet there for a little while."

"Oh, I just, um, I forgot the words." She composed herself and looked at Gracie with a smile. "You were fantastic, though. More, um, masculine than I expected."

Gracie gestured at the radio. "It's Bing! You gotta go low with Bing."

"Sure," Evelyn muttered. "Sure, sure..."

"Hey..." Gracie looked at her again, longer this time. "You sure you're okay?"

"Yep." She managed a smile. "All aces."

Gracie didn't look convinced - Evelyn didn't blame her - but she stopped looking at her, and that was good enough for now.

***

Once Gracie started singing with the radio, she found it hard to stop. Harry Richman's 'Puttin' on the Ritz' was almost impossible not to sing when it came on, and she had a feeling she made a fool of herself with it. Luckily, but worryingly, Evelyn seemed to have given up making fun of her a few miles back. She was back to humming the songs, but she was staring out the windshield and Gracie knew she wasn't really seeing the road in front of them.

"Are you okay?" she finally asked.

Evelyn looked at her, as if surprised to be spoken to. "Uh-huh, yep. I'm okay." She gave a fake smile and then adjusted herself in her seat. "I'm just, oh, distracted, I guess."

"We're getting closer to Chicago. Is that it?"

"No, no," Evelyn said. And then, after a moment, she shrugged. "I don't know. Maybe."

Gracie said, "If all goes according to plan, we'll get there tomorrow night, and I still don't know why we're going. Now might be a nice time to fill me in."

"It would," Evelyn agreed. "But I think... I think I won't. If that's all right."

"Okay. I'll be ready when you're ready."

Evelyn nodded. "Thank you. I think I might take a nap for now, if you don't mind a little silence."

"Mind?" Gracie said, teasing. "I've been praying for some alone time since this trip started."

"You hush," Evelyn said. "And try to keep the crooning to a minimum."

"No promises. You created a monster."

Evelyn sighed heavily and slid down so she could use the rolled back of the seat as a pillow. Gracie reached down for the radio and turned the music down so it wouldn't keep her awake.

"Wake me up if you see anything pretty."

"Present company excluded?"

Evelyn smiled without opening her eyes. "Fresh."

Gracie chuckled. "Sweet dreams, Evie."

Once they left Denver, it seemed they'd also left behind any kind of elevation. She knew that Denver was right in the foothills of the Rockies, but she'd expected the landscape around the "Mile High City" to be a bit more mountainous. Plains stretched out on either side of the road for as far as Gracie could see. She let Evie sleep for an hour before nudging her awake to appreciate all the wide open spaces around them. She had twisted around in her seat to look for any indication of the mountains they'd just driven across, but everything behind them looked just as flat and barren.

"Guess we're on the other side for real now, huh?"

"Looks like it," Gracie said.

Evelyn stretched the best she could, groaning and

grunting as her bones popped. "How long 'til Lincoln?"

"About four more hours at this rate."

"Criminy," Evelyn said. "Who knew this country was so damn big?"

Gracie smiled. "How'd you get to LA the first time?"

"I took the train, like any self-respecting starlet. I wanted the whole experience, including stepping onto the platform with a bag in each hand, hat on my head, gazing around in wonder at everything. I might have looked like a damn fool, but I did it."

"Good for you."

Evelyn repositioned herself in her seat. Whatever had spooked her earlier seemed to have been dispelled by her nap, and she seemed much more at ease.

"What about you? How'd you get to California? Do you have parents? Do they know about..." She gestured at Gracie's outfit.

"I was born in California. Fillmore. You've never heard of it. Hot as hell, smelled like oranges all the time. I had parents, of course, but they died when I was a teenager. So they never knew about Simon Grace. They knew I wanted to be a writer, though."

"I bet they would've been proud."

Gracie smiled. "I hope so. Are your parents proud of you?"

She could almost see the shutters close on Evelyn's face. "Not really. Hard for a dead man to be proud of anything."

"Oh, damn it." Gracie let the smile fade off her face. "I can't believe I forgot about your father. I'm sorry."

Evelyn shook her head, then searched the seat for the notepad she'd been using earlier. She found it and took the pencil out of the glove compartment.

"No, this is part of the profile. Daddy killed, Mama bitter about it. She hated that Daddy died for something as silly as an election. She figured all the politicians were corrupt in one way or the other, so what did it matter who won. At least the guys with guns were honest about it. So she became cynical and cold. She did not like her daughter 'wasting time' playing pretend on a stage. But my teacher kept encouraging me to nurture my talent. And theater class met after school, so the more time I spent there, the less time I spent at home. It was win-win for me."

She wrote a few words in the notebook and then rested her pencil across the page.

"I came to Hollywood to get away from her. Being in the movies was part of it, sure, but it was also a way out. It didn't matter if I ever made it big as long as I wasn't in Cicero anymore." She took a deep breath and let it out slowly. "That's where we're going, like I mentioned. Cicero. My mother is still there. She's sick. I've gotten a few letters over the years but I never..." Her voice trailed off. A few seconds later, she said, "Anyway, sometimes her neighbor sends me letters. I've been told that she doesn't have long left. She isn't on death's door or anything like that. But it was implied I shouldn't dawdle."

"I'm sorry."

"I'm not sure you should be. Who knows, I might chicken out as soon as we get there."

Gracie said, "Whatever you decide. And nothing goes into the profile without your say-so."

"I appreciate that. Thank you." She brushed at her cheek, striving for casual but it was obvious she was trying to wipe away any tears that might have slipped free. She sniffled and looked down at the pad again. "Okay, uh, what's the next question?"

"You know what?" Gracie took the pad and tossed it into the backseat. "There will be plenty of time for that later. The radio might not be reliable out here in the plains, so let's take advantage of it while we can."

Evelyn smiled at her. "I think that's reasonable."

"Find us a station, then."

"You got it, Captain."

It was dark when they arrived in Lincoln, but the town

hadn't closed down for the night yet. Evelyn suggested finding somewhere to eat that also had some kind of entertainment, so Gracie drove around the town limits until she found a bar with a sign that promised the BEST BURGERS and LIVE MUSIC. It had a pretty full parking lot, so she figured it had to have something going for it.

Inside, a scarecrow in a cowboy hat three sizes too big for him was strumming a guitar on a stage for a group of ten or twelve people. The other patrons were mostly men, most of them as worn-out as their clothes. Evelyn led the way inside so Gracie saw the way every head turned in her wake to watch her go up to the bar. Even the two women present seemed transfixed, though Gracie didn't blame them. Evelyn's blouse was sleeveless again and her skirt swayed around her legs in a way that now seemed sultry and inviting.

Evelyn planted her elbows on the bar and leaned forward, wiggling her fingers. The bartender was the only person in the place who hadn't already given her his attention. Even the guitar player missed a chord and had to start the verse over. Gracie arrived at the bar seconds after a man in a thick flannel shirt moved to sit on the stool at Evelyn's side.

"Well, hello there, sweet thing."

"Good evening," Evelyn said, giving him the bare minimum. The bartender came over and Evelyn flashed her teeth in a smile. "Hi there! Can I get a couple of those 'best burgers,' no onions, please, and a big order of French fries, and two Cokes?"

The man said, "Put it on mine, Clark."

"Oh, that won't be necessary," Evelyn said quickly, already going through her purse. "My friend and I can swing it, but thank you so much."

"Friend?" He turned and finally noticed Gracie. He exhaled through his nose and turned his back on her. "Please tell me you don't mean that string bean."

Evelyn waved her finger at him like a schoolmarm. "Now, now, there's no call to be rude. I appreciate your offer, but we're just grabbing a quick bite before we mosey along."

"Why such a hurry?" the man said. "I think we can all be friends."

Gracie stepped forward. She was surprised at the anger boiling in her. She wasn't prepared for the way it made her arms tremble, or how her hands were suddenly like their own separate creatures. All she could think about was the gas station clerk in Las Vegas, hundreds of miles ago but feeling like it had only been seconds. Her hands had formed fists but she didn't remember telling them to do that.

"The lady said we're only interested in dinner, *friend*." She struggled to keep her voice from wavering.

The man twisted to look at her again. "I don't recall inviting you into the conversation."

Evelyn had turned as well. "Simon, leave it alone."

For some reason, the man found that hilarious. "Yeah, *Simon*, leave it alone." He put his hand on Evelyn's bicep and stood up. His grip didn't look particularly tight or painful, but seeing his dirty fingers on the pale skin made Gracie hear whistles in her head. "Come on, honey. Let's go have a seat in my booth and we can all get to know each other. You never know, you might really like us."

Evelyn had tensed and hunched the shoulder of the arm he was gripping. "You know what, I think we're just going to find somewhere else to get dinner..."

"Your dinners are already on my tab."

"I didn't ask you to do that, sir."

A few others in the bar laughed at the 'sir.' The man's face darkened, probably because of the laughter, and Gracie saw something switch off in his face. The whistles in her head turned to alarms.

She was standing next to a table. There was a little dish still half-full of pretzels. Gracie took one step toward it, held the bowl with one hand as she fired a series of rapid punches into the snacks within. The pretzels were smashed into shards and dust. Gracie pivoted on the ball of her foot and swung out with her free hand, slapping the local on his shoulder with the backs of her fingers. He turned to look at her and she threw the bowl at his head. The remnants of the pretzels hit him full in the face, temporarily blinding him with clouds of dust and tiny shards.

"What in the tarnation," he spluttered. He let go of Evelyn's arm and fell back against the bar. He clapped one hand over his eyes, teeth bared in anger.

Evelyn jumped down off the stool and grabbed Gracie's arm. "*Simon,*" she said through gritted teeth. "*Let's go.*"

Gracie pulled her arm free and advanced on the local. She pulled his hand away from his face, then punched him as hard as she could. She heard gasps, shouting, and she punched him again. His arm shot out and grabbed the collar of her shirt, holding her in place as he brought his other fist around to club her on the side of the head. Stars danced in Gracie's vision and her legs went rubber, but the man held her upright by the collar of her shirt. He clubbed her again, then again. On the third blow, she was on her knees.

Someone shouted, "Hank, you're even! All right? Call it a draw! Don't you dare kill someone in my bar, gah'dammit. Just call it even and let it go."

Gracie could barely follow what the man was saying. A moment later, she was shoved backward and went sprawling, too confused to stop her fall. Someone wrapped their arms around her, helped her upright. She smelled shampoo and skin cream and knew it was Evelyn, so she didn't fight.

"Just get the hell outta here, 'fore I change my mind. Lousy dirty fightin' son of a bitch..."

Gracie managed to get her arm around Evelyn's waist and let herself be guided out of the bar. They were most of the way across the parking lot before she realized Evelyn's hand was digging around in the pocket of her slacks. She frowned and looked down. "What're you doing?"

"I'm trying to find your keys."

"You can't drive my car."

"At the moment, neither can you. I'll take my chances.

We've gotta get out of here before that jerk comes out and sees what we're driving. We don't want to wake up tomorrow to find him waiting outside the motel for us."

"Hope you weren't very hungry," Evelyn grunted.

"Their burger's're prob'bly lousy anyway..."

CHAPTER ELEVEN

GRACIE'S HEAD had mostly cleared by the time they found a motel and Evelyn checked them in. She was a surprisingly good driver, only fumbling a little with the gearshift. There was a fried chicken restaurant just across the road from the motel so, once Evelyn made sure Gracie got into their room without any problem, she walked across to get them something to eat. While she was gone, Gracie went to the bathroom and examined her face in the mirror. No actual broken skin or blood, which was a relief. There might be bruising, a little swelling, but that would go away quickly enough. And her head was already much clearer, making her think her earlier discombobulation was due more to emotions than getting her bell rung.

Evelyn came back with the food and tossed a bag onto one of the beds, then sat down at the desk with her back to the room to open her own. Gracie looked at the bag, looked at Evelyn, and waited for her to say something. Eventually, Gracie stepped away from the mirror and broke the silence herself.

"What, you're mad at me?"

Evelyn huffed and took a bite of her food.

"Seriously? You're not even going to say thank you?"

"Thank you?" Evelyn spun in her seat. "You want me to be grateful for, for that...? If it wasn't for you, we could've been having a nice meal, listening to some music..."

"You're blaming *me* for that? I didn't hallucinate that asshole grabbing your arm, right?"

Evelyn rolled her eyes and turned away from her again. "Oh, please. Do you honestly think that's the first jackass who's grabbed my arm in a bar?"

"That doesn't make it okay."

"Of course it doesn't," Evelyn sighed. "But if I started a fight every single time, I'd never go out anywhere."

Gracie said, "It wasn't right. You're not his property to just... to just manhandle!"

Evelyn stood and stormed toward her, raising her voice to a yell. "And I'm not *your* property to defend! I can stand up for myself!"

"Can you? You waited for me to come along to write the article, you waited for me to offer you a ride to go home and confront your mother. Maybe you need someone to hide behind, and I'm just a convenient punching bag."

"That's not fair," Evelyn said. "I'm putting my career on the line."

"So am I. Maybe I wouldn't have been so quick if I'd known how much you liked the attention."

Evelyn rocked back on her heels, eyes wide. "How dare you. *How dare you?* If you really were a man, I'd... I'd..."

She looked like a child on the verge of a tantrum. Gracie stepped forward, further closing the distance between them. "You'd what? What would you do?"

Evelyn stared hard at her for a moment, then pulled back and slapped her hard across the face.

The crack of contact seemed to take all the sound out of the room. Gracie could no longer hear the hum of the air conditioner, voices from other rooms seeping through the walls, or the hum of the light bulbs. The look of rage on

Evelyn's face transformed into shock.

"Oh my god."

"What the hell," Gracie mumbled.

"Oh my god!" Evelyn lurched forward and cupped Gracie's right cheek with her hand, letting her right hand hover over the rapidly-growing sting on her left cheek. "I slapped you."

"You slapped me," Gracie repeated.

"I *hit* you," Evelyn said, her voice suddenly sharp. "I'm so sorry. I'm so sorry." She stepped in and pressed her lips to Gracie's cheek. "I'm sorry, Gracie." She kissed again, but Gracie had shifted her weight just enough that the kiss landed on the corner of her mouth.

This time the sudden stillness was shorter, and it ended with Evelyn moving her head to properly press her mouth against Gracie's. It was an awkward kiss; Gracie wasn't prepared and only parted her lips after Evelyn had already pulled away. Evelyn moved her hands so they were on the scruff at the back of Gracie's neck and she curled her fingers so the nails rasped against the whiskers. Gracie took a deep breath, let it out, and then they were kissing again, properly this time, with Gracie's tongue slipping across Evelyn's top lip as Evelyn walked her back toward the wall.

The door rattled when Gracie's shoulders hit it, which startled her. Evelyn's hands were still on the back of her head. Gracie's hands were held out to either side, her thumbs tucked against the palms, fingers curled, and she had no idea what to do with them. Her tongue was in Evelyn's mouth, and then Evelyn was gently sucking on it, and Gracie was glad the door was behind her because otherwise she would've fallen over.

Evelyn ended the kiss with a trio of small pecks on the corners of Gracie's mouth, but she didn't step back.

"Do you want me to go?"

"What? I don't... what?" Gracie was blinking, still wondering why her mouth was unoccupied. "N-no. Why? Where?"

"I don't know. But right now you're stiffer than a reverend in a brothel." A blush rose in her cheeks. "I didn't mean... I-I meant you're... you're tense. I didn't ask. If you'd prefer I leave~"

"I want you to do it again."

Evelyn didn't hesitate. This time Gracie didn't bother thinking about what to do with her hands, and they simply gravitated to Evelyn's hips on their own. It was as if they'd been itching to get there all along. She pulled Evelyn closer, and Evelyn's hands met on the back of Gracie's head and moved up to where she could grab a handful of hair. Gracie moaned approvingly. Evelyn pressed her hips forward, rubbing herself against Gracie's body in a very appealing manner.

Neither of them could catch their breath when the kiss ended. Gracie's eyes were closed but she could tell Evelyn was staring hard at her. The room felt like it was a thousand degrees, even though she still felt the arctic blast from the vents on her.

"What..." She swallowed the next words. She pressed her lips together, and then forced herself to say them. "What else would you do to me if I was a man?"

"I can show you."

"Show me."

Evelyn moved her hands down, brushing them over Gracie's flat chest, over her stomach, finally hooking them on her belt. She bit her bottom lip as she worked out how to undo the buckle, then looked up. Gracie had been watching her hands but met her gaze.

"Still okay?"

"Yeah, uh-huh."

Evelyn swept her tongue over her bottom lip and sank to her knees. She unfastened the belt, unbuttoned Gracie's pants, and then tugged down the zipper. Gracie was again wearing Y-front men's briefs. Evelyn took Gracie's right hand and moved it so the heel was pressing against the cotton of her underwear. She gently uncurled Gracie's thumb until it was sticking straight out, and then she pressed a gentle kiss to the tip.

"Oh sweet Jesus," Gracie moaned. She leaned hard against the door and moved her free hand to the back of Evelyn's head. Evelyn parted her lips enough to take most of the thumb into her mouth, closed them, and pulled back slowly. She circled the tip with her tongue and then kissed down its length.

Gracie moved her hips forward, which pressed her hand against her mound, which sent electric signals throughout her lower body and threatened the stability of her knees. She wanted to close her eyes but she also wanted to see every second of what Evelyn was doing. Her tongue circled and teased the tip of her thumb, and the feeling of her lips moving over the knuckle made her gasp every time. Now there were smears of bright red lipstick from the knuckle to the nail. Evelyn's lipstick, smeared on her skin, staining her.

The next time Evelyn's mouth wasn't on her, Gracie turned her hand and tucked her thumb away. Evelyn looked confused until Gracie extended her first two fingers instead. Evelyn smiled and reached up to stroke them.

"Oh, it got bigger..."

Gracie tried to laugh but it came out wheezy and strange. Her face was burning. It was hard for her to catch her breath. Her hair had fallen forward over her right eye, and it was sticking to the sweat that had started to build up on her brow. She knew what it looked like, what Evelyn was mimicking, but that wasn't what was driving her crazy. It was her hand against her underwear, it was the warmth of Evelyn's mouth and the slickness of her tongue, the direct line from Evelyn's mouth to her sex. She used these fingers to touch herself, and now Evelyn was kissing them and looking up at her and sliding them back into her mouth and—

"Fuck," she groaned and threw her head back so quickly that it banged off the door.

Evelyn stood up and slipped her hand into Gracie's, squeezing it. A handshake pinned between their waists, and Gracie shuddered and forced her eyes open.

"What would you do to me?" Evelyn asked, wide-eyed and flushed. There was a bead of spit on her bottom lip. "If you were a man?"

Gracie didn't give her brain a chance to consider the possibilities. She grabbed Evelyn by the shoulders and shoved her back toward the bed. Evelyn went where she was directed and even allowed Gracie to spin her around. She bent over the side of the mattress and looked over her shoulder with a smile. Gracie didn't see it because she was too distracted by pulling up Evelyn's skirt and slip, exposing her pale pink thighs.

Evelyn stretched her arms out, smoothed her hands over the blanket, and arched her back. Gracie reached between Evelyn's legs with the hand Evelyn had been using, stroking with her first two fingers. She felt wetness and her cheeks burned, more sweat dripped down the side of her face, and with a grunt, she rocked her hips forward and pushed the fingers inside.

"Oh, fuck!" Evelyn shouted, dropping her face onto the blanket.

"You like that?" Gracie was surprised by the aggression in her voice, but she assumed all the frustrations of the trip and every minor irritation Evelyn had caused her were boiling over now. She put her hips and shoulder into each thrust, the bed creaking under them but the sound was almost drowned out by Evelyn's cries. Gracie grabbed Evelyn's hip with her other hand to hold her in place and thrust harder, moving faster, droplets of sweat falling off and landing on the back of Evelyn's dress.

Gracie's head was swimming, so it took her a few seconds to finally realize Evelyn had gone limp. Her head was pillowed by one arm, her face turned to the side but obscured by her hair. Gracie stopped thrusting but kept her hand where it was, her extended fingers resting against the wet and twitching skin between Evelyn's legs.

"Are you okay?"

Evelyn nodded but turned her head away, pressing her

head into the blanket. Gracie realized she was crying and went tense, on the verge of panic as she pulled her hand away.

"Oh no. Did I hurt you? God, I didn't mean to be so rough..."

"It's not you," Evelyn said. "You were perfect. You were absolutely perfect."

Gracie relaxed and put a hand on Evelyn's shoulder and stroked it down to her hip. "O-okay."

Evelyn pushed herself up on her elbows, shifted to one side, and climbed up onto the bed. She curled up against herself, knees drawn to her chest. She patted the mattress next to her, and Gracie joined her. They lay on their sides, staring at each other, neither saying anything. Evelyn brought her hand up and gently brushed two fingers over Gracie's cheek.

"Does it still hurt?"

"No," Gracie said, and it was the truth. Her entire body was so overcharged that there were only a few parts her brain seemed aware of, and the cheek was nowhere on the list.

Evelyn said, "I have to admit... I don't know what the hell happens now."

Gracie nodded.

It was a damn good question.

What happened next, at least in the short term, was sleep. Evelyn didn't know which one of them succumbed first but, when she opened her eyes some time later, she was looking straight at Gracie's face. Evelyn blinked and stared for a few seconds to see if Gracie would move or show signs of being awake, but her features remained slack. Evelyn eased away from the other woman, grateful they hadn't fallen asleep tangled in one way or another. She eased off the edge of the bed and looked down at the tangled sheets and blankets before focusing on the woman laying on top of them.

Gracie was still completely dressed. Her belt and trousers were undone, and her shirt rumpled, but otherwise she looked like she'd just come in from the car and collapsed into bed. Evelyn stared at her long enough that she became worried

Gracie would wake up and catch her in the act, so she stepped away from the bed to turn off the overhead light. The lamp between the two beds would be enough if Gracie woke up during the night and needed to see.

Once she was undressed down to her slip, Evelyn knelt by the foot of the bed and untied Gracie's shoes. She slipped one off, looked to see if it had woken her up, then took off the other. Once that was done she crawled back onto the mattress and stretched out next to Gracie, holding her breath, still watching to see if she would wake up. Her eyelids didn't even flutter.

Was that a good thing? Evelyn furrowed her brow, suddenly a little worried. That fool had hit Gracie in the head a couple of times. She might have gotten a concussion. What if she wasn't waking up because she *couldn't* wake up?

Evelyn blew in Gracie's face.

Gracie wrinkled her nose and brought a hand up to swat at the disturbance. "Wuh'rer yo'oing," she slurred without opening her eyes.

"Do you have a concussion?"

"I'm sleeping," Gracie said.

They were both whispering, though Evelyn didn't know why. "I just heard somewhere that if you have a head injury, you should have someone~"

"Evelyn." Gracie's voice was a little louder now, though she still hadn't opened her eyes. "I have to drive eight hours tomorrow. I'm fine. Please let me sleep."

"If you're sure..."

"Mm-hmm."

Gracie put her hand on Evelyn's upper thigh and left it there. Evelyn looked down at it, then reciprocated by putting her hand on Gracie's hip.

She meant to stay awake to watch her, just to be sure everything was okay, but she lost the battle quickly. When she woke again a little later, Gracie had moved closer and had a leg hooked over Evelyn's waist. She was gently thrusting, and Evelyn's brain fog cleared enough that she angled her body to make it easier for her. Gracie made a quiet noise in her throat and rolled on top of her. Evelyn put her hands on Gracie's hips and pulled her close, listening to the soft grunts coming from on top of her. Gracie suddenly stopped mid-thrust, a moan dying in her throat, and Evelyn felt her stiffen.

"It's okay," Evelyn whispered. "It's all right. Don't stop."

"I'm... I-I wasn't..."

"Please don't stop."

Gracie hesitated but then began to move again. She raised one arm and braced it against the headboard, pressed her knees down into the mattress, and thrust forward again with determination that made Evelyn cry out in surprise. She moved one hand to Gracie's shoulder, reaching down with her other to pull up her slip so that Gracie was pressing against bare skin. She ran her hand over the material of Gracie's slacks and started trying to tug them out of the way.

"I don't have anything," Gracie said, half-whisper and half-growl. "I don't want to use my hand again, but I-I don't..."

"It's okay. I just want to feel you."

Gracie helped her after that, tugging her slacks and briefs down to mid-thigh. Evelyn whimpered in anticipation and buried her face in Gracie's shirt as they began moving against each other. The bed groaned worryingly, and the headboard knocked the wall each time Gracie thrust forward. Neither of them cared particularly much about the ruckus they were making.

Gracie went stiff when she came, clinging to Evelyn with desperation, her whole body trembling. Evelyn pressed kisses to whatever part of Gracie was available to her, only rarely kissing skin. They both caught their breath and became aware of the sweat on their faces.

"Did you finish?" Gracie whispered.

"I don't have to," Evelyn said without judgement. "Are you okay?"

Gracie sat up and pushed her hair out of her face. "I'll be okay when you finish."

Evelyn smiled and shook her head. "It's okay."

"It's not."

Before Evelyn could argue further, Gracie was scooting down her body. Evelyn retreated toward the headboard, bringing her legs up. Gracie kissed her stomach, then her thighs, and then put her head between Evelyn's legs and kissed her there. Evelyn croaked a sound and pressed the heel of her hand against her lips, eyebrows raised. She bit down on her own hand, mimicked the movements of Gracie's tongue with her own, and wrapped her legs around Gracie's head to draw her in.

When Evelyn finished, her fingers were laced together in the back of Gracie's head, the hairs poking like weeds, and she pushed Gracie down with enough strength to risk suffocation. She reached the crest of her orgasm silently, then rode out the plummet with a shaky groan that transformed into the words, "O-o-oh, Mr. Grace..."

She couldn't catch her breath, but she felt Gracie kissing her breasts, moving aside the slip to kiss and suck her nipple before nuzzling her cleavage. She finally moved higher and rested her cheek against Evelyn's throat.

"That shouldn't have happened."

Gracie's voice was too quiet for Evelyn to analyze the tone, so instead she just kissed her hair and stroked her hands over Gracie's back.

"Well, it can keep on happening as much as it needs to until it feels right."

She fell asleep waiting for Gracie to respond to that so, if she did, she never heard it.

CHAPTER TWELVE

GRACIE WAS already out of bed and pulling on a fresh pair of trousers when Evelyn woke up. The sun was shining in through the window, rays of yellow light so bright they almost looked solid. She knew Evelyn was awake because the rhythm of her breathing changed, and then the mattress shifted under her weight with a groan. They might have done some real damage to the springs during the night, and her cheeks burned at the memory of it.

She glanced back to see Evelyn watching her. "I was thinking we could just have dinner for breakfast, if that's all right. It would save us time on the road. But if you're not feeling up to cold chicken, then we can find somewhere–"

"Cold chicken is fine," Evelyn said.

"Okay." Gracie tucked her shirt into her pants and tightened the belt. "I was, um, thinking we could get a real early start. If we leave by six and don't lollygag in Iowa City, we can get to Chicago by early afternoon. It would give us a little extra time to do, um, whatever needs to be done."

"Sounds good."

"Good." Gracie turned back toward the bed. Evelyn

looked like she wanted to say something, so Gracie spoke before she could. "You have time to take a shower and get freshened up, if you'd like."

Evelyn looked at the bathroom, then at Gracie, then nodded. "All right." She got out of bed and rearranged her slip. Gracie looked away, though she got a peek at some curves that should've remained covered up. She kept her eyes averted until she heard the bathroom door close, and only then did she drop down onto the mattress and clap a hand over her face.

What in the hell had she been thinking? She should have stopped herself, should have stopped Evelyn, should have run as fast and as far as she could. The second she realized what was happening, she should have gone out to the car and camped out in the backseat. But she knew that would never have happened. The second she felt Evelyn's lips on hers, she was lost. Everything that came afterward - the touching, that thing with her fucking hand, every moan and grunt and whimper - had just been another anchor dragging her under.

Now all she could do was try and justify it. Was it really so bad, what they'd done? Sure, in some states it might have been illegal, but she'd never held to those laws. Evelyn knew exactly who she was in bed with, had even confirmed that in the middle of the act. So at the very least there was no guilt over lying. Evelyn knew without a doubt that it had been a woman named Grace Simon doing those things to her, and she'd been extremely willing to go through with it.

But agreeing to something at night, in the heat of the moment, was so much different than accepting it in the light of day. It would be awkward in any situation, but now they were supposed to spend the rest of the day in the car together. It was going to be absolute torture.

The shower shut off and Gracie stood up, fastening the buttons of her shirt. The bathroom door opened, and Evelyn strutted out wearing nothing but what she was born with. Her hair was gathered up in a towel but she was otherwise starkers, all wet curves and pink skin. Her nipples were hard and standing up proudly.

Gracie couldn't help but track her across the room. Evelyn opened her suitcase, casually plucked out a few things, then spun on the ball of her foot and walked back to the bathroom with the clothes draped over her shoulder. She looked back just as she crossed the threshold, one hand on the door.

"Care to join me?"

Gracie clenched her teeth, ignoring the dimples over Evelyn's ass. She shook her head. "No."

Evelyn's face twitched with her reaction, then settled back into an indifferent mask. She shrugged and continued inside.

"Be out in a minute."

The door shut.

Gracie let her legs give out and fell back onto the bed, covering her face with both hands. It was just over five hundred miles to Chicago... and then two thousand miles back to Los Angeles. They technically weren't even at the halfway point yet. Gracie moaned into her hands.

She had no idea how she was going to get through the rest of this damn trip.

***

Gracie had a very bad feeling the moment she stepped outside and looked at the sky. They were only ten minutes outside of Lincoln before the clouds opened up and proved her feeling was correct. She and Evelyn had been driving in silence before the first drops of rain splattered on the windshield, though she could tell Evelyn was itching for a chance to talk. Up ahead Gracie could see sheets of it sweeping across the highway. Flashes of lightning occasionally lit up the unnaturally dark countryside.

Evelyn sat up straighter as they drove into the storm, twisting to see if any of the windows showed anything different.

"Is this safe?" she finally asked.

"We'll probably just drive right through it," Gracie said.

Evelyn looked at her, skeptical, but Gracie kept her eyes

on the road. Another few minutes passed and the intensity of the storm had only grown. There wasn't much distinct thunder, but every minute or so, the whole ground seemed to shake under the tires. The windshield was completely awash by that point, and the wipers weren't doing much at all to help visibility.

"Gracie." A note of sincere worry had crept into Evelyn's voice.

"Yeah," Gracie said, agreeing without acknowledging they were in trouble. She leaned forward a bit and got the lay of the land thanks to a flash of lightning. "We're on a straightaway right now. Keep an eye out for an off-ramp. And fasten your safety belt."

Evelyn did as she was told. Gracie slowed to a crawl, alert for signs of any looming shapes in the deluge that might be other cars on the road. Thunder crashed right above them and Evelyn jumped, hands going over her head before dropping back down. She saw her hands were shaking and realized the car was even more enclosed than it had been in the mountains. She couldn't see past the hood. There was no road, nothing on either side, just a curtain of water, endless water, cascading down the windows~

"No no no no no," Evelyn murmured.

"You're okay," Gracie said calmly. "Do you need to close your eyes?"

Evelyn swallowed the lump in her throat. "I h-have to watch for the, the, um, thing."

"Just breathe like I showed you."

They'd been driving mostly blind for almost fifteen minutes when Evelyn suddenly pointed. "There! An off-ramp!"

Gracie saw it, too. She pulled off the highway onto a side road, pulling off into a wide parking lot that hosted some kind of large white building. She got as close as she could to the barn-like structure, hoping it would provide some kind of protection against the wind and the heaviest rain. Cutting off the engine made the interior of the car become deathly silent, leaving only the sound of rain battering the roof. It sounded like they were in a tin can being held under a tap.

"Damn. This is~" The rest of the sentence died in her throat when she saw Evelyn, pale and trembling in the seat beside her. "Are you okay?"

"Is it going to be a tornado? Could there be a tornado?"

"No," Gracie said, though she honestly had no idea. "It's not the right time of year for that."

"Are you sure?"

She absolutely wasn't. "Positive. It's all right. Just try to breathe, okay? It's going to pass soon." She reached out and took Evelyn's hand. "Look at me. Hey. Look at me."

Evelyn stopped scanning all the windows and locked eyes with Gracie.

"It's just a thunderstorm. We were in a little bit of danger when we were still on the road, but we're safe now. Okay? We just have to sit here and let it pass."

"And no tornado?"

"No tornado."

Evelyn closed her eyes and took a deep breath. She squeezed Gracie's hand and then let it go. "Thank you."

"Sure."

Gracie brought Evelyn's hand up and kissed the fingers. Evelyn tensed, but didn't say anything.

They sat silently, watching the rain wash down the windshield like it was hypnotizing them.

"Look," Gracie finally said, "I'm sorry if this morning was... w-weird for you. It was weird for me, too. I don't really... ever... do..."

"Do what?"

Gracie gave her a half-smile and shrugged. "It's not like I can just blurt out my whole deal to anyone I'm interested in. How am I gonna meet anyone? What am I going to do, go out to a queer club?"

"I'm sure they have clubs for people like you. I mean, people who dress... the way you do."

"Sure. And I could go to those places a hundred times

with no problems, but all it would take is one raid at the wrong time, or one person seeing me walk out with my arm around a woman..."

Evelyn said, "So you've never...?"

"I have," Gracie said, blushing. "A few times. Once or twice." She rubbed the pad of her thumb against her fingertips and chewed her bottom lip. "There have been times I've been close to women who think I'm a man, women I'm attracted to, and it's taken everything in my power to not do anything. To not s-say something. Last night felt like a failure. Even though you were the one who kissed me first. We fell asleep, and when I woke up and saw you next to me, I just... I went... a-all my instincts just... wanted you. So I took you."

"I didn't mind," Evelyn said softly. "I thought it was amazing, really. And since you were honest with me, I want you to know..."

Her voice trailed off and she looked out the windshield. She was silent for so long that Gracie thought she'd forgotten what she was going to say, or had simply changed her mind about saying it.

"You're the first person I've chosen."

"Chosen how?"

Evelyn looked at her like a teacher who was disappointed in a prized student. "I told you I was twenty when I decided to be an actor. And I told you how the whole process involved... favors. The first person I ever had sex with was someone who said it was the cost of getting in the door. After that, sex was just, um... just, um, something I did for work."

Gracie was stunned. "That's horrible. I'm sorry. I didn't know."

"You don't have anything to be sorry for. Last night wasn't what I expected when we met, but it was definitely something I wanted. And there are no regrets, if that's something you're worried about."

"You're sure?"

"I'm positive."

She slid her hand across the seat and turned it palm-up,

inviting Gracie to take it again. Gracie looked at it, then looked up into Evelyn's eyes.

"Come here."

"What?"

Gracie moved the bench seat back a little, putting more room between her and the steering wheel without looking away from Evelyn. She patted her lap.

"Come here," she said again.

Evelyn looked at the windows of the car, which were still veiled by rain. She started to get up and was pulled back by the safety belt. She swore under her breath, and Gracie laughed quietly as she fiddled with the buckle. It finally came free, and Evelyn scooted across the seat toward her.

"Straddle my lap," Gracie said. "Sit facing me."

"Okay..."

Evelyn's voice shook as she threw one leg across Gracie's lap. Gracie put her hands on Evelyn's hips to guide her, gently lowering her until she was sitting down. She leaned back slightly to use the steering wheel as a backrest. Gracie kept her hands on Evelyn's waist but she didn't keep them still. She rubbed in wide circles, drifting up to her flanks and down to her thighs, sometimes moving around to cup her buttocks through her skirt.

"I liked seeing you naked this morning," Gracie said.

Evelyn beamed. "Yeah? I was trying to be a brat."

"You succeeded. But I really liked it."

"Thank you," Evelyn said softly.

"I'd like to see your body again. Will you take off your blouse for me?"

Evelyn immediately started unbuttoning her blouse, staring down at Gracie with an intense, unblinking stare. She shrugged out of the shirt, letting it fall back to drape the steering wheel, and pulled her arms up to free them from the sleeves. She cupped Gracie's face in her hands and leaned in, kissed her hard. Gracie's hands did some exploring of their own, focusing on the skin underneath the slip Evelyn was wearing. While they kissed, Evelyn reached up and pulled the straps of her slip down, letting them hang over her biceps like rings.

"I want you." Evelyn's lips moved against Gracie's mouth, the words riding out on a gasp. She wet her lips and inadvertently licked Gracie's lips as well.

"Here I am for the taking," Gracie said.

Evelyn angled her body so that her sex was pressing against Gracie's stomach. Gracie reached down to cup her ass and guided her, rising to meet her, their bodies grinding hard against each other. The car lurched slightly with their movements. Gracie was briefly aware that Evelyn had been fumbling with the buttons of her blouse for some time, and the realization made her tense up. Evelyn pulled back and examined her face. She was so close that Gracie could see the subtle shade of green in her blue eyes.

"What is it? What's wrong?" Evelyn pulled the now-sagging sides of Gracie's blouse shut again. "I just wanted to see. I'm sorry. If you don't want me to~"

"It's okay. I want you to see."

Gracie swallowed and moved Evelyn's hands away. She pulled her shirt open, then tugged up her undershirt until her breasts were bared. Evelyn's eyes dropped and looked at her. Gracie's heart thudded. Her breasts were small and easy to conceal with regular clothes, but they were unmistakable in a moment like this. Evelyn cupped one with her hand, curving her palm to take its weight before she brushed her fingers over it. The skin erupted in gooseflesh, and Gracie trembled.

"Still okay?"

"Yes." Gracie closed her eyes. "I haven't been touched like that in a long time, Evelyn."

Evelyn cupped the other breast, then hunched her back to lean down and take the nipple into her mouth. She sucked, nipped with her teeth, and then circled it with her tongue. Gracie squirmed under her, put her hands on Evelyn's shoulders and squeezed before pushing up into her hair. She twisted the curls around her fingers and lifted her hips up off the seat to rub herself against Evelyn's crotch.

"That feels so good, Evelyn."

Evelyn kissed a wide arc across Gracie's chest, moving up toward her throat before coming back down to her other breast.

"I hope it feels as good as your mouth felt on me last night," Evelyn said before she kissed the nipple. "I've never felt anything like that. I want to feel it again."

"Yes..."

"I want your mouth on me," Evelyn said.

"I'll eat you up."

"Put your tongue in me."

Gracie moaned and pulled Evelyn back up for a kiss. "Fuck me," Evelyn said into Gracie's mouth. "Fuck and fuck me."

"I hate that word," Gracie said, "except when you say it."

Evelyn giggled. "Fucking fuck me."

Gracie was sure the whole car had to be rocking with the force of their movements, but hopefully the storm was keeping any witnesses inside.

"Where's your camera?"

Gracie couldn't fathom the meaning of the words Evelyn had just said. They didn't fit what they were doing, so she might as well have been speaking French.

"What?"

"Your camera."

Gracie looked around, reluctantly pulled back to reality, and then remembered. "Backseat."

Evelyn craned her neck, and then stretched. Gracie sank into the seat as Evelyn's breasts pressed into her face. She closed her eyes and kissed, then managed to use her lips, teeth, and tongue to pull the underwear out of her way. She felt the warm, soft, pliant skin of Evelyn's breast against her cheek and turned her head, took the hard nipple into her mouth, and sucked eagerly on it. Evelyn cupped the back of Gracie's head with her non-searching hand.

"Oh, that's very nice," she purred. "Keep that up, sweetie. I've almost got it."

"Don't rush."

Evelyn chuckled and leaned back. She let her fingers trail along Gracie's jaw as she leaned back. She settled her weight on Gracie's thighs and held the camera out to her.

"Take my picture again."

Gracie put her hands on the camera but didn't take it. "Now...?"

"Now." Evelyn let go of the camera, forcing Gracie to take it. She shrugged her shoulders to make the slip fall further down her arms. She put one arm across her stomach and lifted her other, resting her hand behind her head and arching her back.

"I don't know if you want a naked picture of yourself floating around."

"It's not floating around," Evelyn said. "It will be with someone I trust. I want you to have it."

Gracie brought the camera up somewhat reluctantly and looked through the viewfinder. Evelyn was too close and the car was too dark. She reached up, clicked on the dome light, and then looked again. Evelyn was bathed in light, framed by the dark and rainswept windshield behind her. She looked absolutely irresistible, like something out of a myth. Gracie snapped two exposures, three, not caring about how much film she was using.

"Want a different pose?" Evelyn asked.

"I don't... Yes."

Gracie held the camera aside. She slipped her hand under Evelyn, pulled her forward, and kissed her hard. Evelyn moaned into her mouth and went limp, sagging against her and submitting to the kiss. Then Gracie pushed her back, brought the camera up, and quickly snapped a series of photos. Evelyn flinched in surprise.

"What was..."

"Now I can always see what you look like after we kiss."

Evelyn grinned, poking her tongue between her teeth. "I might want a copy of that. I'll get it framed."

"What if someone asks who took it?"

Evelyn narrowed her eyes and pushed the camera away, moving in for another kiss. "I'll tell them it's none of their damned business."

They kissed. Gracie didn't know if it was a single kiss or a series of small ones, but she and Evelyn both seemed to understand that the moment was over. The storm was letting up. Soon they wouldn't have the cover of the rain on all the windows and they'd have to get on their way.

Still, Evelyn stayed on top of her and Gracie didn't even try to shift her off. Evelyn's head was like an anchor on her shoulder after the kissing ended, and Gracie crossed her arms in the small of Evelyn's back, looking past her out the windshield. The glass was completely fogged up, but she could tell the downpour had dwindled to a weak shower. The sun had found a break in the clouds and was shining with an unbelievable brightness.

"The storm is over," she whispered against Evelyn's shoulder. "Someone is bound to come outside in a second..."

"Shoot," Evelyn muttered.

She climbed off Gracie's lap and dropped onto her side of the seat. They rearranged their clothes, Evelyn craning her neck to use the rearview mirror to check her makeup.

"You made a mess of my hair, Mr. Grace."

"Don't expect me to say sorry."

Evelyn smirked and returned the mirror to its original position.

Gracie checked the now fogless windows to make sure the spot they'd parked was as abandoned as it had appeared during the storm. The rain that had been left behind shined like diamonds on the grass and every flat surface, catching the sunlight and sending it sparkling back into the clearing sky. A few cars were butted-up against the white barn, but there were no sign of the drivers. She started the car and drove in a wide arc to get back on the main road.

Next stop, Chicago.

CHAPTER THIRTEEN

THE STOP in Iowa City only lasted as long as they needed to use the restroom, stretch their legs, and get some food to eat on the run. When they got back in the car, Evelyn scooted across the seat until her thigh was pressed against Gracie's. She answered the quizzical look with a shrug and said, "Anyone who notices will just think it's a gal and her fella out for a ride. Besides, this way I can feed you." She demonstrated by pressing a curly fry against Gracie's lips. Gracie shrugged and used her tongue to guide the fry into her mouth.

When they finished eating, Evelyn remained where she was and rested her head on Gracie's shoulder. Gracie looked down at her, but didn't say anything about it.

Evelyn was grateful for the silence. She felt like the actual storm she'd just been through was just a hiccup compared to the two storms going on inside her head. On one side, she had everything that had happened in the past twenty-four hours. The fight with Gracie, the slap, the unexpected feel of Gracie's lips on hers, and then the... the...

Sex. Sex with another woman. Gracie's mouth on her.

Evelyn's cheeks burned at the memory. No one had ever

done that for her, and she'd never thought it was something she would want. But she wanted it. Oh god, she wanted it. She wanted it again and again. And she wanted to do it in return. She glanced down at Gracie's lap, so innocent in its khaki, and ran her tongue over her bottom lip. She could do it to a man, but with a woman... she didn't think her neck would bend that way.

She put her hand on Gracie's thigh instead. She kept it there for a mile or so, then moved it higher. Gracie tensed, but didn't say anything. Evelyn bit her lip and looked up without raising her head, trying to see Gracie's face through her lashes. She twisted her wrist and rested her hand on the crotch of Gracie's slacks. When she thought she felt Gracie's legs ease apart, she started to massage.

"Don't."

Evelyn moved her hand back to the thigh. "Sorry."

"It's okay. It's not... objectionable. I just don't really trust myself."

"Okay," Evelyn said.

"Stay on my shoulder, though. I like that."

Evelyn smiled and settled in.

She honestly didn't mind being rebuffed. It was probably for the best, considering Gracie was driving. But that meant she had to focus on the other storm in her mind. It was the bigger storm, the hurricane and typhoon swirling around at the back of her skull. She looked at the odometer, then at the clock, and tried to calculate how long it would be until they were back in Chicago and she was forced to confront what she'd left behind seven years ago.

"You can't just abandon me here all on my own."

"I'm not abandoning you, Mama."

"You're leaving. Walking away, leaving me alone."

Evelyn shook her head. "This is my dream."

"Dream. Everyone has a dream. Just because you have a dream doesn't mean you'll get it. No one in this whole building dreamed of being here, but here they are. Just like you."

"I have to at least try."

Her mother came forward and took her hands. "You're setting yourself up for heartbreak and sadness, doll. You'll go out there and they'll knock you down, and you'll wish you had stayed here. You're happy here, right? Doing your little plays."

Evelyn lowered her head and looked at the floor. "Yes. But I'm good, Mama. I know I am. And if you have talent and you're willing to work hard, the sky's the limit. I know I can be something."

Her mother pulled her hands away. "You're choosing a fantasy over your own mother. It's going to be a disaster."

"I don't believe that."

"Then go." Her mother turned away from her. "At least your father was taken from me. You're choosing to abandon me. I won't forget that."

Evelyn's eyes burned with tears. "So you'd rather I was dead?"

"It would hurt less."

Evelyn still felt that last jab like a butter knife jabbed between her ribs. It was a constant sharp pressure on her heart but it was too dull to cut. Cutting would have been a relief, would have let the blood flow and the healing begin. This way, the knife was always there, digging in, sending shocks of pain whenever she was on the verge of moving on or letting it go.

Under ordinary circumstances, she would never have gotten this close to home ever again. Her debut picture being called *Chicago Canary* was as near as she wanted to come. They hadn't even filmed that one in the city. But then six months ago, she'd gotten a letter. It was addressed to the studio, thrown in with all the other fan mail so it had been a shock when she saw the familiar handwriting.

The letter was short and to the point. Cancer. No need to come running. It had actually been diagnosed the year before, but now the treatments had stopped working. The doctors couldn't say exactly how long she had left, and it wasn't as if Evelyn could actually do much to help. "You might as well just stay in California, nothing for you to do here." The neighbor secretly kept her updated once a month, like clockwork, and it seemed like things were getting progressively worse. But still there was nothing she could do, even if she had the strength.

And then Gracie showed up with a car, a chance to change the industry for the better, and a week when it would be very convenient to disappear. All the pieces had lined up so perfectly that not coming home would have been a distinct and unmistakable choice. She would have been choosing to not visit her mother, and she didn't know if she would've been able to live with that.

But now she actually had to go through with it. They were a few hours, a couple hundred miles, away from the moment of truth, and she had absolutely no idea what she was going to say. She had no idea what to expect. What if her mother just kicked her out? Told her to turn around and go back to La-La Land? Would she be relieved or disappointed? Would Gracie be mad?

Evelyn sat up and rearranged herself on the seat. Gracie glanced over at her.

"Do you need to pee?"

"No," Evelyn said. "Not that a lady would ever use such language. I'm just nervous."

Gracie nodded. "You haven't really told me what to expect up ahead, but I get the feeling it's pretty rough. Anything I can help you work through?" Evelyn shook her head. "But you're sweet for offering. I just need to prepare myself for it to go badly and work from there."

"I suppose that's best. I'll be there for you if you need me to be. And I can make myself scarce if that would be better."

"I'm not sure which one I want right now. But thank you."

They drove the rest of the way in silence. The rest of the country had felt like vast open expanses between large cities, but this final leg seemed to go by in a flash. They had just barely left the storm behind them when suddenly they started passing through all the suburbs and villages clustered around Chicago's outskirts like a protective barrier. Soon enough, much too soon in fact, Evelyn caught sight of those dreaded words on a sign.

CICERO. NEXT EXIT.

Her hand had drifted during the drive, but she reached out and grabbed Gracie's. She squeezed, and Gracie squeezed back.

"We can always just turn around and go back."

Evelyn actually laughed. She leaned in and kissed Gracie's cheek. "Thank you. But I think we better see this through to the end."

"Okay. Here we go."

She signaled the lane change and pulled off the highway, following the long curved road that would take Evelyn back home again.

***

Evelyn directed her to a squat three-story building on a main street that was flanked by a wooded area on one side and a church on the other. Evelyn had explained everything during the last few miles. The reason Evelyn left, the letter, everything. She understood why Evelyn had left, but was also surprised. She didn't think she would've been strong enough to leave under the same circumstances. When Gracie pulled into the parking lot behind the building, her tires bumped across broken concrete and deep potholes that splashed up wide waves of dirty rainwater.

Gracie found an empty spot near a dumpster and stopped the engine. She turned to look at Evelyn. "I can stay out here if you want, or I can come in to offer support. Whichever you think would be best."

"I think I'd prefer you in there with me."

Gracie nodded. "Okay. Just let me know if you want me to go at any point."

Evelyn smiled. She looked pale, but she nodded. "Okay. Might as well get this over with."

They got out and Gracie let Evelyn lead the way to the building. Grass was sprouting up through cracks in the courtyard pavement, which the centerpiece of which was a fountain full of algae-infested water. None of the apartment windows they passed had been cleaned in quite some time, and the brickwork was crumbling in places. Gracie tried not to notice the decay for Evelyn's sake, didn't want her to think she was judging the place she'd come from. Anything she said would've sounded false or patronizing, so she just remained silent as they stepped inside.

She pointed at the first door to the right. "Here we are. Home."

"I'm right here," Gracie said softly.

Evelyn took a steadying breath and smoothed a hand over the front of her blouse. She waited one more beat, then brought her fist up and knocked just below the peephole. She stepped back so she was standing beside Gracie, her hands folded in front of her. Gracie could still see her out of the corner of her eye, and it seemed like she'd pulled a cloak around herself. For the entire trip, she'd been nothing but bubbling energy. Now she was still and silent. It was like someone completely different had taken control of her body.

They waited close to a minute before Gracie started to wonder if anyone was coming. "She could be out. Or maybe she's in bed."

"Maybe she went to the hospital," Evelyn said. "God, I mean, I'm not hoping~"

"I understand." She put a hand on Evelyn's shoulder. "Maybe we should go get something to eat, unwind, come back a little~"

The door swung open and a woman glared out at them. She was tinier than Evelyn, with an angry expression etched into her wrinkles, but Gracie could clearly see where Evelyn's looks had come from. Bright eyes shined out from behind thick glasses, and the ends of her hair were still the same color as her daughter's. She was matchstick thin under a white blouse and black slacks, her feet wearing giant pink slipped. Evelyn had said she was in her late fifties, but the disease made her look two decades older than that, at the very least. Her spirit, however, was apparently undiminished. She jutted out her chin and narrowed her eyes at them both.

"Well. There she is. Huh."

She turned and shuffled back into the apartment. She left the door open behind her, which Evelyn seemed to take as an invitation. She walked in, and Gracie followed her, shutting the door behind them. The apartment was sweltering and smelled like a strange combination of peppermints and fried onions. Gracie felt beads of sweat popping out on her upper lip and forehead almost immediately.

"Hi, Momma." Even her voice had changed. It was softer, more compliant. Gracie wouldn't have recognized it if she hadn't seen Evelyn's lips forming the words.

Alma Wade finished the exhausting trek back to her recliner. She turned and dropped into the cushion, resting her hands on the plush arms of the chair and glared up at them. She looked like a queen ready to be disappointed by her loyal subjects.

"Well?" Alma said.

"How are you?"

"I'm dying of cancer. I assume you already knew that. Only reason you'd put your whole life on hold to come back here. How are *you?*" Cynicism dripped off her words. "Drinking a lot of champagne with Cary Grant? Must be nice."

Evelyn shuffled her feet and looked down at the carpet. "I'm making a movie now. I got the time off to come and see you~"

"Who's he?"

Evelyn looked at Gracie, who stiffened under their combined attention. She swallowed the lump in her throat and fought the urge to straighten her collar.

"This is Simon. He's my boyfriend. He drove me."

Gracie's cheeks reddened. "It's nice to meet you."

Alma twisted her upper lip and looked away. "So. I don't suppose you're here to become my nursemaid. Take care of me in my final days."

"Uh, I-I'm actually just on a break~"

"Of course you are. So you're just here to gawk? Get a look at the old woman before she turns to dust, mm?"

Evelyn flinched. "No, ma'am. I just... I-I wanted to see you. To let you know that I'm doing okay."

"Well, isn't that fantastic."

Gracie said, "Your daughter is a very famous actress, ma'am. She's incredibly popular. The movie she's making right now is going to make her even more well-known."

"What does that do for me?"

"It gets you care," Evelyn said. "Whatever you need. Money isn't an object. That's another reason I came here. If you need medicine or if you need to stay in the hospital, you can just send the bills to me and I'll make sure they're paid."

Alma snorted and shook her head. "They're not paying you enough for *that*."

"They are, Mama. I promise."

Gracie said, "Have you ever seen any of her movies?"

"I don't have time for that nonsense."

"Your daughter is a movie star. One of her movies is playing downtown. Why don't you let us drive you down there and you can see for yourself."

Evelyn looked at Gracie, surprised. "How do you know what's playing downtown?"

"We passed the theater on our way into town. *The Night at Sea*, right there on the marquee." She looked at Alma. "Her movie is on the marquee. It's not quite her name in lights, but it's close."

Alma chewed on her lip, still glaring. "Who are you again?"

"Simon Grace. I'm Evie's boyfriend."

Alma muttered something under her breath and shifted in her seat. "Well, I'm not about to have you rifling through my things while I get ready. Give a dying woman her privacy, at least."

Evelyn was already halfway back to the door before Alma finished talking. Gracie followed her out into the hallway and closed the apartment door. Evelyn walked to the foot of the stairs with her hands over her face, then turned and dropped down onto one of the steps without looking. Gracie walked closer the same way she would have approached a skittish cat.

"How do you feel?"

"I don't know." She wiped at her eyes. "It was pretty much what I was expecting."

Gracie sat down beside her. "That doesn't make it any easier to actual experience it." She put a hand on Evelyn's knee and squeezed. "You did well."

"You think?"

"Hell, I don't know." That got a smile out of her. "But I think you handled it better than I would've. Better than I *did*. Sorry I got all defensive. I guess it's the, uh, boyfriend in me."

Evelyn winced. "Sorry."

"No, don't be sorry. I didn't mind. No one's ever called me that. It was nice."

Evelyn took Gracie's hand off her knee and brought it up to her lips, kissing it. "Thank you for being there. And for giving me a chance to be here. I never would have gotten up the courage to actually do this without you and that article and three days in a car to brace myself for the moment of truth." She looked down at Gracie's hand, noticing her watch. "What if it's hours until the movie starts?"

"The marquee said there was a showing at five." Gracie looked at her watch as well, then nodded. "We should be able to make it, depending on how fast she gets ready."

"That was always a worrying topic even before she got sick." Evelyn sighed. "But we can go in late if we have to. I'm not in the first few scenes, anyway."

They sat next to each other on the stairs, waiting, their arms not quite touching. Someone on an upper floor shouted, a door slammed. Footsteps pounded on the floor, but no one appeared on the stairs. Evelyn saw Gracie looking up and smiled.

"I remember all this noise," she said. "Constant, endless noise from the other apartments. I eventually learned to tune it out, because it was ignore it or go insane."

"Wow. I don't know if I'd ever get used to that."

Evelyn shrugged. "Ignoring it is the only way I ever got

any sleep."

The door to Alma's apartment opened and she came out. She looked a little more spry and was moving faster than she had been earlier, but Gracie was certain it was just an act. There were lines of pain around her eyes, and her lips were pressed tightly together to suppress a grimace. She had changed into a black wool housecoat, her hair pinned up under a small hat, and she was carrying a small purse.

"You said he drove you, so I assume he has a car. I'm not walking all the way to the nickelodeon."

"Right this way, Mrs. Wade."

They took position behind Alma, one at each shoulder, and escorted her out of the building to the parking lot. When they reached the car, Evelyn volunteered to take the backseat. It was really the only option since Gracie couldn't imagine the older, much sicker passenger being forced into such cramped riding quarters. She folded the seat forward to Evelyn could get in, then gestured for Alma to follow.

"Some car," Alma muttered as she took her seat.

"Thanks. I'm pretty proud of it."

"Boys and their toys," Alma said. "Ridiculous."

Gracie glanced at Evelyn and raised an eyebrow. Evelyn covered a smirk with her fingers.

The theater was a mile back the way they'd come. Alma didn't say a word during the drive, but Gracie noticed her examining the car with a calculatedly uninterested expression on her face. She had a feeling the older woman was looking for something to complain about, but the Desoto didn't give her much to work with. Gracie smiled proudly and left the woman to her examination.

They arrived with ten minutes to spare before the movie began. Evelyn opened her luggage and took out a hat and a pair of sunglasses in case any of the employees recognized her, and Gracie bought tickets for the three of them. She was surprised to find there were about a dozen other patrons despite the odd time of day.

Gracie had to admit she wasn't a big movie-goer. She'd

seen *Wizard of Oz* and *Snow White*, and they were fine. But then there were films like *Gone with the Wind* which to her just seemed like a waste of a good afternoon. The idea of seeing one of Evelyn's films, however, had her more excited than she'd ever been walking into a theater.

Alma insisted on sitting alone. "If I have to sit through a whole film, I'm not going to do it with you two looming over me the whole time."

She found a seat in the center of the room, halfway down the row so the screen would be centered for her. Evelyn and Gracie sat next to each other a few rows farther back.

"How are you feeling?" Gracie asked. "Nervous about your mother seeing the movie?"

"More nervous for you to see it, actually." She reached for Gracie's hand. Gracie took it and squeezed. "I hope you like it."

"I'm glad I'll be with you for it."

Evelyn smiled and faced forward. The lights dimmed.

The movie began.

CHAPTER FOURTEEN

The Night at Sea was about an ocean liner making the trip from London to New York along the same route as the *Titanic*. The first half hour introduced the main cast: a rich man heading to America to check out his latest investment, the rich man's wife, the man she was having an affair with, a ship's steward, the captain, and the newly-rich heiress the steward eventually fell in love with. Evelyn played the heiress, of course, the perfect combination of naïve innocence and Hollywood glamour.

Once the characters were established, the rest of the movie took place during a single evening. While on an after-dinner stroll the rich man's wife spotted a smaller boat following along in their wake. It only had one light swinging from its hull, but she could hear voices coming from the deck. She raised the alarm, and soon the passengers decided they were being haunted by a ghost ship that intended to curse them to the same fate as the *Titanic*.

Gracie thought the story was absolutely ridiculous, but the love story was actually not bad. Evelyn was, obviously, gorgeous. Her hair was done up to make her look like Marlene

Dietrich, only much prettier to Gracie's eye. She had only just inherited her wealth, and she looked uncomfortable in every fancy outfit and with every amenity the ship offered her. She ended up wandering the decks, which was where she met the steward and struck up a conversation with him.

It was strange to see Evelyn playing someone so meek and quiet. Not just because of the last few days, but it boggled Gracie's mind to think of how she'd gone from this to playing a vengeful goddess armed with a bow and arrow. She lit up in every scene with the steward, a man who was truly enraptured by her but worried she would only think he was after her money.

She looked at Evelyn and saw that she had her eyes closed. "What are you doing?" she whispered.

"What I do in all my movies."

Gracie looked at the screen. "But you're gorgeous."

Evelyn turned toward her and cracked one eye open. "How would you like seeing yourself blown up that big on the side of a building? With all these people staring at you?"

"Oh." Gracie sunk lower in her seat. "Well, I hadn't considered that."

"I can't stop thinking about it," Evelyn said, closing her eye again. "So I just close my eyes whenever it gets too much."

Gracie patted Evelyn's hand. "I'll tell you when it's safe."

"Thank you."

The movie continued with the passengers becoming increasingly terrified of the ghost ship while Evelyn and the rich man fell in love. It all culminated in a scene where the rich man's wife and the man she was cheating with tried to kill the heiress because she had caught them. They couldn't risk her telling the rich man about the affair and causing a divorce. There was a fight that ended with the steward saving the day. He rushed in and threw the would-be killers over the railing, rescuing Evelyn and finally earning a kiss that would've seemed passionate if Gracie hadn't experienced the real thing. They managed to blame the missing couple on the ghosts, who had vanished with the sunrise.

"You couldn't have been saved by the rich man's wife?"

Evelyn snickered. "Now that's a movie worth seeing."

The credits rolled and the audience applauded. Alma stood up, a dark shape against the screen. Evelyn and Gracie got up and met her in the aisle.

"You weren't the star," she said.

Evelyn looked too shocked to reply, so Gracie did it for her. "Of course she was the star. The whole movie was about her."

"The movie was about the steward. And those ridiculous ghosts. They never explained what the other boat really was. So I suppose they expect us to believe ghosts exist. Ridiculous."

"At least you can admit Evelyn was great in the role."

Alma sniffed. "That hair. If they wanted Dietrich, they should have just gotten Dietrich. I guess you were cheaper."

Gracie resisted the urge to slap the woman. "How dare you? She's your daughter."

"Can we go home now?" Alma asked, looking around as if to see if anyone had overheard.

Gracie was tempted to make the old battleax walk. Evelyn turned and walked away without saying anything. Evelyn glared at Alma for another long moment, then followed her. She caught up with her in the lobby and touched her elbow before falling into step next to her.

"Can *we* go home now?" Evelyn asked.

"That's up to you."

Evelyn sniffled and kept staring ahead, eyes shining. "I tried. No one can accuse me of not trying."

"No..." Gracie looked back. Alma was trailing behind them, close enough to keep up but not so close she could overhear their whispers. "But we scheduled a day. Maybe she's just hurt and angry. Maybe we can give her some time to get used to you being here and try again in the morning."

"I'd rather see the Grand Canyon on the way back."

"The Grand Canyon will still be there the next time you take a road trip. Will she?"

Evelyn sneered, curling her lip. Gracie decided not to point out that it made her look adorable, not scary. "Fine."

"Whatever happens," Gracie said, "you tried. That's all anybody can ask of anybody, right?"

Evelyn made a noncommittal noise and Gracie rubbed her shoulder in solidarity.

They drove Alma back to her apartment in the same arrangement as before, with Evelyn folded uncomfortably in the backseat. Gracie wanted to just dump the bitter old woman out on the sidewalk but decided to play the boyfriend role into which she'd been inadvertently cast. She went around the car and opened the door, offered a hand to Alma, and helped her get up from the seat. Alma pulled her hand free as soon as she was out of the car and started walking away.

Evelyn's shoulders slumped and she shut the car door to follow her. "We'll say goodbye at the door," she whispered to Gracie. "Then we'll find somewhere to spend the night and try again in the morning."

"Sounds good."

They were halfway across the courtyard when a man came out of the building. He wore a polo shirt and slacks, his black hair plastered against his skull like a helmet. He had a square jaw and tiny snake eyes. When he approached them, he smiled in a way that made Gracie automatically want to punch him in the nose. That feeling was amplified when she realized he was looking at Evelyn, who had stopped walking to stare back at him in shock.

"Max? What are you doing here?"

His grin widened to show his teeth. "Hello, Evie."

"Who is this guy?" Gracie asked.

"My agent, Max McNeal," Evelyn said, still staring at him like he was death. Her face had gone deathly pale.

Alma had passed Max but stopped on the walkway, half-turned to watch what was unfolding behind her. There was no surprise on her face, and Gracie immediately knew what had happened.

"She called you while she was getting ready," she said.

"But there's no way you could've gotten here from LA in two hours."

"No, I was already in town. Since yesterday, actually." He shrugged, acting like a humble athlete trying to explain how he'd won. "When Evie vanished, a couple of us got together and decided there weren't many places she could've been running to. I figured this was the most likely place for you to end up. So I hopped on a plane and got here as soon as I could. I got in touch with your mother..." He turned to find her, waved, and then turned back to them. "And I asked her to call me if you showed up. So she did. Told me you were taking her to the movies, so I had time to get here from my hotel."

Evelyn said, "Well, good for you."

"Thank you. Now if you'll get your things, I think there's another flight back to LA tonight... The studio is footing the bill, so we don't have to worry about how much it costs. We should be able to make it if we hurry." He checked his watch.

"I'm not going home yet. And I'm certainly not going with you."

He looked up. "Oh, you definitely are, Evie. You caused quite a hubbub with that little article of yours. Having you back on-set as soon as possible would go a long way to putting out all the fires you started."

Gracie said, "You mean the fires she started for the producers? The directors? Everyone who was named and shamed in the article hope having her back at work will take the heat off of them."

Max shifted his attention to her. "Mr. Grace. There's no need for this to be confrontational, is there? Surely we can all come to an agreement."

"When Hell freezes over," Evelyn said.

Max was still looking at Gracie. "Is that how you feel, Simon? Because I think you should insist on Evelyn coming back with me."

"Why the hell would he do that?" Evelyn said.

"It would show that he isn't holding you against your

will."

Evelyn stuttered over her response to that. "Against my will? What? Holding..." She furrowed her brow and looked at Gracie. She must have seen something in her expression, because her face changed from confusion to worry. "Simon? What's he talking about?"

Gracie swallowed the sizable lump in her throat. She looked at the ground. "When the article came out," she said softly, "the studios tried to cover their asses by saying I was an obsessed stalker. I made up the whole thing, then kidnapped you and ran off."

"Well, that's poppycock!" Evelyn laughed. "All anyone has to do is ask me and I'll set the record straight. It was *my* idea to come to Chicago. She won't actually be *charged* with *kidnapping me.*"

"But they can hold me in custody until we get it all sorted out." Gracie's voice was flat, completely devoid of emotion, as she realized the trap she'd been backed into.

"So, a few hours in a jail cell won't..." Evelyn realized the danger in that. If Gracie spent any time in police custody, even just an afternoon, her true gender would quickly become public knowledge. "Oh."

Gracie swallowed the lump in her throat. "You sh-should go with him, Evelyn."

Evelyn's eyes were filled with such betrayal that Gracie had to look away. "Gracie..."

"I'm sorry."

Max let the awkward, painful silence drag on for a moment before he cleared his throat. "I think we're all in agreement that going back is the best course of action, Evie."

"Well, I'm not!" Evelyn snapped. "Shouldn't I get some sort of choice in where I go?"

Alma said, "You seemed eager enough to leave here for California once before."

Evelyn pivoted to her. "*I* don't have anything to say to *you* ever again. I tried. I *tried.* And this is what you do? This is how you respond to me finally coming home? Message received. I could have stayed behind. And then, what, gotten a job at the supermarket? Some silly desk job just because it resulted in a paycheck, the whole time wondering if I could have made it? Well guess what. I made it. I'm famous, Mama. I got my dream. I worked hard for it. I'm not going to make myself feel guilty because I chose a good life. A better life, one that I actually love."

She turned and looked at Gracie. "And you." Her voice was softer, but still hard and cold. "I understand why. Honestly. I really do. But that doesn't make it hurt any goddamn less."

Gracie flinched and looked away.

Max had listened to the entire exchange in silence. When Evelyn finished, he held out a hand toward the parking lot.

"Shall we retrieve your things?"

"Fine," Evelyn muttered. She brushed past Gracie, who remained planted to the sidewalk, unable to lift her feet enough to follow. The car was unlocked, she could get her things easy enough. She just couldn't bring herself to be there to watch it play out and see the anger and hurt in Evelyn's eyes as she unloaded her bag. Alma also remained on the walkway, smoothing her hands over the front of her dress as if she was waiting to be dismissed.

"She might have been wrong when she left," Gracie said quietly. "I don't think she was, but I know there are two sides to every story and I don't know yours. So who knows. Maybe she didn't leave the right way. But she tried to make amends before it was too late. That's what matters. And what you did today... that's something unforgivable. I hope you can live with knowing that."

She turned her back before Alma had a chance to respond. She was almost back to her parking spot when a car sped by, almost clipping her. She was too startled by its sudden appearance to think about whether Evelyn was in the passenger seat. It was gone out of sight before she thought to look.

***

Evelyn was devastated. The only thing she could think about was Gracie looking away, her voice saying 'you should go.' She thought they'd shared something. She thought what they'd done during the storm, if not everything that happened the night before, had been the start of... she didn't know what. But something. She couldn't process being pushed away like that. Even though she logically understood why Gracie made the decision. Her secret was at risk. Even spending one hour with the police endangered her secret being revealed one way or another. That discovery would have destroyed her entire life.

Still. For one moment, she thought she'd found someone willing to take that kind of risk for her.

"...all the same to you."

Evelyn snapped back to real life, back to the passenger seat of Max's car. She looked at him, and he seemed to be waiting for an answer.

"I wasn't listening," she said quietly.

Max sighed. "I *said* we'll go back to my hotel so I can get my things and check out. I'll return this car to the man I borrowed it from, and then we'll head to the Air Park. There's another flight tomorrow morning, but I'd prefer to catch the earliest one possible so we can put an end to this whole escapade. If that would be okay with you."

"Fine. I don't care."

Max looked at her, surprised. "Really? After all this, all the trouble you caused, you're going to give up, just like that?"

"It doesn't matter," Evelyn said, staring out the window but not seeing anything they passed. "There's nothing for me here anyway. Might as well get the heck out as quickly as possible."

Max shrugged and faced the road again. "Works for me. No point in wasting any more time."

"None at all," Evelyn agreed.

She put her head back against the seat and closed her eyes, hoping Cicero and everyone in it would be gone by the time she opened them again.

Chapter Fifteen

After Max drove off with Evelyn, there was no reason for Gracie to stay in Cicero a minute longer than absolutely necessary. She made the decision to leave as soon as she was back in her car. She would start the trip back to Los Angeles immediately. She would find somewhere to stop when she got hungry or tired and spend the night there. It didn't really matter anymore. She didn't even know if Evelyn still approved of the profile or not. She didn't know if Bill would print it. The studio had effectively hijacked the whole narrative.

It was over. And she wouldn't have anything to show for it except six thousand miles added to her odometer and some memories that were going to be too painful to revisit.

Her eyes filled with tears and she whipped off her glasses to rub at them. When she blinked them back into focus, she saw the road sign informing her how far she had before she was officially out of the city. She stepped on the gas to get out faster.

As she started retracing the route she'd spent the past few days drawing, Gracie came to a decision: she would still write the profile. She owed it to Evelyn to see their plan through, even if it was doomed to failure. After that, she had no damned clue what she was going to do.

She had two thousand miles of road to figure it out.

The seats on the plane were more luxurious than Evelyn expected. They were extremely comfortable, and she had plenty of room to stretch her legs out in front of her. Not that she cared about being doted on right now. She would have much preferred whatever motel Gracie found for them and the cramped seats of the Desoto. Sadly it seemed as if she might have taken her last ride in that silly green car. She already missed the creak of the seats, the smell of greasy fries and hamburgers.

She had barely paid attention to the trip from her mother's apartment to the air park. Now that she was actually in the plane, she realized the incredibly loud rumbling noise making the floor rattle under her feet meant they were about to take off. She looked past Max out the window, then twisted to look down the aisle. The stewardess was a few rows away talking to a man in a suit.

"Everything okay?" Max asked.

"I've never flown before," Evelyn said. "I was hoping to get something to take the edge off."

"There's nothing to worry about," Max said, but he raised his hand to signal the stewardess.

The blonde ended her conversation and approached them, the baby-blue skirt swishing around her knees when she crouched down next to Evelyn's seat. She flashed them a smile that was artificial enough to have been photographed for a cigarette ad.

"How can I help y'all?" she asked in a chirpy Southern accent.

Max smiled. "My friend here would like something to calm her nerves."

"Oh of course, hon." She opened a metal tin and took out a cigarette, pinching it between her fingers to offer it to Evelyn.

"She doesn't smoke," Max said.

Evelyn took the cigarette. "Don't speak for me, Max."

The stewardess pressed her lips together to suppress an unprofessional smile. She produced a lighter from the pocket of her blazer and used it to light the cigarette. "Let me get you something to drink, hon. Do you have a preference?"

"Alcohol."

"A popular choice. I'll be right back."

She stood and walked away. Evelyn twisted in her seat to watch her go, focusing on her pale white stockings. The legs were very shapely, and the curve of her hip was certainly intriguing, but Evelyn didn't feel the same twinge of desire she felt when she looked at Gracie. Did that mean she didn't like women after all? Was she only attracted to Gracie because she wore the disguise of a man so well? She thought about wrapping her lips around Gracie's thumb and sucking it. Surely that wasn't something those sorts of women enjoyed.

Although Gracie certainly seemed to enjoy it.

And they *had* used their fingers a lot. So maybe that made it just as sexual.

She held her hand up and spread the fingers out, examining them, wondering how Gracie might have seen them the night before. She thought of the lewd gestures people could make with the hand, symbolism that most people learned by the time they were teenagers. And using her hand certainly came naturally to her with Gracie.

She caught Max looking and curled her fingers into a fist and tucked it into her lap as if she'd just been caught touching herself.

The stewardess returned and held out a glass of amber liquid. "Here you go. My personal favorite." Their fingers brushed when she handed over the glass, and Evelyn had to tighten her shoulders to prevent herself from shivering. The stewardess must have felt something, too, because she locked eyes with Evelyn and this time her smile was natural and sincere. "Let me know if you need... anything else during the flight."

"I will. Thank you."

Evelyn watched her walk away again. Surely she'd imagined that pause before 'anything.' She wasn't being propositioned by a woman so soon after her experience with Gracie.

The stewardess stopped at the front of the aisle and looked back over her shoulder. She smiled when she caught Evelyn staring. She raised an eyebrow, wet her lips, and then ducked out of sight into the plane's galley.

Evelyn brought the glass up to her lips and drained it. An ice cube bumped against her lips and she used her tongue to draw it into her mouth, holding it against the inside of her cheek in the hopes it would cool her down a little. She didn't know if she was imagining the flirtation or not, but given the way her fingers had tingled when the stewardess touched them, she definitely had her answer about the sexualization of hands.

When she was an hour outside of Cicero, Gracie saw a plane overhead, flying west. She tried to focus on the road but her eyes kept betraying her, drifting up to track its progress. She knew it wasn't Evelyn's plane. It couldn't have been. But what if it was? What if Evelyn was up there in that thing, looking down, and she saw the car? She hadn't seen any other green cars in quite a while, so maybe it would be visible from the air. And if they looked at each other at the same time, maybe they would feel something.

Eventually the plane was too far away for her to see it anymore. She welcomed its departure, glad she wouldn't have the distraction. She was already dealing with the fact the car was too empty, too silent. She glanced in the passenger seat and tried to imagine what Evelyn would've been doing if she was there. Humming a song. Pointing things out as they passed. Fiddling with the radio.

Her smell lingered in the car. Gracie had tried to ignore it, but it was too strong. She thought about rolling down the windows, but she wasn't entirely convinced she really wanted to dissipate it. As long as the perfume remained, she could pretend she wasn't really on the road alone. That she hadn't abandoned Evelyn at the first sign of trouble. Just handed her back to the people she was supposed to be protecting her from. But no, protecting her own secret had been more important.

"Damn it!" She smacked her fist against the steering wheel, surprised by her own shout. Pain flashed up her wrist from the punch, and she hissed, shaking the hand. "Damn it," she said again, this time through gritted teeth.

The trip to Illinois had only been tolerable because of Evelyn. Now the thought of a return trip along the same roads through the same boring stretch of country exhausted her. She switched on the radio so she would at least have some company while the signals were still strong enough.

From the moment they were off the ground, Evelyn was in agony. Her ears popped, which made her briefly terrified that she had gone deaf, but that horrific and constant rattle-rumble of the engine was still like a spike to her brain. She tried leaning forward to put her head between her knees, but that only made it worse. The shaking felt like a hand was holding onto her belly and wrenching it back and forth. She heard someone retching somewhere behind her, and she didn't think it would be long before she joined them in purging.

A gentle hand rested on her shoulder and she jumped, turning to see the stewardess offering her a compassionate smile. And, even better, a pair of earmuffs that looked like metal cans. The blonde leaned in until her lips were almost touching Evelyn's ear. The move was necessary, but it also meant the woman's body was stretched along the length of Evelyn's arm, her breasts on Evelyn's shoulder, and when she spoke her breath was warm on Evelyn's skin.

"These won't help everything, but they might turn down the volume on the worst of it."

Evelyn turned her head and her lips met a wall of heavily-sprayed hair. "Thank you." She shouted the words, but their position made it feel more intimate than it was. They were practically necking. She hoped she wasn't blushing.

"Let me know if you need anything else," the stewardess said. "My name is Emma. I'm a really big fan."

"Oh!" Evelyn pulled back and managed a smile. "Thank you," she said again.

Emma nodded, winked, and handed over the earmuffs. Evelyn took them and clamped them on, immediately lessening the amount of noise by a huge degree. She closed her eyes and sank back into the plushness of the seat. Maybe she could fall asleep. Maybe she could spend the rest of this godforsaken trip unconscious and wake up back in the real world where she only had to be herself a little bit of the time. Constant honesty was exhausting.

She was on the verge of falling asleep when they hit a particularly bad patch of air and her stomach heaved again. She lurched forward, startling Max, and grabbed for the bag attached to the back of the chair in front of her.

It was going to be a long, long flight.

Gracie stopped at the first motel she saw after sunset. She just didn't feel like pushing on any further, and she was technically a day ahead of schedule anyway since they'd only spent the afternoon in Cicero. She checked into her room and dumped her bags, the exhaustion of the day catching up to her. She sat on the edge of the bed, took out her notebook, and flipped through it to find the first blank page. She stopped when she saw blocks of unfamiliar handwriting.

Evelyn's contributions.

Gracie ran her fingers over the large looping letters. It wasn't quite cursive, but the letters were bold and leaned into each other in a pleasing, elegant way. She hadn't pressed down hard enough to leave imprints in the page the way Gracie did, so the ink looked like it had been painted onto the page. There were smears where Evelyn's hand brushed over words before it was fully dry. She read what had actually been written and noticed little notes in the margin.

"Hi Gracie (when you read this later)" followed by a smiling face.

"I am ENJOYING this CAR RIDE!"

"You just ate my doughnut! I didn't say anything because I'm not really mad but I wanted you to know I know and you owe me a doughnut now."

Gracie laughed and bit her bottom lip. She barely even remembered having doughnuts, but she knew it was one of the snacks they'd picked up in Vegas. She'd been sure she only ate her fair share of all the food, but maybe she'd been mistaken. She certainly wasn't going to dispute the accusation.

Not that she *could* dispute it.

Her smile faded at the thought of Evelyn in the air somewhere, maybe already past the Rockies. She knew planes made a lot of stops on cross-country trips. Even so, she would probably be back in California by morning. The space between them was growing with every passing second, and even if Gracie drove non-stop there was no way she could ever catch up. It would be days before she saw Evelyn again, at the very least. There was a chance they'd never see each other again, and that idea made her heart ache. She closed her eyes and pressed her fist against her forehead as if she could keep the idea from escaping and becoming reality.

"I wouldn't want to see me, either," she muttered. "I was supposed to keep her safe. But I abandoned her to the people she was running from at the very first opportunity. To protect *me*. To keep *myself* safe. Call yourself whatever you want, Grace Simon, the simple fact is that you're a coward above anything else."

She got off the bed and went to room's desk. She switched on the lamp and sat down, turning to a fully blank page of the notebook, and started writing.

Ordinarily Evelyn would've been livid about Max wrapping his arm around hers to lead her off the plane. But having spent the last ten hours alternating between throwing up and nursing a headache caused by the constant drumming of the engine noise, she welcomed the crutch. She had no idea why anyone would want to fly anywhere. Cars and trains took a lot longer, obviously, but at least a person still felt like a person when they got to their destination.

Max escorted her to the parking lot where his car was waiting. Night had fallen, and the air was so much colder than she'd expected. She shivered and kept her head down. The only consolation was that soon she would be in her own bed, comfortable and warm, and she could start putting this whole dumb week behind her.

She was aware Max was speaking but had ignored everything until she heard "set" and "tomorrow" in the same sentence. She raised her head and swept her hand out in front of her.

"Hold up, fella. What's this talk about going back to set? Sol gave me a full week off. I've got a couple of days left."

"That's before you went and dropped that article. We've done a pretty good job keeping things calm and normal for now. But telling people you're back to work would go a long way toward getting us back to normal."

Evelyn pulled her arm away and took a step away from him. She wobbled on unsteady legs, but managed to stay upright. "Maybe I'm not interested in going back to normal."

Max looked at the ground. He took such a deep breath that his shoulders rose and then sank down. He raised his eyes up to her and he spoke in a measured tone.

"You wouldn't like the alternative to normal, Evelyn. Trust me."

"Sol wouldn't fire me. Not this late in filming."

"You're right. He probably wouldn't. You've filmed too much of *Olympus* to do a recasting at this point. He's stuck with you. But the next director might not bother. And the next. It won't matter how good you are at auditions if they associate you with all this trouble. If you make yourself a headache, this could be your last movie."

Evelyn closed her eyes. She heard the hum of cars on the

road nearby. It made her think of Gracie, now on the road all by herself.

"The choice is yours, Evie. I'm sure Sol will give you another few days, but you need to think about what they'll cost you in the long run."

She opened her eyes. "What time do I have to be at the studio tomorrow?"

Chapter Sixteen

THE CALL was for five in the morning, which felt like another layer of punishment. She was so exhausted that she couldn't even appreciate being home. Safe and sound, back in her own four walls, sleeping in her own bed. Or at least trying to. She knew there were gaps in her memory where she must have slept, she spent the majority of the night fretting. She tossed and turned and looked toward the window. She wondered where Gracie was. Tried to tell herself she didn't care. Told herself she was a liar.

When her alarm went off, she went to the bathroom and took her first real shower in almost a week. She drowned herself in the steady, powerful spray but still didn't quite feel like she'd gotten all the road dirt off her skin. She wasn't entirely sure she wanted it all gone. She wanted to feel the grime, to remember she'd gotten away from this town if just for a little bit.

She brought her hand to her face while she was still under the spray. She knew there was nothing left of Gracie to smell, but she closed her eyes and tried anyway. She touched her fingertips to her lips and curled them, brushed them across her cheek, and shivered at memories.

A car was waiting outside her house to take her to work. When she had delayed as long as possible, Evelyn finally dressed and went downstairs. She climbed into the backseat and the driver headed off without a word. Evelyn shrank into the corner of the backseat and watched the neighborhood through her window.

The sky was pale violet-blue, the sun still blocked by the hills, but the town was already buzzing with activity. The apartments she passed blazed with light, and there were enough cars on the road to provide a steady stream of traffic to escort her to Universal. It was a stark change from the long and lonely highways she'd been getting used to with Gracie.

"Fuck," she said under her breath, irritated with how often her thoughts had been swinging back to Gracie since she got home.

"Ma'am?" the driver said.

"Nothing. Never mind."

He faced the road again.

Evelyn had to get Gracie off her mind. As far as she knew, she was never going to see 'Simon Grace' again. It was probably for the best. Too much pain there. She'd let herself be open and vulnerable. She had tried something, possibly discovered something about herself in the process, and then got the rudest of all possible awakenings. She knew it was wrong to hold Gracie's actions against her. Was she supposed to risk her entire life for Evelyn? Someone she hadn't even known a week? The Simon identity was Gracie's job, her livelihood, her entire public persona.

But it had cut her to the bone. Maybe it was because of what they'd started to find with each other. Maybe it was the fact it happened after spending time with her mother again. God, all that toxicity, all that blame and anger she thought she'd put behind her came boiling to the surface. And while the wound was still raw, Gracie came along with a salt shaker and just—

"We're here, ma'am."

Evelyn blinked and sat up straighter. They were parked outside the open door of Stage 7, various crewmembers visible within.

She mumbled a thank-you to the driver and slipped her sunglasses on as she climbed out of the car. Activity slowed to a halt as she passed, every head turning toward her as the chattering turned to poorly-concealed whispers. She ignored them and walked confidently toward the corner where she knew the dressing rooms would be found. She was almost there when Howie, the production assistant, intercepted her.

"Sol wants you ready in thirty."

"Okay," she said, not bothering to slow down or look at him.

Howie trotted to keep up. "He, uh, he's... he also..." Howie was fumbling with a handful of papers that he was trying to get out of a binder without wrinkling them. "He has, uh, some new pages. Today's scene is all new."

"Fine."

She took the papers from him and continued into her dressing room. Howie stopped at the threshold like a vampire who needed an official invitation, and he was forced to hop back so he wouldn't get smacked in the face with the door when she slammed it. She dumped her bag on the couch and glanced at the pages before she started to get ready. Half an hour was ridiculous. With hair, makeup, and costume, she would need at least...

Her eye caught on a word in the new script pages and every thought process in her head grinded to a halt so she could process it.

Evelyn stood in the middle of the room and found the first page. Her face grew hotter as she read the scene, and she was already moving back to the door by the time she got halfway. Her rage was so powerful, so potent, that she ignored the voice of Howie as he tried to rein her in. She stormed onto the set, which had been transformed an ornate Olympian throne room, and shoved anyone who didn't get out of her way fast enough.

She spotted Sol standing near one of the cameramen and zeroed in on him. He saw her coming when she was only a few steps away.

"Evie! Welcome back!"

Evelyn planted her hand in the center of his chest and shoved. He stumbled backward a few steps, eyes wide in surprise. She held up the script pages which were now wrinkled by her fist.

"What the hell is this bullshit, Solomon?"

He dropped his phony smile so the rest of his face matched his dead eyes. "New scene. Your friend isn't the only one who did some writing this week."

"This isn't what I signed on for. I didn't agree to anything like this."

"Maybe if you'd been here instead of flitting off to wherever, we could have discussed it. As of now, though, the scene is scheduled for today."

Evelyn unwrinkled the pages and looked down at them. She had to force her eyes to focus on the words so she could read them out loud.

"'Artemis attempts to leave. Ares grabs her arm, stopping her. She struggles, but he is stronger. He sits down and pulls her onto his lap *where he proceeds to spank her.*' You can't be serious with this."

The screenwriter, Daniel Scott, had approached during the tirade. "Hey now," he said, far too amused. "The actor doesn't read the stage directions. You should know that by now."

She threw the script at his feet. "We all know why you added this shit."

Daniel gave her a look of pure innocence that made her want to throw up. "To show there's a hierarchy with the gods. Artemis and Ares have a disagreement about what to do with the mortals and he shows dominance."

Evelyn narrowed her eyes and shook her head. "You know that's not what this is about."

"Dan decided this scene was important to the movie as a

whole, and I have to agree with him."

"Oh, I'm sure you did."

Sol sighed wearily and stepped closer, lowering his voice. "There are a lot of people watching this happen," he said quietly. And, sure enough, she noticed everyone on set had surrounded them to witness the fight. "You wouldn't want word to get around that you're a troublemaker."

Evelyn's eyes burned with tears. Either of anger, sadness, or just plain resignation, she couldn't say. Max had said the same thing. The article had only resulted in her becoming a potential problem. She was trapped. She could walk off the movie, but the movie would suffer, and everyone would say it was because of her. Sol would control the narrative just by talking to his friends over drinks and cigars. She would become 'that pain in the ass,' or 'that loudmouth.' She hadn't solved anything. She had just put herself in a cage where she would have to let someone spank her ass on camera just to keep working.

"I—"

"I won't do the scene."

Evelyn looked at Sol, then turned toward the voice. She recognized who was speaking but she needed to double-check before she believed it.

Barry Denton was standing a few feet away in the crowd of rubberneckers who had gathered to watch the fight. He was fully in costume, a toga that revealed one side of his chest and both muscular arms. His dark goatee was trimmed in a sharp, neat style. He was olive-skinned and gorgeous and had exactly the sort of face someone pictured when they thought of Greek gods, and right now those pitch-black eyes were staring unblinkingly at Sol.

"What are you talking about, Barry?" The director sighed, exasperated. "Of course you're doing the scene. We discussed this."

Barry stepped forward, officially entering the conversation. "Yes, *we* discussed it. And you're just telling me *now* that *she* didn't even know about it?"

Sol said, "When were we supposed to have told her?"

"I'm not doing a scene like that without her go-ahead. And it sounds an awful lot like she's not okay with it. If she's out, so am I."

The wind seemed to go out of Sol. He had turned fully toward Barry and was almost pleading now. "Come on, Barry. You read that stinking article..."

"Yes, I did." Barry's voice had gone very low, and his body had become very still. Evelyn felt like she was staring at a panther about to strike. "A lot of other people read it, too. And those people will go see *Olympus* knowing we were filming it when she gave that interview. Do you think the public is stupid? They're going to see this damn spanking scene for exactly what it is. And you want me to be the one doing it. I don't want to see another article saying I'm the sort of actor who would do something like that. Because I'm not."

Sol and Daniel looked at each other. It looked like both were waiting for the other to speak. Barry didn't give them the chance.

"If you want to label someone as difficult, make it me. If your version of what just happened starts to circulate, I'll make damn sure to set the record straight. I killed the scene. Not her."

Evelyn's cheeks were burning. She didn't dare look at Sol, she couldn't look at Barry, and the idea of locking eyes with a stranger was too much to contemplate. So she looked between the director and the writer and waited for someone, anyone, to break the silence.

"Go home, Evelyn."

She looked at Sol. He looked angrier than she'd ever seen him. "Go..."

"Go home," he snapped, then ran a hand down his face. "We'll shoot the, the seduction scene today with Joe and Adora. We'll do the Artemis stuff tomorrow like we had planned." He looked at Evelyn but his eyes skipped over her like he was afraid of making Barry angry just by looking at her. He started to walk away and motioned for Daniel to follow him. Over his shoulder, he told Evelyn, "Get the hell out of here. Tomorrow. Five am."

Evelyn didn't give him the satisfaction of acknowledging what he'd said. The crowd had started to disperse and she hurried to catch up with Barry.

"Thank you for that."

"I was only standing up for myself," he said without looking at her. "Trying to make me do a scene like that with an unwilling partner is extraordinarily bad behavior. They should never have tried it."

"Right," Evelyn said. "I... of course I understand that. But I wanted to thank you anyway."

He finally looked at her. His eyes were so kind that she almost cried. "I would have just assumed it had been okayed with you if you hadn't spoken up. So thank *you*. For letting me know."

She understood that what had just happened wouldn't be brought up again. She nodded. "You're welcome. We have to look out for each other, right?"

"Sure do. I have to go get ready for the new scene, though."

"Don't let me keep you."

He bobbed his head once and turned away, leaving her behind.

She stood there on the set, alone, and watched as the rest of the crew returned to their duties. She was in her street clothes on a stage made up to look like Olympus, feeling like a complete idiot, wondering if this job was even worth all the hoops she was jumping through to keep it. She felt right in front of a camera. Once someone called *ACTION!*, all the stress and frustration felt worthwhile. And there was nothing like seeing herself on a big screen.

It wasn't until that moment when she realized seeing the movie in Cicero hadn't been about her mother at all. She'd said it at the time, but it didn't really click in her brain until this moment. That damn woman had never been proud of her, and the stupid boat movie was never going to change her mind. It was about Gracie seeing the movie, seeing her, and being right next to her when she did. Gracie was important to her. She could admit that now. She didn't want to put a name to the feeling, but she'd be lying if she said Gracie was just some reporter she'd gone for a long car ride with.

A male voice behind her softly said, "If we can get you to clear the set, please..."

"Right, sorry."

She walked away, leaving Olympus behind. She wondered if the driver was still around. Probably not. But that didn't matter. She would get her things and catch the damn bus if she had to. She wanted to get home, shut all the windows, and spent the next few hours thinking long and hard about what her next steps were going to be.

Evelyn had fallen asleep on her couch when she realized the knocking on the door was real and not part of her dream. And what a dream it had been. Gracie, hair long and flowing, shirt open to reveal her breasts, lips parted. She was glorious and fully feminine, and Evelyn wanted her as badly as she had wanted her in the 'Simon' get-up. In her last moments of grogginess, between the nap and returning to the world, she felt the knowledge she was actually, undeniably, and sexually attracted to a woman finally sink in.

She didn't have time to process the discovery because the knock came again. She stood up, smoothed down her skirt, and made sure her hair wasn't too a-shambles. The visitor knocked again just as she reached the foyer.

"Criminy, give me a second," she called.

She hadn't realized she was expecting it to be Gracie until she swung the door open and saw Barry Denton on the stoop.

"Hiya, Evie. Sorry. Not really a fan of dropping in myself, but I thought we needed to talk."

He had changed into his street clothes, but somehow still managed to project the energy of a Greek god. Evelyn didn't really want him in her house, but she felt like she owed him one for sticking up for her on-set. He might have saved her career. Besides, she was damned curious about what he had to say. She stepped back and ushered him inside.

"Nice place. I'm in the Palisades."

Evelyn shut the door. "Is Sol on the rampage?"

"What? Oh, no. Not really. I think the scene was his petty little attempt to get back at you for everything. He didn't think it would be that big of a deal until you blew up at him. Now he's mostly trying to save face. 'It really was just for the movie! Honest!' He's hanging as much of it on Daniel as he can. The crew seems to think you were just sticking up for yourself. The cast is trying to think of themselves in that situation, so they kind of think you're a superhero."

"That's a relief. And a shocker." She walked past him and nodded at the kitchen. "Something to drink? I don't really know what I have."

"Water's fine." He followed her as far as the counter. "I started thinking about what happened today, and what the perception of it might be. Not just on set, but when word gets out."

She brought him a glass of water. "Why would word get out?"

"You screamed at a director in front of the entire production. It's going to be talked about. And the fact I stuck up for you is going to be part of the conversation."

She shrugged. "You come out looking like the white knight. Is that a problem?"

"No. But people might start wondering *why* I stuck up for you. I know, the obvious answer is because it's the right thing to do. Ask any actor to strike an unwilling scene partner in front of a camera, I hope everyone in town would have ripped the script to shreds. I'm just wondering if there's maybe an unexpected benefit we can take from it. Well. Mainly me. If we told people that I stood up for you because we're an item."

Evelyn furrowed her brow. "Why would we do that? Wouldn't people believe you did it just because you're a good person? Saying it was just because I'm your girlfriend makes you come off a little less well, actually."

Barry nodded slowly. "That's true. It's less altruistic this way. But it helps in other ways."

"What ways?

"I'm queer."

Evelyn blinked and took a step back. She had no idea how to categorize her reaction. She was scared he had sensed something about her, worried someone might overhear what he'd just said and think it applied to her. Somehow her dreams and the things she'd done with Gracie on the road had already caught up with her. They knew, whoever 'they' were, and her punishment would be swift and cruel.

Barry held up his hands. "Whoa, whoa. I'm sorry. I didn't think I'd throw you into a panic. We can just forget I said anything..."

"No," she finally said, her brain spinning in her head. "W-why, why would you t-tell me that?"

"Because I feel like I can trust you. You stood up for what was right for yourself. Not just today, but with that article. Hopefully you're willing to do the same for someone else. Sometimes tabloid people sniff around and ask why an eligible bachelor like me has been single so long. There are only so many excuses I can give. I don't remember hearing about you dating anyone, so I thought maybe you could just play the role a little to get them off my back."

Evelyn relaxed. "Oh. As a thank-you for sticking up for me."

Barry's eyes widened, and then he looked away. "Well, I kind of thought of it that way. But you can say no. It's not... I'm not saying you have to do this because I stuck up for you. You don't owe me anything for that."

"What would it entail?"

"Dinner a couple of nights a week. Being seen out in public. Going for walks. Nothing untoward. Nothing you're uncomfortable with. And all paid for by me, of course."

Evelyn poured herself a glass of water and took a sip. It would be a good way to deflect from the bad press about her flying around. And she did owe him for risking his own job, even if it wasn't an official one-for-one exchange. He stuck his neck out for her. The least she could do is repay the favor, especially if it was as easy as letting him pay for a few of her meals.

"And you're sure they'll believe you'd settle for someone like me?"

Barry laughed. "Are you kidding? Any guy would jump at the chance to be on your arm. I feel a little guilty keeping you from them."

Evelyn thought about Gracie's arms, then dismissed the thought. "What the hell. I'm sure people are saying terrible things about me out in the world. It would be nice to pepper in a little good stuff."

He sighed, his shoulders sagging. "Thank you, Evie. You're a lifesaver. Truly, just playing along for the rest of the shoot would go a long way to taking the heat off."

"You're welcome. A couple of dinners with a handsome, polite man who isn't going to try and get in my pants. There are worse favors you could've asked me for."

Barry smiled. He was completely relaxed now, and it made him even more handsome. "Can I ask you something, though? And you can choose not to answer."

"Go on."

"When I first told you, I thought I'd terrified you. I thought I had completely misread you completely. But now you seem fine with the idea of me being... the way I am. So what was that initial panic about?"

Evelyn took a drink of her water to buy time before she had to answer. Then the put the glass down and looked him in the eye.

"Because I think I'm queer, too."

Barry stared at her. Then he picked up his glass and held it out to her. "To finding each other in the strangest ways."

Evelyn laughed and clinked her glass against his, then downed the rest of it in a single swallow.

CHAPTER SEVENTEEN

GRACIE WALKED up to the barrier, a chain link fence which seemed absurdly inadequate for the job. She didn't even want to risk resting her hands on it for fear the whole thing would collapse. It was better to stay a few feet back, because it gave her a chance to take in the truly marvelous site spreading out in front of her for as far as the eye could see: the Grand Canyon at sunrise.

This experience almost hadn't happened. She had all but decided she wasn't going to take any side trips on her first night back on the road. She had called Bill to let him know she'd have the profile ready as soon as she got into town. Her plan was to spend every day composing in her head, then writing it down when she stopped for the night. That would give her plenty of time to get the necessary length and edit out anything extra. She wanted Bill to know she could drop it at the offices for proofreading before it went into the Sunday edition.

"Forget it. Profile's canceled."

Gracie had dropped down onto the edge of the motel's bed. "What do you mean, canceled?"

"You're a writer. You should understand small words like that." She heard him crunch something between his teeth. "Evelyn Wade is poison right now. She's toxic. The phones have been ringing off the hook this whole week with advertisers wanting to pull out."

"That doesn't make any sense." She closed her eyes and rubbed her forehead. "Why would advertisers care about–"

"Because they got calls from people a lot more powerful than Bill Swain, editor of the *Merc*. They wanted us to retract the whole thing, say you lost your mind and made the whole thing up, but I'm not going that far. I told everyone I'm standing by the article, because I know it came direct from Evelyn Wade's lips to your pen. And once you get back to town, we'll sort out this whole kidnapping hoo-hah. She's back in town, none the worse for wear, and apparently she's back at work on the movie. So the cops are starting to get bored. You'll be fine. The paper will be fine."

"And what about Evelyn?"

"That's really up to her, isn't it?"

Gracie had tried to sleep after that, but her brain refused to shut up. So after an hour of tossing and turning, she threw her things back into her suitcase, checked out, and got back onto the road. She wanted to get home. She wanted this whole damn road trip behind her. The farther she got from Illinois, the easier it was to not think about what happened in the motel, to not think about the thunderstorm. She made the decision to just drive straight through.

She only stopped when she got tired. She got off the main road and found side streets and parking lots of stores that had closed for the night and slept. The method got her across the plains and into the mountains in what felt like no time at all.

The first sign pointing the way to the Grand Canyon made her remember Evelyn pushing her to take a side trip. It had probably just been a stalling tactic, a way to postpone the ugliness in Cicero, but there had been real interest in her voice when she talked about it. Gracie had never felt very strongly one way or the other about the Grand Canyon, but maybe it was worth seeing... maybe...

She finally decided there was nothing to lose and pulled off the highway so she could change her route. Once she'd gotten everything figured out, she took the next exit and headed south.

The trip had been made in absolute darkness. No ambient light from nearby towns, no moon, nothing but the headlights of her car cutting a relatively meager wedge out of the black. She caught quick glimpses of wildlife on the edge of the road. Elk, rabbit, foxes. They ran up, eyes shining with reflected light. They froze in their tracks, then twisted and vanished as quickly as they had appeared. She drove more carefully after that.

She slept in the backseat again, setting an alarm to be sure she was awake for dawn. Her alarm buzzed much too soon, and she stumbled from the parking lot to find a good place to watch.

It would be a huge compliment to call what she found a walkway. It was an arm of rock with fencing on either side to give the illusion of safety. She eventually arrived at a wider observation point and settled in. She didn't have to wait long.

Light poured in from the east. The sky changed colors, and the clouds expanded and began rolling as if someone had thrown a switch. She could see for what seemed like a thousand miles, the entire sky laid out in front of her as the shape of plateaus and rocky cliffs appeared out of the darkness. It was like the stone was glowing from within, purples and pinks and blues to match the sky.

Gracie knew she was holding her breath and let it out slowly through pursed lips. It was only when the sun was fully in the sky that she realized she'd forgotten her camera. She wasn't too concerned about that, though. There was no way her camera could possibly have captured what she'd just witnessed, and trying to get the right shot would have distracted her from the experience. She would much rather have the memory than a flimsy piece of film.

She stayed as long as she could justify, then made her way

back down the winding path to her car. She was grateful she hadn't been able to see the steep fall on either side when she had ventured out. Given how scared Evelyn had been on the mountain pass, she might not have even wanted to risk it. Those wide open views would have helped, though. And Gracie would've been there to help her, hold her hand, keep her steady...

She stopped at the end of the path and turned back to look one more time. Everything was lit now. She was angry at herself for describing it as a "big hole" in the ground. Now she understood what made everyone flock here, why everyone said it was a thing that had to be seen to be believed. She knew her camera would never do justice to the magnitude. It was like standing on the edge of the Earth and finally *seeing* it. The world stretched out in front of her and, above it, a wider expanse of sky than she could ever remember seeing.

"Are you okay?"

Gracie turned toward the little old woman who had spoken. The lady's eyes were hidden behind big oval sunglasses, but there was an understanding smile on her face.

"I'm fine." When she heard a tremor in her voice, Gracie realized she was crying. She touched her cheek to confirm it, and laughed quietly as she rubbed her thumb against her wet fingertips. "Sorry."

"Don't be sorry, dear. First time?"

"Yeah."

The lady nodded. "My twelfth. We live in Vegas, so it's not a huge trek. But it still gets to me that way sometimes."

Gracie inhaled slowly to get her breathing back under control. "I'm sad, too. I could have shared this moment with someone. Someone who... I... guess means more to me than I realized."

"Is she still alive?"

Gracie was startled, then realized the woman thought she was a man. Of course her 'someone special' would be a woman. She nodded.

"Yeah. She's still alive."

The old woman gestured at the canyon with both hands. "Well, *this* isn't going anywhere. Go get her. Bring her back. Second time is just as impressive, especially if it's with a 'someone.'"

Gracie nodded. "Thank you."

The woman waved, already walking away. "You're welcome, dear. Don't wait too long. The canyon will always be here, but we won't."

Gracie arrived back in Los Angeles in early afternoon. She'd only stopped once to get something to eat, a hamburger which remained half-eaten in its wrapper on the passenger seat. Before this trip, she would have been apoplectic about anyone doing something so potentially messy in her car, but getting back home was more important than the upholstery. She intended to spend the time planning what she would say when she arrived.

She had seven hours from when she left the canyon, plenty of time to compose the perfect speech, but she passed the city limits sign without even the slightest idea of how to start. She decided to hope and pray that the words would come to her in the moment.

It was the third day since Cicero, since they'd last seen each other. Evelyn had been home for two days at that point. Two days of thinking about the trip and everything that happened on it, what she wanted it to mean, where she wanted to go... if anywhere.

Gracie drove to Silver Lake and spent a few minutes driving in circles because she couldn't remember Evelyn's exact address. She finally consulted her notebook and drove there, parking across the street, and sinking back into her seat to stare at the unassuming front of the house.

All she had to do was get out, walk up to the front door, ring the doorbell...

Then what? Wait for Evelyn to say something first? She couldn't put that kind of pressure on her. She had to at least try to start a conversation.

"Here I am"? "Sorry about throwing you to the wolves"?

She had been parked long enough to feel conspicuous when the front door to the house opened. She tensed, torn between jumping out of the car and diving onto the floorboard so she wouldn't be seen. Hiding wouldn't help anything anyway; it's not like there was a fleet of green Desotos floating around town. It turned out it didn't matter what she did, because she didn't immediately recognize the man who had come out of the house.

He was ridiculously handsome. His hair was mussed. He was wearing a white undershirt, a more formal shirt draped over one muscular arm.

Gracie felt her cheeks burning as she watched him walk to his car. He pulled out of Evelyn's driveway and zipped past her without so much as a sideways glance, even though he must have seen her sitting there like an idiot. Her fingers were shaking so badly that she could barely turn the key to start the engine, anger and embarrassment filling her whole body to bursting. She didn't want to be anywhere near Evelyn Wade when it exploded.

She drove away. She held the wheel in a two-fisted death grip, her arms as rigid as oaks, eyes locked on the road ahead. Her driving was completely mechanical and without destination or intent in mind. She just wanted to get away.

It was clear what had happened. Her brain put the pieces together even though she wanted it to shut down, to ignore everything.

Evelyn had panicked. She came home, realized what they'd done, and jumped on the first male specimen that presented itself. She wanted to put as much distance between herself and Gracie as possible. She'd seen it before, and it was never anything less than heart-shattering. She refused to cry this time. She refused to admit she'd believed her time with Evelyn was anything more than a lark, some fantasy, a hiccup in both their lives. She'd had her fun and now...

And now.

She drove until she saw the ocean and found a place to

park. She was at the Santa Monica Pier, and the idea of being among a crowd of strangers felt like the safest thing in the world at the moment. She took off her shoes and walked out onto the scorching sand. Her feet adjusted to the temperature in due time, and she let herself sink in a little with every step, focused on the stretch of blue and the waves crashing against the shore. Finally she dropped down, sitting on a small rise, and folded her arms across her knees.

The ocean was still terrifying. It was huge and endless and she felt her heart racing just being this close to it. But somehow it was a little more bearable after standing on the edge of the Canyon. And the beating of her heart could just be emotions struggling to get out. Her face was hot and she pressed her hands against her cheeks. The tears there surprised her, but part of her knew they'd been falling since she stopped moving.

She buried her face in her elbow, hoping no one else on the beach noticed the sobbing woman in their midst. She hoped they would just let her be alone in her misery.

***

She finally forced herself to go home. She'd only been gone for a week, but all the familiar trappings of her home felt like things she'd dreamt once. Her usual parking spot had a different car in it. Her living room felt cold and abandoned. The only thing that seemed to have remembered her was the bed. The mattress welcomed her, and she was half asleep by the time she pulled the blankets up over her fully-clothed body. She woke several times during the day but always managed to drift off again. She considered it a full-body reset after everything she'd just been through. Four thousand miles of monotonous roads and the endless hum of tires on asphalt had apparently made her brain weary in a way she couldn't understand.

Besides, it wasn't like there was any reason for her to get up. No profile to write, and Bill would probably be glad if she just stayed away from the office for as long as possible given the trouble she'd caused for him. Maybe she'd spend another week in bed and then the road trip would be the thing that felt like a dream. That seemed like the best bet. Sleep until Evelyn was just a face on a poster.

Someone was knocking on her front door. She ignored it the first two times but it started again just as she was falling back to sleep.

With a growl, Gracie kicked away the blankets and forced herself off the mattress. She felt like death warmed over, too groggy to even walk straight without relying on the wall for balance. The knock came again.

"Give me a second, damn it." She pushed her hair out of her face with one hand as she pulled the door open with the other. She squinted at the sun, which seemed to be shining like a spotlight from just behind her guest. All she could see was a gilded silhouette in the shape of a woman. "What do you want?"

"Wow, you look like wet toast."

Gracie held up a hand to block the light. "Verity? What are you doing here?"

Verity stepped around Gracie and came uninvited into the apartment. "I've missed you around the office the past week, Simon. It's been absolutely *dreadful.* Boring. So when Mr. Swain told me you were back in town I decided to swing by and let you know your absence was noted. That's a nice feeling, isn't it? To know someone missed you?"

"Yeah," Gracie said with a sigh. "Yes, Verity, i-it's very sweet that you missed me while I was gone. But I've just spent seven full days driving, and I'm exhausted..."

"And...?"

Gracie stared at her. "And?"

Verity held her hands out to either side. "And *you* missed me...?"

"Of course," Gracie said, resigned. "Yes, I missed you, Verity."

She beamed and brought her shoulders up in an expression of glee, then spun on her heel and headed toward the kitchen. It was only then that Gracie noticed she was carrying a large paper bag. She hurried to catch up with her.

"What, um, what are you doing?"

"Cooking you dinner, silly." She put the bag down on the counter and started unloading groceries. "You just said yourself you spent a week on the road. Everything in your icebox is probably spoiled or growing mold." She tilted her chin down and looked reprovingly at her. "I know how you *men* can be, especially when it comes to feeding yourselves. I thought what better way to welcome you home than with a nice homecooked meal."

Gracie closed her eyes. "That's very sweet of you, Verity. Thank you. But it's really not necessary. I'm..." She suddenly realized she didn't know what food she had in the apartment. And, in all fairness, there was a good chance Verity was right about the level of expiration. "I, I'm fine, I can... I can take care of myself."

"The point is that you don't *have to*," Verity said. "You're welcome."

There didn't seem to be a dignified or polite way to get out of it, so Gracie just surrendered. "Thank you. I, um, I can at least help."

Verity waved her off. "No, no. Don't you dare." She came around the counter and brushed something off both of Gracie's shoulders. "You just rest. Go take a shower, change out of these road clothes, get feeling a little more at home."

"That actually doesn't sound so bad."

"Of course it doesn't. I know what men need." She winked, then tilted her head slightly. Her chipper expression changed into one of vague confusion. "You know, I don't think I've ever seen you without your glasses on. You were even wearing them the last time I saw you. The night I, um... stayed over." She grinned suggestively.

Panic spiked in Gracie's chest. She'd left her glasses on the nightstand. Stupid. "I-I was taking a nap. Just, um..." She backed away and ducked her head in a useless attempt to keep Verity from looking too closely at her.

"Aw, I didn't mean to make you self-conscious. I think

you look dashing without them. It makes your eyes look, um. I don't know. Softer."

Shit, fuck, damn it. Gracie nodded and kept her head down. "I-I'm just, I'll go take that shower... Everything you need should be in the kitchen..."

"Go on." Verity waved her away, chuckling at what she apparently thought was just standard male nervousness. She went back into the kitchen. "I can take care of myself out here."

Gracie was almost to her bedroom door before Verity called her again.

"Simon?" Gracie looked back and Verity smiled at her. "You're home sweet home, handsome. Time to put that silly road trip behind you."

Gracie swallowed the lump in her throat and nodded. "You've got that right, Verity. And I'm certainly going to try."

CHAPTER EIGHTEEN

THE ARTICLE was quickly forgotten. Gracie didn't know how she felt about that. Evelyn had seemed resigned to the fact it wouldn't be the explosive revelation it should've been, but it was still shocking to see how little impact it had. Maybe there were invisible ripples behind the scenes that no one was seeing, but there was no way to know that without contacting Evelyn. Maybe even she didn't know if anything had changed yet. Gracie was back at work, assigned to the same dull stories as always. No political news. Definitely no entertainment coverage. She felt like she'd gotten her fill of that world, and Bill had decided it wasn't worth the trouble to force it on her again.

Verity was a much more immediate problem. After the welcome-home dinner, which was perfectly platonic and ended with a kiss on the cheek, she'd started lingering around Gracie's desk at work. She'd somehow managed to get Gracie to agree to have dinner with her on three days out of the past week. They also had lunch together more often than not. It didn't seem possible to get out of the lunches, but Gracie had been trying to think of a polite way to stop the dinners.

She tried to never think about Evelyn. But reminding herself not to think about Evelyn - the long miles, the motels, a mouth around her thumb - only kept the memories bouncing around in her mind. One morning she woke up to the sound of rain on her window and had such a visceral memory to that storm, the car, Evelyn's weight on top of her, a hand on her breast... she had to masturbate before she could go back to sleep. She spent the rest of the day furious at herself for being triggered so easily.

For the most part, though, life was back to normal. She was convinced Verity would lose interest or get fixated on someone who actually returned her affections.

She fully believed that would happen until the lunch when Verity casually asked what Gracie was planning for their anniversary.

Gracie stared, her sandwich halfway to her mouth. Verity was sitting across from her in the chair she always pulled over from Mort's desk, poking through her salad to spread dressing around.

"Our what?"

"Our anniversary. One month since the big..." She lowered her voice to a whisper. "Sleepover."

Gracie sat up straighter in her chair. "That's not when we started da~ We're not *dating*. We're just spending time together."

Verity rolled her eyes. "Oh Simon. You're not still playing that game, are you? It's one thing to be coy. It's another thing to be charmingly oblivious. But now you're just being hurtful."

"Honestly, I'm not trying to be." Gracie sagged back in her chair. "Verity, you're an amazing woman. You're gorgeous. You're brilliant. But we're not right for each other."

Verity twisted her lips, brow furrowed, and jabbed her fork into her salad. "You've never even tried. Don't I deserve at least *trying*?"

"Yes. Of course you do. That's what I'm saying. You deserve someone who will try. I'm not that person."

"So you want me to believe you're not attracted to me?"

Gracie closed her eyes. "No, I'm not saying that..."

"Because I can tell, you know. I can tell you're holding yourself back. You want me. Is it because we work together?"

There it was. The perfect way out. Gracie opened her mouth to pounce on it, but Verity continued before she could.

"It's a bullshit excuse."

"Verity..." She looked around, grateful the rest of the office had gone out to lunch. "There... there's... someone else. Someone I care about. Okay? A-and it wouldn't be fair to her or *you* if I pursued something with you."

Verity crossed her arms over her chest. "Who."

Gracie winced. "It's not that simple. I can't just—"

"Good grief," Verity grumbled, rising from her chair and spinning on the ball of her foot. "You're unbelievable, Simon Grace."

"Wait." Gracie stood, almost tripped over her chair, and pursued. "Wait, don't storm out."

Verity spun to face her. "You don't want me here, and now you don't want me to go. Which is it, Simon? Hm? Maybe you want to just keep me on the hook in case this 'other' thing doesn't work out." She raised an eyebrow. "Is that it? Am I your backup?"

"No." Gracie rubbed her forehead and looked at the ground. "I wish I could just..."

Verity was a good person. She was kind. She was beautiful and Gracie would legitimately be interested in a relationship with her, but there was absolutely no chance of that happening with such a huge secret between them. Verity didn't even know who she was, and therefore couldn't want her. She deserved someone who returned her feelings. Gracie had no idea how to explain that without hurting her.

She looked up, then scanned the room to make sure they were alone. She took Verity by the arm and pulled her into a storage room. She found the light switch for the single bulb hanging in the center of the room and flipped it, revealing a space full of boxes stacked taller than they were.

Gracie weaved through the mess to a spot that would still be out of sight even if someone opened the door. Verity's heels clicked on the floor as she followed Gracie.

"You're scaring me, Simon."

"I know, I'm sorry, but I need to tell you something and I don't want anyone walking in on us."

She reached the corner and put her back to it, turning around. The light was pathetically dim here and cast strange shadows on Verity's face. Gracie was sure her glasses were doing the same, so she took them off. She pushed her hair back as well.

"I'm a woman."

Verity's nose wrinkled, her eyes narrowed, and she hunched her shoulders. "Pardon?"

"My name isn't Simon Grace, it's Gracie Simon. I'm a woman. I just put a man's name on my submissions so I could get a job. And then it kind of snowballed into this."

"You must think I'm insane to believe this."

"Verity~"

"*You* are a *man*," Verity said. Then she stepped forward and clapped her hand hard against the crotch of Gracie's slacks.

It was such a sudden, unexpected move, that Gracie didn't have time to retreat. She wouldn't have had the room to escape anyway, given how she was crammed into the corner. Instead she just went rigid, arms out to the side, back hunched, and clenched her teeth as she watched Verity's expression change. Anger seeped into confusion, then became shock. Her eyes widened and she looked down. She spread her fingers wider and pressed harder.

Gracie grunted. "Could you, um... not..."

Verity pulled her hand away like she'd just seen a spider. She backed up until she was pressed against the shelves.

"Y-you're a... you..."

"Verity, please. I'm begging you..."

"Oh, God." Verity clapped a hand over her mouth. Then, realizing where it had just been, dropped it. "Oh, God!"

She turned and fled the room. Gracie started to pursue, but then realized how it might look to anyone who witnessed the situation.

She took a step back and slumped against the wall, put a hand over her face, and tried to imagine the worst possible scenario following Verity's discovery. If she could imagine it, then maybe it wouldn't be so bad. Maybe whatever actually happened would be a relief by comparison. She grunted in frustration and thumped her head against the wall.

Or maybe she should just resign and save Bill the trouble of firing her and quit. Make things easier for everyone.

Gracie stayed in the storage room until she heard voices outside, indicating others were coming back from lunch. She smoothed back her hair, put her glasses back on, and went out to try finishing the day.

Gracie got takeout chicken on the way home even though she doubted she could stomach it. Verity had never come back to work after the big reveal. Gracie spent the entire afternoon waiting for the axe to fall. Maybe it would be a phone call to Bill, who would then call Gracie into his office. Maybe Verity would come back in and stand on a desk to let everybody know at the same time. And just because it hadn't happened today didn't let her off the hook. It could happen tomorrow, or really any time at all. Verity could hold onto the information until she was having a bad day and wanted to cause a ruckus. There was no safety now. No letting her guard down. She would just have to wait and hope she got used to the feeling of dread in her belly.

Or, she thought as she approached her apartment to discover Verity was sitting with her back to the door, *I could just get all the dread out at once.*

Verity looked up at the sound of Gracie's approach, then quickly got to her feet. Gracie finished her approach carefully.

"Hi," she said.

"Hello." Verity stared hard at her, seemed to realize how rude that was and looked away. She must have realized that also came off as rude, because she started shifting her weight from one foot to the other. "I'm not planning to stay. You don't have to worry about that."

"Okay," Gracie said, still cautious. "Do you want to come in anyway?"

Verity shook her head. "No. I think I still need to do some thinking. But I've done a lot of thinking already. Enough to at least come here and talk to you about what you said."

Gracie looked around. The walkway was empty, and she didn't see anyone in the parking lot, but she'd overheard enough conversations of people passing her door to be cautious.

"Maybe we should talk about that inside."

"I'm not staying."

"No, I know, but... even thin walls are better than thin doors with peepholes."

Verity's eyes widened. "Oh shoot. Right. I-I'm sorry."

Gracie stepped past her and fumbled with her keys. She opened the door, ushered Verity inside, and shut the door behind her.

"I'm not going to tell anyone at work. I never was going to tell anyone, but I realized you were probably really worried about that. So, um, I wanted to make sure that was the first thing I told you."

"Thank you." Gracie felt the tension rise from between her shoulders. "I really appreciate that."

Verity nodded. She was still looking at her feet. "And I understand why you did it. Of course I do. I did the same kinds of job interviews you did, and it's a little miracle that I've gotten as far as I have. So to get to your position, it makes sense."

Gracie said, "I never meant to deceive you."

"No, no, of course you didn't. In fact, on that account, I probably owe *you* an apology. You tried to let me down as politely as possible and I just kept pushing."

"I didn't want anything to happen under false pretenses.

You didn't really know who I was."

Verity said, "Yeah. A-and if I'd known the truth I would never have... I-I'm not saying... There are women out there who are, um, supportive of that sort of thing? I guess? But I'm not one of them. I w-would have had a real problem if you'd let anything happen. I'm a little upset about how much actually *did* happen. But that's my fault. You were a perfect gentlema- uh, uh..."

Gracie said, "I got it."

"When I think of what I almost did-"

Gracie held up her hands. "Okay. You can stop. You're verging on offensive, okay?"

Verity flinched. "Sorry." She wet her lips and looked around the apartment. "I just wanted you to know that your secret is safe with me. And I'm not going to bother you anymore."

"We can still be friends."

"You, um, you mentioned something about finding me attractive, though. Was that true?"

Gracie nodded slowly. "Yeah. Of course."

Verity made a face. It was gone in an instant, but Gracie saw enough to bristle. Verity cleared her throat and smoothed down the collar of her blouse.

"I don't think being friends would be a good idea."

"Right." Gracie stepped out of the way so Verity could get to the door. "I really will miss having meals with you. Outside of the whole... flirting... I've enjoyed getting to know you."

She could tell Verity had no idea how to process that. She smiled tightly, eyes darting anywhere except for Gracie.

"I'll see you at work," Gracie said, taking pity on her.

"See you at work," Verity said, fleeing without a backward glance.

Gracie stood in the silence of the apartment after she was gone. She decided to focus on the positives. She was safe. She wouldn't have to live in fear of Verity trying to seduce her, which was almost the biggest relief of all. It was sad to lose a friend, obviously, but her overall peace of mind was going to improve. So there was that benefit.

But she'd gotten used to the company. They had good conversations when Verity wasn't trying to turn them into something they could never be. It had made her feel less alone, and now the crushing silence was back. The loneliness was back. It never bothered her before. She'd had hundreds of meals by herself with a book, or the radio playing, or just people-watching out the window. But now, because of the road trip...

...because of Evelyn...

She put her chicken down on the table and went into the kitchen to get a plate. Talking to Verity had also been a way to distract herself from other thoughts. Like the fact that she'd heard through various sources that Evelyn had officially and publicly started dating Barry Denton. Filming was complete on *Olympus*, and they made the relationship public by going out to dinner at the Brown Derby and making sure they were seen by the photographers camped outside the exits.

The picture confirmed Denton was the man Gracie had seen leaving Evelyn's house upon her return to Los Angeles. It was easy enough to figure out the timeline on what happened. Evelyn let her guard down, fucked a woman, panicked about what that made her, and went out to prove she was 'normal'. It was a classic story. Verity was probably on her way to find the first willing red-blooded male a ten-mile radius.

Gracie sat down and put her head in her hands. It was an old story and one in which she was sick of playing a starring role.

CHAPTER NINETEEN

THERE WERE men having sex in Evelyn's guest bedroom.

She was trying not to think about it. But this entire night had been built around the event, so she couldn't separate their activities from her current situation. She was sitting on the back porch, smoking a cigarette, looking at the part of the sky not obscured by neighboring houses or palm trees. Lillian Irwin was on the lounge chair beside her, also smoking, also most of the way through the bottle of wine she had brought.

Lillian was there as the date of Edward Prinz, the man who was currently defiling - or being defiled by - Barry. She wasn't entirely sure how it worked. She definitely knew she didn't want to know the details of how it worked. This was the fourth of their "entertaining nights" since they publicly announced their so-called relationship, and the fourth couple who had been their guests. It was easy for her, and she didn't mind it. She was content to just set up the evenings, have a nice meal with some charming guests, and then spend an hour or so pretending to bond with whatever woman tagged along for the ride.

"Does this happen often?" Evelyn ashed her cigarette in

the tray next to her chair.

Lillian smiled at her. "I don't think we're supposed to ask that, dear. In fact it's probably best not to ask any questions at all. Barry pays for the meals and everything, right?"

"Of course."

"Well, then just enjoy yourself."

Evelyn said, "I don't mind the dinners. Or the conversations. But just sitting here while we know *that* is happening..." She nodded toward the house. "It's more than a little awkward. I'm surprised they're able to perform at all knowing we're basically down here just waiting for them to finish."

Lillian said, "You know we don't have to just sit here and wait."

"What do you mean?"

Lillian shifted on the chair so that she was lying on her side. "I mean maybe we could have a little fun of our own. Sometimes the girls and I take advantage of being left to our own devices and... get to know each other as well as the boys are."

Evelyn was grateful for the dark so her blushing wouldn't be visible. "Oh."

"Have I scandalized you?"

"No," Evelyn said too quickly. "I've... I know what Barry is and I don't have a problem with it. So obviously I know there are others... the other... the opposite..."

Lillian chuckled softly. Evelyn couldn't help but feel like she was being laughed at.

"I've had sex with a woman."

Lillian sat up straighter. "*Really.*"

Evelyn squeezed her eyes shut and cursed her big, stupid mouth. "Uh huh."

"Tell me everything."

"Um, I... No, I shouldn't betray her confidence..."

"I don't need her biography, dear. Just the broad strokes. So to speak. Give me something to picture tonight when I'm alone in my big bed."

Evelyn's blush deepened until she was sure she was glowing. "We, um, were in a car. There was a storm. I got on top of her. We kissed. She, um, she was in the driver's seat. And we kissed some more. And she put her fingers in me."

She heard a sharp intake of breath and looked over. Lillian had dressed for the night in a pair of black slacks and a silk blouse. The slacks were now undone, and her finely boned fingers were tracing along the edge of what appeared to be a pair of lacy underpants.

"Don't stop there," Lillian said breathlessly.

Evelyn was worried about her neighbors overhearing. They were outside, exposed, but she was pressed against a wall of indecision. She wanted to stop and run from this. She wanted this to last for the rest of the night. She watched as Lillian's hand disappeared into her underwear, then ran her eyes up over the curves of Lillian's breasts. She was breathing hard, and they rose and fell under the silk.

"I kissed her breasts," Evelyn said. "I licked her nipples until they were hard enough to suck."

Lillian moaned. Evelyn looked at her parted lips. Lips that were painted bright red. She imagined kissing them. Everything about Lillian was so feminine, everything soft and curved, so unlike Gracie.

"Where else did you put your mouth?"

"On her n-neck. We were in a car." She couldn't remember if she'd established that yet. She was finding it hard to catch her breath enough to speak. She put a hand between her legs and squeezed her thighs around it. "But she put her mouth on me the night before. Her lips and her tongue."

"Did you like it?"

Evelyn hissed, "Yes."

"Did you want to do it to her?"

"Oh fuck yes."

Lillian groaned. "Such language, I love it."

Evelyn bit her bottom lip and moved her hips against her captive hand. The chairs groaned under them. The legs scraped against the patio.

"I want to do it to you."

Lillian opened her eyes and stared at her, and then her lips parted in a wide O. She lifted her chin, hunched her shoulders, and gave a tiny, choked howl that Evelyn knew could only have been an orgasm. Evelyn's face burned and she used her fingers against the crotch of her pants, pushing herself to the edge to follow Lillian over. She managed to remain silent when she came, but her face contorted into a strange and unflattering mask until the tremors stopped.

"My, my..." She looked over to see Lillian licking her lips, limp in the lounge chair. She had one hand flung over her head, and her eyes were half-lidded. "You're quite the storyteller."

Evelyn fell back against her own seat.

"Do you really want to use your mouth on me?"

"My god," Evelyn muttered.

She was saved from answering by a clatter on the stairs inside the house. They turned to see Barry and Edward had reappeared. Their hair was wet from the shower. Edward was wearing the same clothes as earlier, though more rumpled with the shirt open at the collar. Barry had only bothered putting on his trousers which were also unbuttoned.

"We'll have to revisit this another time, I suppose."

Lillian got up, smoothed her hands over her clothes, and went inside. Evelyn gave her nerves a second to settle down. Her face was burning hot and she fanned her cheeks with her hand before she followed.

The two couples made idle chat for a few minutes before Edward suggested they call it a night. The men embraced by the door, nothing untoward beyond a slightly too-long brush of hand over shoulder. Lillian kissed Evelyn on the cheek and lingered just long enough to whisper, "I would devour you if you let me." Evelyn shivered and found herself struck mute until the door was closed.

Barry had gone back into the kitchen. "I can wait a bit and head home after your neighbors go to sleep. Or I don't mind spending the evening on your couch if that's better. I'm fine with either option."

Evelyn followed him. "Is it worth it?"

He shrugged. "The couch makes my back a little stiff in the morning, but otherwise~"

"No, not that." She took a seat at the kitchen counter. "Doing all of this just for sex. Is all this running around, keeping secrets, being constantly terrified of being exposed… is it worth it?"

"Oh, that." He filled a glass with water and took a drink as he considered the question. "Well," he finally said, "what's the alternative? Spending life alone? Becoming a monk? Settling for insufferable sex with a woman just because that's socially acceptable? No offense."

She smiled at that. "No offense taken."

He twisted his lips and narrowed his eyes at the wall as he considered it. "The simple answer is yes. The danger has always been there, you know? It's always been risky even before I became an actor, but I never let it stop me. I think…" His voice trailed off and he shifted his weight. "I guess a better question would be 'is it enough?' And I think my answer to that question is also yes. It's not everything I'd want. It's not a real relationship. But it's better than nothing."

Evelyn considered that. "Thank you. For a real answer and not just making a joke."

He shrugged. "I could tell you weren't just making conversation. What's going on with you?"

"I told you I thought I was maybe, um, like you. But part of me thought maybe it was both. I could be with both. But that doesn't feel right. I think I just want women. I-I mean, want to be with them. Or, or one of them." She covered her face with both hands. "God. Never mind."

"Don't be so hard on yourself," he said, chuckling. "It's not something you can just admit all at once. And you shouldn't. You should be sure how you feel before you go around saying anything out loud. You never know who you can trust."

She moved her hands so that she was cupping her chin. "I

can trust you."

"Only because you have a bazooka aimed at my head if I ever make you mad. I have to behave and stay on your good side."

"Behave? Stay on my good side?" She sat up straighter and looked at him with feigned shock. "Do you mean you've been on your best behavior? Goodness, man!"

He chuckled again and finished his water. "What's the verdict on where I'm spending the night? I'm honestly okay with either, but if I'm staying here I need to let my assistant know."

She waved vaguely toward the couch. "Stay here if you want. As long as you're serious about the couch being a suitable alternative to your actual bed."

"You don't know how crappy my bed is."

Evelyn came around the kitchen island and kissed his cheek. "Thank you, Bartholomew."

"Oh, lord, throw that ugliness in the trash, please, I beg you."

"It makes you sound refined." She patted his arm. "I'm going to bed."

"Goodnight, Evie."

She waved at him over her shoulder as she went upstairs. Her mind was filled with thoughts of Lillian, and as a result she spent longer in the shower than she otherwise would have. Afterward, her face scrubbed of makeup and her favorite robe brushing against her sensitive scrubbed skin, she sat on the edge of her bed and took out the latest copy of the *Mercury*. There still hadn't been a profile of her. She'd scanned every page of every edition that had come out since her return from Chicago. The article never showed up, but Gracie was still showing up in bylines. She was writing stories like POLICE SEARCH FOR PROWLER IN BEL-AIR and STOLEN PROPERTY RECOVERED; SUSPECTS STILL AT LARGE, nothing associated with Hollywood at all.

At first she thought maybe Gracie hadn't gotten back in time to print it on the day they originally planned. But then the next issue was also silent, and the one after that. She finally had to admit the profile wasn't going to happen.

She didn't know why she was surprised. Their whole plan had gone to hell the second Max showed up. It had been a risky play from the beginning and they'd gotten a lot farther with it than she really expected to. The important article had made it to print. That was the only thing that mattered. Even if it had turned out to be a dud.

She'd never expected a nuclear explosion in the middle of Sunset Boulevard. She didn't think studios would march their naughty boys out of the building and replace them with good men who knew how to behave like adults on set. If she was completely honest with herself, she didn't know *what* she had expected to happen once the dust settled. But for everything to just go back to normal was extremely disheartening.

Evelyn fell back onto the bed and crossed her arms, pinning the newsprint to her chest. She was the only one who had been in danger. She was the only one suffering. She should have just kept her stupid mouth shut.

Of course if she'd done that, she never would have met Gracie or gone to Chicago. She never would have finally confronted her mother. And as painful as that had been, she was grateful it happened. It was the closure she hadn't realized she needed. She'd always been holding the door open with one hand just in case. Now she could let it go and move on.

The problem was that she wanted to move on with Gracie. She had been tempted by Lillian, and yes it would be amazing if Lillian was lying in bed next to her right now, but she knew anything they did together would just be an experiment or a substitute for what she really craved. She didn't want a girly woman in silks and lipstick. She wanted a woman who strutted in slacks and short hair. She didn't want to taste lipstick. She wanted to taste *lips*.

Evelyn closed her eyes and touched her mouth, imagining it was Gracie's hand. She had just started teasing the fingertips with her tongue when the phone jangled on the nightstand, scaring her half to death. She sat up and let the paper fall, fluttering to the floor as she crawled across the mattress and stretched to grab the receiver. She fumbled with it and exhaled a quick, "Hello," as she flopped onto her belly. "This is Evelyn Wade."

"Hello, Evelyn? This is a bad time."

She wasn't sure if the second phrase was a statement or just a poorly worded question. "No, it's only..." She looked for a clock, couldn't find one. She knew it was terribly late, though. She recognized the voice on the other end but it was out of context and strange in another way she couldn't pinpoint. "To whom am I speaking?"

"Oh, I'm so rude. I'm sorry. This is Adora Bell."

Evelyn arched an eyebrow. "Oh. Well, this is a surprise." She tried to move into a more comfortable position without making too much noise. "How did you get this number?"

"I asked someone on set. I don't want to get them in trouble. I swore I would only use it for something of the utmost importance."

Evelyn was definitely going to circle back around to the identity of the informant. Only a handful of people on the *Olympus* set knew her well enough to have provided her private number, and she was willing to cut any of them out of her life for such a transgression. She was more concerned about Adora's tone of voice. It was completely uncharacteristic. Flat, almost dull, as if she was struggling to find the energy to form the words. It could just have been the late hour. Or...

"Okay," Evelyn said. "Does this fit the bill?"

"I don't know. I think so. But I think that's something you have to decide." She sighed heavily, and then Evelyn heard the unmistakable clink of ice cubes against a glass as she took a drink. "After we wrapped on *Olympus*, Solomon called to congratulate me on my work in the movie."

Evelyn closed her eyes to brace herself for what was bound to come next.

"He said he had a couple of producer friends who were looking for someone just like me. He said he could name six films off the top of his head that I'd be perfect for. I could have my choice, just like a kid in a toy store. But he said it would have to be unofficial because it was unfair for the other actresses if they knew I'd just been handed whatever role I ended up taking. No one likes to think they're the second choice, you know?"

"What happened?" Evelyn asked. She listened to the wind outside, but it was hard to hear anything over her own rapid heartbeat.

"Nothing. I mean, nothing yet. But probably... nothing. I don't know." There was a long silence where she didn't even take a drink. "There's going to be a party at Solomon's house this weekend. The other producers are supposed to be there. Just to get a look at me. Get to know me a little better. Pitch themselves and the movies."

Evelyn said, "Adora, you--"

"I read the article," Adora said. "I mean, this isn't my first rodeo, Evie, I know what goes on in this town. But I didn't know how... I-I didn't know it happened to everyone all the time."

Evelyn sat up. "Adora. I can't tell you not to go to that party. I can't say your career won't suffer if you turn Solomon down. But you know what's going to happen at that party, and it's not going to have a damn thing to do with how good you are on-screen."

Adora's voice was tiny. "I know."

"You called me because you want me to talk you out of it. But that's not my place. I'm sorry."

"Would you go?"

Evelyn rolled her head from side to side, listening to her neck pop. "I don't know. But I didn't know I would refuse to film that spanking scene, either. Sometimes you just have to go with what your gut says in the moment. And your gut told you to call me. I think that's enough of an answer."

"What if I can't get hired on another movie?" Adora's voice wavered.

"What if this became the only way you *ever* got cast in a

movie? Directors and producers lining up to offer you a script just because they figure it's the easiest way to get in your pants."

Adora sighed heavily. "God damn it."

"It's a harder road, going the other way," Evelyn admitted. "You might not get the level of fame you deserve. Because you *are* talented, Adora. You can be a star on your own merits."

"You think so?"

Evelyn said, "You're younger than me and you're prettier than me. If I admit you're talented, you better believe it's the gospel."

Adora laughed. "Thanks, Evie."

"If you want to give me a call when it gets really rough, I'll be there for you. Even if you just want to talk."

"Really?"

"It's what I wanted someone to do when I was first starting out."

Adora sniffled. "I'll keep that in mind. Thank you."

"You're welcome. But for now I'm tired and I want to go to sleep. I think you should sober up before you make any decisions about Sol's invitation, okay?"

"I promise. Goodnight, Evie."

"Goodnight, Adora."

She hung up and slumped against the padded headboard. "Damn it, Sol, you piece of garbage. A girl that young... you had no right to put her in that position. Damn you."

But there was a bright side. Adora Bell, young and impressionable and so very endangered by the predatory wolves who used soundstages as a hunting grounds, had read the article. She'd made a smart decision to keep herself safe because of what Evelyn said, because of what Gracie wrote. She was enormously grateful to the ingenue for calling her. It was like she was a sign sent from Heaven to ease her mind at her moment of doubt.

They had done good in the world. Even if Adora was the only girl they ended up protecting, she felt like that was enough of a success. She smiled and slid down until she felt the pillow under her head. She was still dressed, and still lying on top of the blankets, but she didn't care. She wanted to drift off to sleep while this feeling of pure, blissful accomplishment was still fresh in her mind. Hopefully she could carry it with her into dreams.

Hopefully Gracie would be there waiting to share in their victory.

CHAPTER TWENTY

A FEW days later, Evelyn stood at the back window and stared out at the patio while Max McNeal prattled on behind her. More accurately, she stared at the lounge chair Lillian had been sitting in during her last visit. To be even more precise, she was trying to remember the color of the other woman's underwear. She thought it was white, but it had been difficult to tell for sure. The backyard had such poor lighting. Which was a good thing, considering what they'd almost done. And she supposed it didn't matter if they were white or baby blue when all she really cared about was~

"Are you even listening to me?" Max asked.

"Yes." She turned away from the lounge chair and went to join him at the kitchen island. "You said something about a script where men play poker and I'm a femme fatale who manipulates them all. Was I supposed to respond to that?"

He held up the script as if seeing it would affect her decision. "Really think about this one before you just say no. They're thinking of getting Gregory Peck for the cardsharp role..."

Evelyn flopped down on a stool across from him and

planted her chin in her hand.

Max sighed and flipped the script upside down. "So we pass on that. Riders of Vulture Canyon."

"Western?" He nodded slowly. "Prostitute or schoolmarm?"

"Prostitute," he admitted.

She took the script from him and placed it upside down on the others. "Next."

Max gestured at the pile. "That's it, Evie. Those are the directors willing to make you an offer. These are your options whether you like it or not. You have to pick one of them. Something here has to be the lesser evil." He sorted through the stack. "The poker one, you get to be a criminal. You get a gun, you can wear amazing fashion..."

"I don't care. Whatever the character is, she's just a prop for the male characters. Find me something like Artemis."

He gave a quiet chuckle. "I hate to tell you, but those scripts don't really exist, Evelyn. If you sit around waiting for another one, you're going to be too old for it anyway."

"There has to be something."

"Maybe there is. But it's not being offered to you."

She held out her hands. "Then *you* offer me to *them*. That's supposed to be your job. Sell me to the directors and the producers. Make them believe I'm the only person who could possibly be in their movie. You found me Artemis, find me the next one."

Max rubbed his forehead. "Evie, I'm sorry, but there aren't a lot of people willing to take a risk on you."

"A *risk*...?"

"You disappeared for a week in the middle of a shoot. You caused a ruckus and refused to film a scene, which required a major rewrite. You gave that interview to the paper that named names. People are reluctant to have you on their set, and honestly, you gave them a lot of reason to be worried."

She said, "So you vouch for me. You back me up, Max. Tell them the scene I refused to film was wedged in at the last minute and nothing had to be rewritten. Tell them I left to visit my dying mother. Tell them they'd be idiots to pass me up. That's why you're my agent, right?"

"It's not that easy."

"God forbid you actually have to work for what I pay you."

He shook his head. "Evelyn, you pissed off a lot of powerful people. It's not going to matter what I say to them, because people higher than all of us are saying you need to be punished. That means you're not getting called for Hitchcock or Walter Lang. You have to work your way back up. Prove you can play ball and be nice on movies like these."

Evelyn leaned back. "Get out."

He started gathering his scripts. "Probably smart. I have another meeting in the Valley in about an hour. We can talk again, go over the pros and cons~"

"No, we won't talk again. Get out and don't come back. You're fired."

Max stared at her. "You're not thinking clearly."

"I have an agent who wants to smack me back down to bit roles. You don't believe in me, so why the hell should I keep you on the payroll?"

"If you think it's hard to find directors willing to work with you, just imagine what it will be like finding an agent. I'm willing to fight, but~"

Evelyn shook her head. "You're done. You chose your side when you came and retrieved me like a dog told to fetch. So bye-bye."

Max shook his head sadly. "You're going to regret this, Evie. I promise you, it's going to be a scary, lonely world out there without me clearing the way."

"Somehow I feel like I'll survive."

Max left.

Evelyn went to the refrigerator and poured herself a glass of cold water. Her hands were shaking, her face burning. She pressed the cool pitcher against her forehead and closed her eyes. Maybe she had acted too hastily. Maybe she let her anger take control. Max had always had her best interest at heart, even when he was at his most infuriating. Hell, especially when he was infuriating. He'd told her to skip that movie about the *Titanic* she'd been desperate for, and it turned out to be a boondoggle. Overbudget and cursed with so many on-set accidents that the insurance finally shut them down.

"I'm going to be so angry at him if he's right," she muttered, staring down into her glass.

It was basically the same thing Gracie was suffering. She was being assigned mundane crime beat stories when her talents would be better served elsewhere. She hadn't been on the front page since the road trip ended. That had to be some kind of punishment.

Evelyn took a drink and tucked her bottom lip into her mouth. She looked into the living room, at the telephone sitting by the couch. She drifted over to it without thinking. She picked up the receiver and told herself she didn't have a motive, but she dialed information and listened to the line buzz in her ear. Another buzz. Then a click.

"How may I direct your call?"

"The Los Angeles *Mercury* office."

"Please hold."

Buzz, then two clicks, then a droning sounds. Evelyn waited. She crossed one leg over the other and sat up straighter. She looked out the window.

"Good afternoon, Los Angeles *Mercury*. How may I direct your call?"

"Simon Grace, please."

"One moment."

Another buzz. Evelyn's heart pounded in her chest. This time the wait was much shorter and ended mid-buzz.

"Simon Grace."

Evelyn's hand twitched at the sound of her voice. She somehow sounded exactly like a man, even though Evelyn knew the truth. It wasn't a parody, some gruff impersonation. In some ways her voice was still soft and feminine, but there was an edge to it. Evelyn couldn't explain it, but she knew that

Gracie could give lessons to quite a few professional actresses about how to alter their voices.

"Hello? Are you still there, caller?"

"I'm here," Evelyn said quietly.

Gracie was silent for a long time. Evelyn didn't count the seconds, but it felt like it should've been long enough for the sun to move across the living room floor.

"Hi."

Evelyn paced as far as the phone cord allowed. "How, um, how are you doing?"

"Fine?" It was a question, followed by a noise that indicated frustration. She was struggling to keep her voice low, and Evelyn was acutely aware that she was sitting at her desk in a presumably busy bullpen. "Sorry. I wasn't expecting to..."

"I know. I don't know why I called. I don't have anything to say."

"The article, the profile... my editor~"

"No, I understand. That's not important."

"I gave you my word."

"You did everything in your power to make it happen."

They were talking over each other, so Evelyn stopped talking. Apparently Gracie had the same idea, so there was just silence on the line.

"I just fired my agent."

"Really?"

"He was only bringing me garbage. He was letting the studios decide where I should work, and how, and with whom, and I wanted to find someone who would fight for me. I forgot to find out if a person like that actually exists."

Gracie said, "Hey, I fought for you."

Evelyn felt a flash of anger. She tried to fight it down, but the words came out anyway. "You just let him take me. You protected yourself and your own secret at my expense. Don't tell me you fought for me, Gracie."

Silence. "At the bar," Gracie finally said. "I fought for you at the bar. Literally. I had the bruises for a while..."

Evelyn put a hand over her face. "Oh, god. Right. No. I-I

remember. God, Gracie, I'm sorry. I was just so hurt by the... A-and of course you fought for me. Of course you did." She pressed the phone receiver hard against the side of her head as if she was trying to shove it all the way through her skull. "I'm sorry. I didn't mean to diminish that."

"It's okay."

"That's not the part of that night I think about."

Gracie laughed. It was a nervous sound. "You think about it?"

Evelyn nervously touched the collar of her blouse. "A lot, actually."

"Me too."

Evelyn rubbed her lips together and rested her shoulder against the wall.

"How, um..." Gracie cleared her throat. "How's, um, Barry?"

"What?" Evelyn had to search her suddenly distracted brain to remember who she was talking about. "Oh, uh, he's fine, I guess."

"The two of you..."

Evelyn realized how it must look to Gracie. She also realized the danger of revealing the truth to a journalist. Of course, this was *Gracie*, a woman with too many secrets to go around blabbing about anyone else's. But it wasn't Evelyn's secret to give away no matter how much she trusted the person on the other side.

"Yeah. I hope you don't think that has anything to do with you. Or us. Or what happened."

"You're a big girl. You can make your own decisions."

Evelyn flinched. "Gracie..."

"I should probably get back to work. I'm sorry."

"No, Gracie. Wait." She twisted the phone cord around her hand and pulled it tight. "Do you want to come over for dinner? You can meet Barry, and–"

"I'm not really, uh, I'm not... no, I don't think so."

Evelyn said, "I'd really like to explain. But I think it would be better to do it in person."

"It's fine," Gracie said, sounding weary. "It's not the first time this has happened to me. It won't be the last. It doesn't make what happened any less special. You don't have to feel bad about it. I said I was fine earlier, and I meant it."

"Gracie..."

"It's okay, Evelyn. Really. But I do have to go. You probably shouldn't call me again."

"Gracie, wait. Please."

There was a click, and the line died. Evelyn slumped against the wall and put the receiver against her forehead. She gave herself a few good whacks with it before she turned and slammed it back down on the hook. Stupid Barry and his stupid secret and stupid her for agreeing to it. If Gracie had just agreed to dinner, she could have had Barry tell the truth and settle everything. For now the best she could hope for is getting his approval to tell Gracie on her own the next time they spoke.

If they ever spoke again, that is.

The photo showed Evelyn sitting on a motel room bed, her lower body drowned in a sea of blankets. The top two buttons of her pajama top were unbuttoned, which put most of her bust on full display. There wasn't any cleavage or decolletage, it was almost entirely shoulder and collarbone, but Gracie couldn't stop herself from running her finger across the lines of it as if she could feel the skin under her fingers.

The picture captured Evelyn in the moments before waking up, in the breath after she dropped her pose and became a real person. Her hair was hideous. The photo wasn't framed well; the sun seeping in around the curtains washed out most of the details but gave its subject a gilded edge. It was perfect in its imperfection, and Gracie felt confident in saying it was one of the best photos she'd ever taken.

That was the only reason she hadn't ripped it up, or burnt it, or otherwise destroyed the photo. It was taken to accompany an article that was never going to be published.

And she had promised to let Evelyn see the pictures before she did anything with it. Since it was unlikely they would ever sit down and go over the roll, the proper thing to do would be destroying the pictures and burning the negatives.

But then they would be gone. She was in her darkroom, and the photo was clipped to a string in front of her, and she felt like it was a window back to that motel room. Before they'd kissed. Before she had felt Evelyn's weight on top of her, or knew how she tasted. She remembered the feel of Evelyn's hand on her breast and was only barely aware of moving her own hand to mimic the caress. She stroked her fingertips across the material of her shirt and closed her eyes. She could almost hear the rain on the roof, feel the heat of their breathing that had fogged up the windows...

Gracie snapped her eyes open, dropped her hand, and turned away from the picture. The attempted escape only made her focus on the other roll of film. The roll that she didn't want to develop.

The roll from the car.

She went over and picked it up. This is the one she should destroy. The film from the car. The photos Evelyn had told her to take. There was absolutely no reason to have it. She should just go back into the main room and expose the film to sunlight to take away the temptation. All it would take was three steps and one twist of her fingers to do the right thing.

It didn't matter if she did destroy it, because she could still see the images crystal clear in her mind. Evelyn's slip falling down to reveal her breasts. Pale nipples, dark. Freckles on pink skin. Lips parted, her tongue poking out.

Gracie didn't notice when she started the process of developing the film. Once the film was out, all she would have to do is turn on the light. One flip of the switch. But she didn't do it. She continued working. She knew she would make prints, which she would then have to guard with her life. She would never forgive herself if they were ever stolen or even seen by the wrong person.

But despite the danger, she wanted to see them again. She wanted to preserve something of that moment that was more substantial than her own memory.

The main reason she'd come into the darkroom was to shut off her brain. The darkness, and the repetitive act of developing prints, was just the relief she needed after the phone call. It was supposed to be a way to stop herself from obsessing over Evelyn. Apparently her brain had a sense of humor. Dinner? With Evelyn and her new boytoy? No way in hell would that ever happen. Gracie understood the relationship just fine already.

She'd felt Evelyn was different. She couldn't say why, exactly. Maybe it was just a case of wishful thinking. Her feelings for Evelyn were deeper than she wanted to admit, and she was having a hell of a time letting go.

She used the tongs to pull the print out of the tub, shaking it gently as she brought it across the room and hung it from a pair of pegs. She took a step back and stared at it. The light had created unusual and intriguing shadows over her chest and made her face look carved from stone. Her eyes reflected the light perfectly. It was maybe the best photo she'd ever taken and she would never show it to another soul.

She was torn away from her appreciation by the phone ringing. She left the darkroom and went back into the main part of her house. It was like stepping out of another dimension, one of blinding sunlight and colors. She blinked her eyes back into focus as she answered the phone. She hoped to hear Evelyn's voice on the other end, even though she knew there was no chance it would be her.

"Hello?"

"It's your lucky day," Swain said. "Wow. That's going to sound crass given the circumstances. Eh, who cares. I have an address. You got your pencil ready?"

Gracie kept a pad and pen next to the phone. "Go ahead."

He gave her an address in San Fernando. "Be there as soon as possible."

"Why is my lucky day in the Valley?"

"Because that Councilman Atwater fella you were so eager to interview a while back lives there. Or I suppose I should say he used to. Got real dead this morning. Some are saying suicide, others are saying he maybe got a little help."

Gracie's pen paused above the paper. "Wait. You're giving *me* this story? This is big."

"Yeah, potentially national shit. Don't screw it up, Simon. This is your way out of the doghouse. You ready?"

A dozen replies rolled through her mind. She had questions about whether this meant the article was already forgotten, if her profile of Evelyn was officially dead, if it was fair that she was getting a chance to move on when Evelyn was still suffering... She didn't ask any of them because she knew the answers and would have hated to hear them out loud.

"Simon?"

"Yeah," Gracie said, tearing off the page with the address on it. "I'm ready."

CHAPTER TWENTY-ONE

EVELYN KEPT her eyes on her plate to avoid looking at Barry, who was in the middle of a story about some script his agent had offered him. It was some Biblical epic and would be great exposure for him, but he wasn't sure he wanted to be in anything so "dripping with religion." This dinner was just another part of their ruse. They were in her private home with no prying eyes to act as witnesses but Barry told her that was the point. They had to maintain the story even when they thought they were the only people in the world who knew what they were doing. Sometimes all his rules made her wonder if this whole thing was just some trick to make her date him without her being aware of it.

But no. She'd seen him with men, and he hadn't shown the slightest interest in doing anything physical with her.

"Are you okay? Evie?"

She realized he'd stopped his rambling a few seconds earlier and blinked him back into focus. "Sorry. I wasn't listening."

"Obviously." He smirked. "I've been holding court long enough. You obviously have something you want to talk about, so I cede the floor."

Evelyn put down her fork. "I need to tell someone our relationship is a ruse."

His smile faded. "I don't think that's a very good idea. It's not safe. If the papers get even a whiff of us being fake, they'll start asking why."

"I know..."

He tapped his fingers on the edge of the table. "Who do you *need* to tell?"

"Simon Grace."

Barry laughed. "The reporter? You have to be joking. You want to tell a *reporter* who just tried lighting a fuse on the whole entertainment industry?"

"You don't understand, we... we had a..." She gestured in the air. Relationship didn't seem like the right word. "We formed a bond with each other. And right now, I think it's eroding. Because of this, because of you and me. And I need to tell him the truth so he doesn't get the wrong idea."

"I'm sorry, Evie. We can't take that risk."

She closed her eyes, regretting it immediately when she felt the tears that her lashes knocked loose. "You mean *you* can't take that risk. You're the one with the secret that can't get out."

"Oh, so you're not attracted to women anymore?"

"I..."

"Is that what this whole Simon thing is about? You want to fight these urges by jumping into bed with a real man?"

Evelyn leaned forward and covered her face with both hands. The heat coming off her cheeks almost burned her palms. How had she gotten tangled up in this mess? How could she be in a position where two different people were making the same damn accusation for different reasons? She needed to just tell Barry. Tell him that Simon was really Gracie. But that wasn't her secret to tell, any more than Barry's. She couldn't betray two confidences, but she was trapped without doing it.

"If I tell him," she said, keeping her voice measured, "I

guarantee that he will give you a secret about *himself* that would be equally destructive. It would destroy his entire life if it got out, even worse than yours."

"What secret?"

"I can't tell you," Evelyn said through clenched teeth. "Just like I can't tell *him* your secret. If I did, neither one of you would ever trust me again, and rightly so. Will you have dinner with him? Just the three of us? We-we can have a... we can talk, we can--"

Barry was already shaking his head. "I haven't come this far in my career just to risk everything by inviting a reporter to dinner and talking about it. I'm sorry, Evelyn."

She wiped at her eyes. "Because, once again, someone else's needs are more important than mine."

"We can... we can discuss... breaking up. But we don't want a situation where one of us comes off looking like the villain. One of us will get a movie on location, long-distance will be a strain, we can end things naturally. Everyone will understand, we'll both look great."

"Do you have a movie coming up?" she asked flatly. "Because I don't."

"No. Not... yet. But it's bound to happen sooner or later. A month, maybe two."

She chuckled flatly and shook her head. "Wonderful. I'll just put my life on hold until we can put on a good show for the public."

"That's our entire life, Evelyn. Just a show for the public."

"Right." She pushed her chair back and stood up, turning her back on him. "I'm going to take a shower. You know where the linens are if you want to crash on the couch, or lock up when you go, I don't give a damn which one."

"You've barely touched your dinner," he said.

Evelyn didn't look back as she headed upstairs. "I'll eat it later."

***

Gracie knocked on Swain's door. It was slightly ajar and swung inward at the touch of her knuckle, but he waved her in before she could apologize for intruding. She stepped up to his desk and dropped the page onto his blotter.

"All ready for the next edition."

"Fantastic." He picked it up and started to scan the words. His expression shifted as if he'd just caught a bad smell, then he went back to the top of the page and read from the beginning. Then he looked at her. "What the hell is this? Evelyn Wade's life story? We shit-canned that when she decided to lose her mind in the last article. Besides, you were supposed to be working on the Atwater thing."

"A politician who was about to be arrested for embezzling and grift decided to kill himself instead of facing consequences for his crimes. That's boring. People will want to read this."

Swain started to argue, drawing in a deep breath before he let it out with a deflated woof. "You're using my own logic against me, aren't you?"

"Yes, I am. Everyone's going to be covering Atwater. We're the only ones who are going to have a full column about the woman who risked everything to take down the studios' casting couch."

"It's going to be controversial." He said it as if that was a perk, not a downside. "Even with the headaches it caused, that edition sold like gangbusters." He kept reading and pursed his lips. "This isn't half bad. Makes her look good, too. Are we sure that's the direction we want to go? Things could turn either way for her right now. That Greek gods thing could be the last movie she ever makes."

Gracie squared her shoulders. "It's the only direction I'm going, Mr. Swain. If you want something negative, find a novelist."

He patted the air. "All right, all right, it was just a suggestion. You're a hard guy to understand, Simon. I would've never expected to see you willingly write for the entertainment page again. Especially with a front-page story dropped in your lap. I'll never figure you out."

"That's how I like it, Bill." She saluted him and headed

out of his office. "I'm taking off for the rest of the day."

She grabbed her jacket as she passed her desk, putting it on as she continued out of the building rather than taking the time to stop.

She hadn't planned to change her story. She was grateful that she would finally get a chance to write the story she'd planned to write so long ago. She still felt like the exclusive, a chance to be on the cusp of what might be the biggest political story of the year, had been pulled out from under her. Getting it back was only the world correcting herself.

Then she found herself in a room with four other journalists waiting for an official statement on Atwater's death. She had taken out her notebook and flipped back to the original notes she had taken when she planned to interview him, looking for anything she might salvage from that original aborted story. As she went back through the pages, she caught glimpses of Evelyn's handwriting that made her slow down. It was ridiculous but she felt like going back before those pages would erase them, rewrite them, make it so those days never happened.

It was only then that she realized how desperately she wanted to preserve that trip. Not just the moments in the last motel or the rain. The entire trip. The frustration, the meals, the silences. She would even relive the fight if it was guaranteed to lead to the same aftermath. She left the other reporters in such a hurry that one of them followed her, certain there was some other big story in the offing that he wanted to get the scoop on.

He must have been surprised when she pulled into a movie theater parking lot and bought a ticket to the matinee to *Over Red Rocks*, a movie that had already been out for years.

Two hours later she left the theater. She bought a newspaper and scanned listings until she knew where she had to go next. She broke the speed limit on the way, risking a ticket in order to make the next showing of *Chicago Canary*.

After the films, she'd gone straight home. She took all the prints from her darkroom, save for the more risqué shots, and lined them up on her desk around her typewriter. Her first draft was done in an hour. She went through the notes Evelyn had given her to give it another pass. When she was satisfied she was finished, she typed up a second copy and put both of them on the coffee table so she would be sure to take both of them when she left the next morning.

Now, having delivered the first copy, she got into her car and drove to deliver the second.

Once again it took her a few minutes to find Evelyn's address. The neighborhood was a maze, and she presumed that the houses were not designed to be easily found by people driving around. Eventually she saw the familiar driveway and pulled into it. She wouldn't let herself be dissuaded. She wouldn't let her spirit be knocked down. She got out of the car, walked up to the front door, and knocked. She didn't give herself a second, not a breath, to hesitate.

She had plenty of time to panic while she stood on the stoop and stared at the stubbornly still-closed door in front of her.

After two minutes had passed, she knocked again. She told herself this was a stupid idea. She told herself Evelyn wouldn't want to see her, let alone talk to her, let alone go along with what she had planned. All her resolve fizzled and faded with each passing second. She twisted her wrists, holding her hands tight against her hips as her fingers typed on an invisible typewriter. She knocked one more time and told herself she would wait a total of five minutes. Surely that would be enough time to—

The door opened and she was looking at Evelyn for the first time since Cicero. She was more gorgeous than Gracie remembered. Her eyes were more green, the eyebrows more arched, the bow of her lips more pronounced. Her hair was pulled back but was still loose enough that it puffed out on one side of her head, and she was wearing a pair of rumpled pajamas that looked too big for her.

"What are you doing here?"

"I need to show you something."

Evelyn shrugged. "Fine."

"No, I need you... to come with me, so I can show you something."

"I'm not going anywhere." Evelyn gestured at herself. She sighed and sagged against the door. "I'm not in the mood for this, Gracie."

"Please," Gracie said. "I know I don't deserve your trust, not after what I did in Cicero. I wish I could take it back. I wish I could tell that asshole you weren't going anywhere with him. The days driving home were the worst hours of my life. I can't make up for that, but I can make one thing right. But it *is* going to require trust."

Evelyn stared at her, eyes half-closed as if she was on the verge of falling asleep.

"I just want a chance to make it right."

"I must be a glutton for punishment," Evelyn muttered. "But you have to wait. I want to wash my hair and put on clothes."

Gracie nodded. "Of course."

Evelyn stepped out of the doorway, still shaking her head as if she didn't believe what she was doing. She gestured toward the living room and kitchen.

"I'll be as quick as I can."

"Take your time."

Gracie didn't think to ask if Barry was home until Evelyn was already upstairs. She decided it didn't matter. If he was there, he would make his presence known soon enough.

She went into the living room and sat down in one of the armchairs. She hated being in anyone's personal space when they weren't there. It always made her feel like an intruder. So she was very careful to keep her hands in her lap and only snoop with her eyes. There were framed posters on the walls for all of Evelyn's movies, even the one that didn't feature her face or credit. She supposed they would have to be rearranged when *Olympus* came out, since she didn't see a place for it.

Her eyes drifted past the couch, then swung back to focus on something that seemed out of place. At first it looked like an ordinary throw pillow, until she noticed it was pressed down behind the cushion. It was a bed pillow, long and wide. That revelation made her see the blanket that had been mostly kicked under the dust ruffle. Someone had slept on the couch the night before. Maybe for several nights, judging by how the pillow was mashed down into the corner.

She was torn away from her speculation by Evelyn's return. She had changed into capri pants and a sleeveless polo shirt. Her hair was hidden under a cloche hat, and Gracie assumed she hadn't even tried to tame it. She crossed to the living room area and crossed her arms.

Gracie stood and led Evelyn out of the house. Evelyn paused on the threshold but then walked to the passenger side of the car and got in.

"I thought I'd taken my last ride in this thing."

"I'm glad to have you back," Gracie said as she slid behind the wheel.

Evelyn didn't say anything to that.

Gracie drove them out of the neighborhood and headed east. Evelyn kept her head turned, looking out the window as if she was in a taxi or riding the bus.

"Can I ask you a question?"

"Sure."

"Why are you mad at me?"

Evelyn whipped her head around. "Why am I—"

"I'm only asking," Gracie said quickly, "because I think there are multiple reasons you might be sore. I just want to have an idea which one I should try and amend first."

"Can we just get this over with?"

Gracie sighed. "Okay. I'll guess. If you're angry that I didn't follow through with the profile in the paper, I'm making amends for that as we speak. It's being edited right now, and it will be in the paper tomorrow. There's a copy in the glove compartment if you want to read it."

Evelyn's posture had slowly eased up while she was talking. When Gracie gestured at the glove box, Evelyn reached out and clicked the latch. She found the paper rolled into a tube and took it out.

"I know I also promised you a chance to read over it before it went to press, but I didn't really have time for that. I hope you approve of it anyway."

"Evelyn Wade didn't choose the world of acting, acting chose her." She read the first sentence and then looked across the seat at Gracie. "What is this?"

"It's your profile. It's going to run in the *Merc* tomorrow."

Evelyn pressed her lips together and looked down again. Gracie could see the page was trembling in her fingers. After a minute, she began to read again.

"We met Evelyn as a wide-eyed ingenue in *Chicago Canary* just a few short years ago, and soon we'll see her again playing a Greek goddess of war in *Olympus*. I found Evelyn on the set of this upcoming epic and can faithfully report that she wears the role with ease and aplomb. Some may be surprised by the range shown in such a short amount of time, but not this reporter. I've spent the past few days watching all three of Evelyn Wade's movies and I can say wi..." She looked at Gracie. "You did?"

"Well, I saw the boat one with you in Cicero. The Aztec downtown was showing *Red Rocks*, and there was a place way out in the middle of nowhere with one daily showing of *Chicago Canary* still on the schedule. It was worth tracking that down." She cleared her throat and kept her eyes on the road. "You're a great singer."

"No, I'm... my voice, it's serviceable."

"You sounded like an angel."

Evelyn didn't look up from the page. She cleared her throat and continued reading where she'd left off. "I can say with certainty that her talent is not a question of range. Rather, her skill lies in finding the humanity in every character she brings to life. Evelyn is a woman who appreciates the beauty in the world and isn't afraid to be afraid. She braves the dangerous and scary things in her life and brings this strength to her roles..." She shook her head, her voice shaking. "This isn't true."

"Of course it is. Keep reading."

"It's fiction."

Gracie sighed. "You risked everything to protect other actresses from suffering the same things you went through. You arranged to go across the country even though you knew exactly how the meeting with your mother would go. You went back because you knew it had to happen. Just like you knew it was worth risking your career to warn women you've never met about the dangers they'll face."

Evelyn sniffled and wiped at her cheeks. "That's really how you see me?"

"Absolutely," Gracie said. "I'm sorry it took me so long to write it."

"I suppose I won't hold it against you." She laughed at the fact she was crying and looked out the window, only now realizing they had left behind the city. "Where are we?"

"There's somewhere we have to go."

"Are you kidnapping me again?"

"Sort of."

Evelyn folded her arms. "This is getting to be a burden, Mr. Grace. Three or four more times and I might stop coming with you."

Gracie couldn't help but smile.

CHAPTER TWENTY-TWO

"BARRY AND I aren't in a relationship."

She hadn't expected to say the words before they blurted out of her mouth. She hadn't planned to say anything. But being in Gracie's car again, the massive and magnificent green beast, had felt like a chance to reclaim what they'd lost in Cicero. Their trip east had felt like something was growing, something was beginning, and then Max had come in and lopped off the bud before it could fully bloom. But here they were, passing through the same scrubland, the same hum of tires on asphalt, and all she could think about was the fact Gracie thought she was taken.

"Okay," Evelyn finally said. "The newspapers certainly seem to think so."

"The newspapers are easy to manipulate. They're all looking so hard for something, it's easy to make them think they've found it. Attractive man and beautiful woman work together in close proximity, sometimes half-naked, they're bound to start a relationship off-camera. Barry and I use figured we would use that to our mutual advantage."

Evelyn said, "I noticed the bedding on the couch. I

assume that's where he's been sleeping."

"You never know when someone's watching," Evelyn said. "We always have to be careful. It's the candid shots that really sell the story. Anyone can have a nice platonic dinner with a coworker. But if a reporter sees Barry come out of my house in the morning, they draw their own conclusions."

Gracie made a peculiar sound that Evelyn didn't try to parse. "I don't understand, though. I know why you would want to look like you're having a cookie-cutter relationship, but what does he get out of it if you're not actually sleeping with him?"

Evelyn tapped her finger against her lips and considered her next words very carefully. "The fake relationship is mutually beneficial... because... only one of us is attracted to men, sexually, and it isn't the one most people would consider correct."

"One of–" Gracie inhaled sharply. "Oh. Wait. You're... you're not attracted to men?"

"Well, not exclusively. Not to the extent Barry is."

"Oh."

Evelyn quickly added, "I'm going to tell him you're a woman. Just in order to keep things fair. If his secret got out–"

"No, I understand, yes. Yes, he... he deserves to feel protected." She groaned and shook her head. "That's why you wanted us to have dinner together. God. You wanted us to tell each other our secrets so you wouldn't be stuck in the middle."

"Right."

"I'm so sorry, Evelyn. I thought... I was..."

Evelyn said, "You don't have to explain. We could have solved a lot of problems just by talking. I could have gone to find you. And you could have come to see me."

"I tried. As soon as I got back to Los Angeles. I went to your house. I saw Barry come out your front door in the morning, and this stupid reporter made an assumption.

Evelyn's eyes widened. "Oh! Oh." She looked out the window at the road. "Oh..." She put her hand over her mouth and then, to her surprise, laughed. "Well, here's to plans that work *too* well."

Gracie smiled and chuckled as well. "You wouldn't have been the first woman who jumped out of a lesbian's bed and ran to find a man."

"I suppose not. I'm sorry I made you think I'd rejected you like that. I was angry at you for what happened in Cicero. But that didn't change anything else. I wouldn't have been so angry if I didn't care."

"Same, about seeing someone else come out of your house."

They were quiet for almost a mile of road. Finally Evelyn broke the silence. "What would you have said? If it had taken you ten more minutes to reach my house and Barry was already gone? If you'd knocked on my door, what would you have said to me?"

Gracie thought about it. "I would have apologized for letting you go. I knew it was the wrong things to do the second it happened. The drive home felt like penance. It was torture. Hundreds of miles of empty road all by myself. In silence. It gave me time to really think about what a fucking mistake I'd made letting Max take you. If I had it to do over again, I'd have fought for you."

Air couldn't get through Evelyn's throat for a moment, which made her choke and cough. Her eyes burned with sudden tears as she hunched forward with a hand over her mouth.

"Evie?" Gracie's voice was panicked.

Evelyn felt the car slowing. "Don't... stop." She couldn't even say two words without coughing between them. "I-it's just... just your... choice of words."

"They're your words. I can't take credit for that." Gracie reached over and touched her arm. "Are you sure you're okay?"

"I will be. I'm sorry."

"Don't be sorry."

Evelyn got her breath back and patted her flat palm

against her sternum. "I'll be fine. I'm fine."

"Did I say the right thing or the wrong thing?"

"The right thing." Evelyn was glad her coughing fit had given her an excuse for the wetness in her eyes. "The absolute right thing."

A few miles later they spotted a diner and Evelyn suggested they stop to get something to eat. She was starved, and she also thought she should use their phone to call Barry and let him know where she'd gone. The last thing they needed was for anyone to really think she'd been kidnapped. She managed to get in touch with him through his agent's office. He was concerned, and more than a little confused, but he was willing to keep it quiet if she guaranteed she was in good hands. She swore that she was, even if she had no idea where Gracie planned to take her. She was certain that, wherever it might be, it was somewhere she'd definitely want to be.

Evelyn went back to the booth Gracie had claimed. Their food had been delivered while she was on the phone, and Gracie was already partaking of their shared order of crinkle-cut fries. She slid into the other side of the booth and unwrapped her patty melt.

"This is the best I've felt since Cicero," Evelyn admitted.

"Me too."

Evelyn took a bite of her sandwich and looked outside. The sun was almost blindingly bright, and the flow of cars on the road caused sparkles and flashes to constantly splash across the diner's window. She had a feeling Gracie was taking her to Las Vegas for some reason. She had heard things about the city - "Sin City," they were calling it - but she couldn't imagine wanting anything there. She wasn't a gambler. She didn't think Gracie was, either. But she was willing to go along for the ride, to see wherever it might take them.

"What if we kept going?"

"Hm?" Gracie wiped some mayo from her bottom lip. When she swallowed her bite of burger, she said, "Keep going where?"

Evelyn shrugged. "Anywhere. What if, after we go wherever you have planned, we don't go back to Los Angeles? We just keep going east and see what we find out there?"

Gracie considered it. "Well. For one thing, you didn't pack for even *one* day..."

"So we'll buy some clothes on the way."

Gracie smiled. "You really want to just drive until we run out of road?"

"Yes!" Evelyn laughed, then put a hand over her face and shook her head, still smiling. "No. I don't know. It sounds lovely, though. Doesn't it? Just the two of us in a car."

"It sounds amazing," Gracie admitted, her voice soft. She looked over at Evelyn. "I'm in if you are."

Evelyn chuckled quietly but didn't answer.

When they were back in the car, Evelyn cranked down the window and put her arm outside the car. She cupped her hand against the wind and Gracie sped up a little to let her ride the current.

"Are you ever going to tell me where we're going?"

"You'll see soon enough. We'll be there by nightfall."

Evelyn watched her hand for a few seconds and then realized. "You're taking me to see the Grand Canyon."

Gracie slumped back against the seat. "Damn it. I wanted a big reveal, I wanted a... a big moment where you didn't know until we were actually there..."

"You wanted to sneak up on the biggest hole on Earth?"

Gracie smirked. "It's more than just a big hole, you know."

"Well, *I* know. How do *you* know?"

"I stopped there on the way home. I thought it would make me feel like you were with me. Instead, it made me realize just how far away you were. I wanted you to be there so bad. So I thought I might as well make amends and take you now."

Evelyn said, "This is an entire day. Two, counting the trip back."

Gracie winced. "Yeah. I-I probably should have warned

you about that. You should have had a chance to pack a change of clothes or at least a toothbrush. I just wanted to surprise you, and~"

"No, that's not what I meant," Evelyn said. "This is two days of your life dedicated to taking me to see the Grand Canyon. Just because I wanted to see it."

Gracie relaxed. "Oh. Well, yeah. You still want to see it, right?"

Evelyn's smile made her cheeks hurt, and she reached up as if she was going to physically push them back down into place. "Yeah. Yeah, I really want to see it."

"Okay. Give me a couple hours."

"So what happens next?" Gracie said after another few miles of silence.

"Next...?" Evelyn pointed ahead. "Next is the big hole."

Gracie chuckled. "No, I meant for you. For your career. What's... what's happening?"

"Oh." Evelyn slumped against the seat. "Another big hole. I just finished *Olympus*, and there's always a bit of an empty period before the next project kicks off. It's hard to tell if this is just a normal lack of offers or if it's something more permanent. At this point, I really don't care. If the only way I can get jobs is keeping my mouth shut and fucking anyone who takes an interest, then they can keep their roles. I'll find something else to do with my time."

"Good for you."

"Mm. We'll see if that morality holds up when my savings have dried up and rent is due."

Gracie said, "I'm sure there are some directors out there who are honest and respectable. Maybe this article will help them find you."

"We can only hope." Evelyn thought back to the late-night call from Adora Bell. "I know it's helped at least one girl. Or at least gave her enough pause to make an informed decision about how to proceed. So I can take comfort in that, no matter what happens. I helped someone. I helped her. I may have saved her some damage."

"That's a huge thing, Evelyn."

"Mm-hmm." She folded her arms over her chest. "Can I sleep? I know we haven't seen each other in a long time. But I've been sleeping awfully ever since I got back from the road trip, and right now I feel like I could just pass out. I don't want you to think~"

"No, please, sleep. We've got a ways to go yet. I'll wake you so you won't miss anything."

Evelyn nodded her thanks and sank down in the seat. She closed her eyes and let the hum of the car relax her.

"And I'm not a dummy," Evelyn said when she was right on the verge of sleep.

"What?"

"I haven't been able to sleep since the road trip. And now, a couple of hours in your car, I'm... on the verge..." She sighed heavily and felt the tension seep out of her. She smacked her lips. "I just... I know what it says. About you. And about... how I feel about you."

Gracie chuckled. "You find me dull as dishwater?"

"It means I'm a cat," Evelyn murmured. "And cats only fall asleep where they feel safe."

Seconds later she was asleep.

"Evelyn?" Gracie hated disturbing her, so she spoke almost too quietly for even a conscious person to hear. Evelyn had slumped over almost immediately after comparing herself to a cat. The next hour had been a serenade of heavy breathing and sweet little snores, with the occasional shift of position on the seat. Once or twice she was pretty sure she'd seen Evelyn wake up, look out the window, and immediately go back to sleep, but her eyes were already closed again by the time Gracie risked looking away from the road.

She'd found a parking spot near a camping area. The ground was rocky and they were surrounded by skeletal trees with bare branches. She considered letting Evelyn sleep for a while longer, but they were so close to sunset that she was worried they might miss it. She rested her hand on Evelyn's shoulder and gently shook her.

"Evie…? We're here, hon."

Evelyn's eyelids fluttered. She looked out the window, and immediately clapped a hand over her eyes. "Oh! Oh no! I don't want to see it for the first time by accident."

Gracie smiled. "We're still about half a mile from the rim. You won't see anything but trees from here, I promise."

Evelyn pushed herself up and rubbed her eyes. "Boy, I was out like a light."

"You sure were. You okay?"

"Yeah. The walk will help me wake up."

They got out of the car. Evelyn stretched her arms above her head, the hem of her polo shirt riding up to expose her belly as she linked her fingers and twisted her waist one way, then the other. Gracie heard a pop and Evelyn sighed blissfully. Gracie came around the front of the Desoto and pulled out a handkerchief.

"If you want to wait until you have a good view, I can blindfold you for the walk out."

"Really?" Evelyn eyed the cloth. "Won't people think that's a little silly?"

Gracie shrugged. "Who cares?"

Evelyn nodded. "Right. Yes! Screw them."

Gracie folded the handkerchief in half, then wrapped it around Evelyn's eyes. She tied a loose knot and then took Evelyn's hand.

"Trust me?"

"Of course."

Gracie squeezed Evelyn's fingers and led her away from the car. They had only walked a little way before Evelyn leaned in close and slipped her arm around Gracie's elbow. Gracie tensed and looked around, even though she hadn't seen any other campers since she parked.

"Relax," Evelyn whispered. "Even if someone sees us, they'll just think we're a couple out on a stroll."

"And if they recognize you, it might cause problems for you and Barry," Gracie whispered back.

Evelyn said, "Oh." After a few steps, she shrugged. "I don't care. Let them gossip."

Gracie smiled and ducked her head. "Are you okay? Not too disoriented?"

"Just keep me away from the... what do they have, guardrails?"

"Fences. They're more than waist-high. You'll be safe."

"Keep me away from them anyway. Gravity is already pulling at me in a weird way."

Gracie tightened her arm around Evelyn's and led her down a rock-lined path. The canyon spread out to their right, as magnificent as it had been the day before, but Gracie was glad it wouldn't be Evelyn's first view. For something like this, spectacle was required, and she was taking her responsibility as guide very seriously. She wasn't going to mess up this memory.

They passed two lookout points that Gracie deemed unworthy. Evelyn had smiled when Gracie dismissed the first one, and laughed at the second.

"It doesn't have to be perfect," she said. "As long as it's pretty, I'll be satisfied."

"But I won't be. It has to be just right."

Evelyn sighed and put her head on Gracie's shoulder.

A few minutes later she found it. The lookout point was in the deep V between two stone walls that sloped almost vertically down to the canyon floor. The angle of the walls seemed to open up the entire canyon to their view, framing the nearby rock formations and a good chunk of sky as well. Gracie positioned Evelyn near the railing and guided her hands to the metal bar.

"Okay, are you ready?"

"Yes." Evelyn's voice and fingers were shaking. "I'm excited."

"I can tell."

Gracie untied the blindfold. Then, before Evelyn could open her eyes, she leaned in and pressed a kiss to her lips. Evelyn made a sound of surprise, and then her mouth relaxed and she tilted her head into the kiss. Gracie put a hand on

Evelyn's cheek, and Evelyn snaked an arm around Gracie's waist. She cupped Gracie's ass through her slacks and moaned appreciatively into the kiss.

Then Gracie stepped back and to the side.

"Open your eyes."

Evelyn opened them. She took a deep breath and instinctively took a step back. Gracie put a hand in the small of her back to keep her from going too far, and Evelyn's grip tightened on the handrail. When she breathed again, she said, "Wow," and let her weight rest against Gracie's arm. "Wow, oh, wow."

"I know," Gracie said. "I saw it at sunrise. Looks like sunset is pretty fantastic, too."

"Look at the colors!" Evelyn gasped. "Oh, Gracie. Thank you."

"You're welcome." She kissed Evelyn's hair. "I'm sorry I said no the first time you asked to come here."

Evelyn shook her head. "Don't be. This is perfect. How long can we stay?"

"Well," Gracie said, "we shouldn't stay until it's full dark. I don't know how well these paths are lit. But I brought a flashlight, just in case~"

"No, no, no, no," Evelyn said, turning to put a finger against Gracie's lips. She looked into her eyes. "How long can we stay? Here."

Gracie understood. She wrapped her arms around Evelyn and pulled her close. "As long as we want, Evie. As long as you'll have me."

Evelyn smiled and stood on her toes to kiss Gracie's lips as the shadows stretched around them.

Evelyn wasn't surprised when Gracie pulled into the parking lot of a campground not far from the Canyon. They'd left when the sun was just barely visible in the distance, using the last bit of its light to follow the path back to the car. It would've been ridiculous to expect Gracie to spend another eight hours driving back in the dark.

She waited in the car while Gracie went inside to reserve a room, which turned out to be a cabin at the end of a short dirt driveway.

Gracie led her into the cabin, pausing to turn on a light. It was a single room with a sitting area directly in front of the door and a queen-size bed behind it. The kitchen was to the right, and Gracie gestured toward it.

"They said the fridge is fully stocked. And, um, the bed... they only had cabins with one bedroom, but I don't want you to think I was presuming anything. I can sleep on the couch or we can~"

Evelyn cut her off by kissing her. Gracie immediately returned the kiss, her strong arms wrapping around Evelyn's waist and pulling her close.

"I really would have," she said quickly between kisses, "mm, taken the couch."

"I know." Evelyn was quickly trying to work the buttons of Gracie's shirt with hands that barely seemed to work. "Can I tear this off of you?"

Gracie reached up to help her. "No, I only have one shirt..."

"Then hurry," Evelyn whimpered. She kissed Gracie's cheeks, jaw, and neck while Gracie unbuttoned her own shirt. The second the felt the material being pulled away, she bent her knees and started kissing lower. Across Gracie's collarbone, down to her cleavage, across to take a nipple into her mouth. She used her teeth and tongue on it while Gracie grabbed handfuls of her hair and made the most delicious noises of encouragement.

Gracie let Evelyn spend some time on her chest before she pulled her away, taking her mouth for another long kiss. They moved across the room like dancers, feet shuffling over the hardwood floor toward the bed. Evelyn tugged her polo shirt out of her slacks and immediately felt Gracie's hands brushing over the newly-exposed strip of hip and the small of her back and left goosebumps in their wake. She leaned back long enough to pull the shirt over her head and drop it, then watched Gracie's face as she reached behind to unfasten her bra.

Once it was gone, Gracie cupped Evelyn's breasts. "I love seeing you naked."

"You do?" Evelyn felt the blush creeping up her throat.

"Yes." She bent down and pressed her lips to Evelyn's chest. "You're gorgeous."

Evelyn closed her eyes and, for reasons even she couldn't explain, lifted her heels so she was standing on her tiptoes. Gracie took it as a hint to move lower, so she did. She knelt on the floor and kissed Evelyn's belly as she unbuttoned her pants and slowly, but with a desperate urgency, tugged them down over her hips. Evelyn held her breath and stepped out of the pants and her shoes at the same time, then let Gracie guide her toward the bed so she could lie down.

"Please," Evelyn said, resting the back of one hand across her mouth.

"This?" Gracie asked, and lightly brushed her lips over Evelyn's thigh.

Evelyn's body twitched and she moved her legs apart. "Yes."

"This?" Gracie asked, angling her head. She kissed skin no one else had ever kissed, and her hair brushed Evelyn's sex.

"*Yes*," Evelyn moaned. "That... more."

Gracie's finger brushed against her. Evelyn grunted. And then Gracie's mouth was on her. Evelyn closed her eyes and opened her lips, slipping her middle finger into her mouth and biting down hard on the knuckle. She pulled her feet up onto the mattress and pushed down with them, lifting herself up to meet Gracie's lips and tongue. Gracie responded with increased force, which made Evelyn's legs tremble.

She came with a force that surprised her, dropping her hand to cry out and then immediately putting it back in case anyone nearby might overhear.

Her brain went foggy for an unknown amount of time, because the next thing she knew, Gracie was climbing on top of her. She'd removed her pants at some point during the blackout. Evelyn felt skin on her skin and reached out for it as she accepted Gracie's kiss, taking the tip of her tongue into her mouth and gently sucking on it, eyes closed and brow furrowed at the strange taste of herself.

"Show me what to do to you," Evelyn said, taking her mouth away from Gracie as little as possible to get the words out.

"You want me to show you?" Gracie asked. She slipped one arm around Evelyn's shoulders, propping her up slightly off the mattress.

"Yes." She was cradled against Gracie's bare chest, and she couldn't imagine ever getting up from this spot. "Show me."

Gracie brought Evelyn's hand to her mouth and kissed two fingertips, then took them into her mouth. She sucked and swirled her tongue, then guided the hand down her body. Evelyn watched its path, even though she knew Gracie was staring at her face. She could feel the intensity of her stare like it was a heat source, but she couldn't tear her eyes away from her fingers tracing a wet path over Gracie's breast, down her stomach, to... to...

"Oh," Evelyn said, then looked up to see what Gracie's face was doing.

Gracie's eyes were closed. Her teeth pulled at her bottom lip, and a line appeared between her eyebrows. Evelyn turned her hand, and Gracie stroked her palm and the inside of her wrist.

"Do this..." Gracie let go and held up her hand to make a 'come here' gesture.

Evelyn did what she was told and watched Gracie flinch. "Good?"

"Great, baby. Press harder..."

"Okay..."

Evelyn stroked and watched Gracie's face. Sweat shined on her forehead and her hair was stuck to it. She looked desperate, maybe even pained. But she only whispered "faster," and "right there," so Evelyn didn't stop. Before long,

Gracie was thrusting against her fingers, and her other hand tightened on Evelyn's shoulder. Gracie moved her leg so that it was between Evelyn's thighs. Evelyn captured it and rubbed against her, matching the rhythm she had found with her fingers.

"I think you're going to let go," Evelyn half-whispered, half-moaned, and then she watched and felt it happen. The muscles moved against her trapped fingers, and Gracie's face twisted into the most hideously gorgeous expression she'd ever seen. When the waves passed, she exhaled twice, very hard, and her arms gave out. She slumped to one side and pressed her face to Evelyn's shoulder, kissing her, trembling so hard that it made Evelyn's breasts shake. She chuckled when she realized this, but she didn't say anything. She just held and kissed Gracie until she came back to herself enough to participate.

"Tell me again, Grace," Evelyn whispered, eyes closed. "Tell me again how long we can stay here."

"As long as we want." Gracie kissed Evelyn's neck, which made her shudder. "As long as you'll have me."

Evelyn smiled and decided it would almost be enough.

EPILOGUE

One Year Later

GRACIE FINISHED tying her bowtie as she came out of the bathroom, giving the two sides a gentle tug to make sure they were even. Evelyn, sitting at her vanity, huffed and rolled her eyes.

"This is completely unfair. Just because you're going dressed as a man, you can get away with a shower and a nice suit. Did that even take you five minutes?"

"Ten. I shaved, too." Gracie brushed the back of her hand over her cheek. "I don't know if it actually makes a difference. But it's a ritual. And sometimes I nick myself, and that makes it a little more believable to people at the office."

Evelyn put a hand on her chest. "Oh, lord, I'm sorry. I had no idea of the sacrifices you were making."

Gracie stood behind Evelyn's chair and bent down so they could look at each other in the mirror. "You could go dressed as a man, too. You'd look amazing in a tux and tails." She teased Evelyn's curls. "Nice top hat."

I'll leave that to Marlene, thank you." She finished with her eyelashes and turned her head. "Kiss me before I start on my lipstick."

Gracie did as she was told, then pressed another kiss to Evelyn's cheek before she went to get her shoes. "I'm glad you have your priorities in check."

"We can't have you showing up with lipstick on your mouth! People will see that, realize you're too beautiful to be a man, and then the whole jig will be up."

Gracie chuckled and sat on the edge of the bed. Their bed. The bed they'd shared since Gracie moved in a few months earlier. Barry understood the situation once it was laid out for him, but he and Evelyn needed time to work out a satisfying end to their so-called relationship that made them both look good. The opportunity came when he was cast in a Western filming in Spain. He would have to relocate for three months. It was as good a chance as any to say their relationship wasn't working and they had mutually decided to part ways.

She was glad they'd been forced to wait. It gave them a chance to get away from the heightened environment of their road trip and see how they felt in their real lives. They got to know each other in real life, and quickly discovered that their feelings were only stronger without the forced proximity of the car. And sex in a proper bed was a completely different creature than motels.

"Are you all ready for tomorrow?" Gracie asked.

"Tomorrow? I just have to be there. You're the one who has to be ready. It's the opposite of tonight. Tonight you're just my arm candy."

"True." Gracie adjusted her cufflinks. "Wait. They're not going to want to talk to me, are they?"

"Who?"

"The photographers. Some of them are going to be from the *Merc.* Or used to be there. God, that would be strange, running into them on the red carpet..."

Evelyn got up and walked over. She petted the top of Gracie's head. "You don't have to come. I know you're not really comfortable with publicity and all that."

Gracie took Evelyn's hand, kissed the knuckles, and pressed it against her cheek. "You're sweet. But I want to support you. Besides, this is *our* movie. This movie is the reason we met. I can't just catch the matinee."

"True, true. But to set your mind at ease, no. They don't really care about the partners unless they're also famous."

"Thank goodness for that."

Evelyn finished her preparations and they headed out. Gracie waited until they were in the car before she asked if Evelyn was nervous.

"Not really. I'm used to these things by now. I know what to expect."

"But this is the movie with Sol and that screenwriter asshole whose name I can never remember. It might be awkward."

Evelyn shook her head. "No, they're like all the other male assholes in this town. They barely even remember that article came out, because barely any of them had to suffer consequences."

Gracie knew the actual number was two. One actor and one producer who had been fired due to their behavior on set, and in the case of the producer, he was only punished because in his case it had been a violent sexual assault and the actress had taken photos of her bruises. They were the sacrificial lambs so the rest of the boys could continue with business as usual.

"I hate that it went away so quickly," Gracie said.

"It didn't go away," Evelyn said. "The men may not have suffered the way they should have, but the women haven't forgotten. Adora hasn't forgotten. The article was proof that none of us have to suffer alone. And it inspired a lot of us to look out for each other."

Gracie smiled at the mention of Adora. "I have to admit, I underestimated her."

"Hell, we all did. Her name is Adora Bell, for Pete's sake." Gracie laughed.

A month after their Grand Canyon excursion, Evelyn got

a call from Adora's agent. She'd been cast in a new noir mystery movie. They were desperate to cast Adora as the femme fatale, but she had a caveat: she would only take the role if they auditioned Evelyn to play the owner of a night club that the detective character frequented. Apparently the tactic worked. They not only called her to read, and Evelyn fell in love with the character. The director offered her the role before she even left the building.

Her career was getting back on track. *Olympus* was already getting rave reviews, and most of the critics were singling out her performance for praise. Adora's agent, seeing the press for her current movie and seeing how she was snatched up for the new one, jumped at the chance to sign her.

Gracie's career was also going well. She was still at the *Mercury*, and her 'failed' excursion into entertainment reporting meant that Swain was keeping her on the 'boring' stuff: politics, both local and national. She made the front page more often than not, and people were starting to take notice of her byline. In her spare time, she was working on a novel. She wasn't serious about it. She wasn't even sure she was going to try publishing it. But she thought it was a fun way to keep her brain engaged between articles. Evelyn certainly seemed to like what she'd read of it, although she said the male lead needed to be a woman, and the two women characters needed to have sexier scenes together.

"Write what you know, darling," Evelyn told her.

"The Queen would never sully herself for a lowly bandit," Gracie insisted.

Evelyn shrugged. "Depends on how sexy the bandit looks in suspenders."

Gracie found a parking spot a block away from the theater hosting the premiere. Evelyn checked her makeup and hair in the mirror, then took Gracie's hand.

"You're not offended by walking, are you? You know I love... well, I've grown to love this car. But it's not exactly the sort of thing I want to arrive in. Do you understand?"

"Sure," Gracie said. "I don't like the idea of handing off

the keys to a valet anyway. You're the one who has to walk a block in high heels."

Evelyn waved off her concern. "I've done worse for longer. Just give me something to lean on and I'll be fine."

Gracie nodded. "At your service, Miss Wade."

"Thank you, Mr. Simon."

"Then what are we waiting for? Your public awaits."

Gracie slipped her glasses on, tucked her hair behind her ears, and winked at Evelyn before she got out of the car.

They made love after the premiere. Evelyn roleplayed as Artemis, and Gracie played the doomed sailor who washed ashore on the island. With all the fun and games, they hadn't fallen asleep until almost two in the morning. More accurately, Gracie fell asleep. Evelyn was still too buzzed from the night and excitement for the next day. She slipped out of bed, wrapped herself in the sheet she'd used as Artemis' chiton, and went downstairs. She left all the lights off and went out onto the back porch, sinking onto the chaise lounge and leaning back until she could see the stars.

There were still going to be directors, producers, and actors who preyed on women in the industry. Her interview hadn't created a horde of pitchfork-wielding villagers that ran them out of town. But the villagers had at least been woken up. Adora wasn't the only actress who had been in touch with her, and she knew there were others who were adding names to the list Evelyn had started. Men you should never be alone in a room with. Men whose party invitations should always be turned down. Women had always watched out for each other to a degree, but it had always run the risk of being labeled gossip, sour grapes, or subtle manipulation of a competitor. Now it was public record. Now there was evidence, and those warnings would be taken seriously.

"Hey."

Evelyn looked over the top of her head. An upside-down version of Gracie in boxer shorts and a tank top lurched out of the house and dropped heavily onto the lounge next to

Evelyn.

"You didn't have to come down here," Evelyn said, playing with Gracie's hair.

"I sleep with you," Gracie murmured, already half asleep.

Evelyn's heart swelled. "Well, there's no need for both of us to be uncomfortable. Come on. Let's go back up to bed."

"Okay..."

Evelyn thought she had just waited a second before she surrendered the soft cushion of the lounge, but the sunlight against her closed eyes told her that much more time had passed. She blinked up at the dawn sky and then kissed the top of Gracie's head to wake her up.

"You fell asleep."

"So'd you." Gracie's mouth was misshapen against Evelyn's breast. "Heard you snorin'..."

Evelyn said, "I only fake snoring so you'll think I'm asleep, then I can watch you sleep."

"That's awful," Gracie said.

Evelyn patted Gracie's arm. "Come on. We really do have to get up. I want to take a shower before we head out."

"Shit. Me too."

They untangled themselves from each other and got up, heading back inside. Over the course of the next hour, they showered and put together their outfits. Gracie wanted to be sure they'd gotten everything they would need.

It had been Evelyn's idea to celebrate the premiere with another road trip. No plan, no real destination in mind, just the two of them in a car going somewhere. "We've gone on two road trips," Evelyn pointed out, "and neither of the destinations turned out being the most memorable thing about them."

"You loved the Grand Canyon," Gracie had said.

"The Grand Canyon is phenomenal," Evelyn admitted. "But that cabin...? Oh my *God*."

Gracie had laughed and leaned across the breakfast table to kiss her.

The car had been inspected by a mechanic, the tank was

full of gas, and two bags were sitting next to the front door, ready to go. While Evelyn was in the shower, Gracie went through the house to make sure everything was locked, shut down, or unplugged. When she was convinced the house wouldn't burn down while they were gone, she put on her fedora and went out to do a walk-around on the car.

She was kicking the tires when Evelyn came out. She pulled the front door shut, gave the knob a firm shake to confirm it was locked, and joined Gracie in the driveway.

"So, have you made a decision about where we're going?" Gracie asked.

Evelyn considered the question. "I've had enough of the desert, I think."

Gracie rested her arms on top of the car. "North?"

"Hm." Evelyn nodded. "North would be cold."

"And trees."

"Rain."

Gracie arched an eyebrow. "Love the rain."

Evelyn smiled. "North it is." She patted the top of the car. "Hop in, my queen."

"Whatever you say, Bandit."

Gracie loaded the bags into the backseat. Evelyn slipped on a pair of sunglasses. With one last look up at the house, Gracie got behind the wheel. She already had a few ideas of where they could go. They couldn't cross the Canadian border, so there was a definite point they couldn't cross, but she didn't mind. There were plenty of places in they could discover along they way. She'd heard great things about Seattle.

She backed out of the driveway and turned to take them out of Silver Lake, away from Los Angeles, into whatever the Pacific Northwest had in store for them.